PROWL
THE NIGHT

Books by Crystal Jordan

PROWL THE NIGHT

CARNAL DESIRES

ON THE PROWL

UNTAMED

PRIMAL HEAT

EMBRACE THE NIGHT

SEXY BEAST V
(with Kate Douglas and Vonna Harper)

SEXY BEAST 9
(with Vonna Harper and Lisa Renee Jones)

UNDER THE COVERS
(with Lorie O'Clare and P.J. Mellor)

Published by Kensington Publishing Corporation

PROWL
THE NIGHT

CRYSTAL JORDAN

APHRODISIA

KENSINGTON PUBLISHING CORP.

www.kensingtonbooks.com

APHRODISIA BOOKS are published by

Kensington Publishing Corp.
119 West 40th Street
New York, NY 10018

All Kensington titles, imprints, and distributed lines are available at special quantity discounts for bulk purchases for sales promotion, premiums, fund-raising, and educational or institutional use.

Special book excerpts or customized printings can also be created to fit specific needs. For details, write or phone the office of the Kensington Special Sales Manager: Kensington Publishing Corp., 119 West 40th Street, New York, NY 10018. Attn. Special Sales Department. Phone: 1-800-221-2647.

Aphrodisia and the A logo Reg. U.S. Pat. & TM Off.

ISBN-13: 978-0-7582-6155-7
ISBN-10: 0-7582-6155-1

First Kensington Trade Paperback Printing: October 2011

10 9 8 7 6 5 4 3 2 1

Printed in the United States of America

For Frank, because you make me laugh, make me think, and make me crazy. Thanks for all the inspiration for my books. Don't ever stop. I love you.

For Michal, because no one could ask for a better best friend. You're still the only girl I'd ever call my "heterosexual life partner." Twelve years and counting . . .

For all the writers who keep me sane in the insane world of publishing: Kate Pearce, Loribelle Hunt, Dayna Hart, R. G. Alexander, Eden Bradley, Karen Erickson, Robin L. Rotham, Patti O'Shea, Rhiannon Leith, Elaina Huntley, and Gemma Halliday. Those critiques, brainstorming sessions, pep talks, and ass-kickings were most appreciated, even if I didn't know it at the time.

For Tim Cahill and Rolf Potts, who both patiently answered my questions about travel writers. I can only hope I did the profession justice with my hero. Any mistakes are entirely mine. Also, thanks for being willing to put in a cameo in the book. You guys were great sports!

Last, but never least, for my grams, because you were the first to challenge me to write. You believed I could do it, even when I didn't.

Contents

Crave Me

1

Want Me

135

CRAVE ME

I
_____

He was inside her, and he'd never felt the distance between them so keenly.

Tomas lay on his side, twined around his wife. He pulled her leg tighter over his hip, driving his cock deeper within her. She gasped, her nails digging in where they gripped his shoulder.

The slickness of her sheath squeezed his dick, and he couldn't keep the snarl from ripping past his throat. He felt the Panther within him grapple for control of the carnal encounter. His fangs slid down to scrape his lower lip, and his heart pounded so loudly it drowned out every other sound in their bedroom.

Every inch of them was pressed together. There was a hair-breadth of space between their faces; he could see the individual lashes surrounding her exotically tilted eyes. But those eyes were closed, the dark wings of her brows drawn together in concentration.

"Ciri, look at me." When she didn't obey him, he sank his cock deep and stopped moving.

She hissed a protest, her lashes fluttering open. Her irises shimmered between Panther gold and their natural dark shade.

Her nails turned to talons on his shoulder, scoring his flesh. "Keep going!"

Their gazes met, locked, and there was a single moment of the connection he used to feel every time they touched. Leaning forward, he kissed her. He wanted it to be sweet, to show how much she meant to him, to let her know she owned his soul and always would.

His mate.

The slice of her claws intensified, the pain ratcheting up his pleasure. She bit his lip hard, then thrust her tongue into his mouth. The wildness in her, the Panther, called to his own feral nature. She pushed her heel against the back of his thigh, urging him to move. He couldn't refuse her.

Grinding his pelvis against her clit made her moan into his mouth. Her wetness increased, the tight slickness of her pussy gripping his cock. He withdrew until he almost slid out of her, then shoved back in, arching his back to power deep into her sex.

She ripped her mouth away from his, throwing back her head to scream. The sound was both woman and Panther at the same time. He worked himself inside her, loving the feel of her, the noises she made, the way they fit together.

He wanted to kiss her again, but she bit her lip, and he couldn't give her as much as he wanted. As usual. His heart clenched at the reminder of how out of sync they were everywhere except the bedroom. He stuffed the thought away and focused on what was good. This. Right here, right now.

Arching her over his arm, he bent forward to suck her nipple into his mouth. When he let it pop free, it glistened with moisture, the color a dark rose. He flicked it with his tongue, nipped it with his fangs. She twisted in his embrace, crying out. He held her close, held her in place as he transferred his attention to her other nipple.

She whimpered, bending her back farther to offer herself up to him. "More, Tomas. *Kudasai.*"

The Japanese word for *please* rolled off her tongue in a breathless rush. It underscored the differences between them. They both spoke Spanish and English, as all Panthers did, but he was from the South American Panther Pride in Brazil, so he also spoke the local Portuguese, whereas she was born in the Asian Pride in Tokyo. There was only one Pride to rule the shifters on each continent, which left both of them a world away from home, here in North America. Neither of them was handling it well.

If only that was the worst of their problems.

Her inner muscles clenched on his cock, milking him, and his thoughts dissolved into lustful cravings. Sweat gathered on his forehead and slid in rivulets down his face. His lungs heaved as his strokes picked up speed and force.

Running his hand down her back, he gripped her ass tight. Burying his face in her neck, he drank in the scent of her. This was the only time he could, the only real closeness they shared anymore. His instincts roared as they always did with her. Mate. The perfect match for him, the only woman who would ever be able to breed with him. He groaned, his fangs extending. God, he wanted her, he always wanted her.

His heart hammered in his chest, base animalistic need warring with the man's control. It took everything in him to hold back, to keep from coming. He wanted her with him. Even if nothing else between them worked, he wanted this to be perfect. He eased his hand inward to part her buttocks. She shivered, her breath catching when he teased her anus. "Do you like this, Ciri?"

"Yes," she gasped. Pushing her hips back, she opened herself to his penetration.

Pressing the tip of one finger to the pucker of her ass, he

5

worked the digit in. At the same time, he kept up a steady rhythm inside her, fucking her deep. When he slid his finger in and out of her anus, he could feel the movement through the thin wall of flesh that separated the two channels.

She closed her eyes, turning her face to bury it in the pillow as she sobbed for breath. Her hips surged frantically between his hand and his cock, her tight nipples rubbing against his chest. He could feel how close he was to orgasm, how it sank its claws in and dragged him toward that inevitable edge. He couldn't fight it any longer. He thrust hard, harder, his hands and hips working her body as fast as they could. The slickness, the friction, it was intense enough to drive him to his knees.

She snarled, her fangs baring as she came. He felt the hot clench of her pussy around his dick. Her eyes flared wide and her irises burned to Panther gold. For a moment, he could see into her soul the way he used to. The passion, the love, was there. But her body gripped his, her voice rising to an urgent scream. "Yes, yes, oh, *yes!*"

That was all he needed, the last slender tether he had on his restraint tearing away. He sank to the hilt, felt the deep contractions of her sheath pulse around him, and he exploded. His body shook with the force of his orgasm, shudders ripping through him as his come jetted inside her.

Every bit of tension leeched from his body, and for the first time in a long time, he felt . . . relaxed. At peace. He sighed as his cock slid from her, their combined moisture still drying on their skin. He loved his scent all over her, loved her scent on him.

Unhooking her leg from over his hip, she pulled back. When she rolled away from him, the gesture gutted him. He had to wonder if that flash of love he'd seen was a figment of his imagination. They'd once lain together after sex, touching and kissing. Her arms around him, her fingers caressing him, a soft smile on her face that was just for him. Where had that tenderness gone? He stared at her slim back and had no idea how to reach her. Everything had once been so easy, and now he could feel her withdrawing by the day.

Rolling onto his back, he threw his arm across his eyes. He was so fucking tired, he couldn't see straight. Working his ass off didn't seem to be getting him any further ahead, but he didn't know what else to do. Letting his family down wasn't an option. His grandfather had instilled too deep a respect for family honor and too solid a work ethic in him for that.

If anything, his father was even more of a workhorse. It had been six months since his *avô* had died and elevated his father to Pride leader. Which made Tomas the heir to the South American Panther Pride.

His stomach roiled at the thought. Everything had changed so damn fast, his head was still spinning half a year later. He'd been sent to tour the Prides after he'd turned thirty, which was the custom of Panthers. Since he hadn't found his mate in his own Pride, he went to see if there was a match for him in one of the other Prides. It had been fun to socialize and flirt with all the single women, but he'd also been there to represent his Pride to the other leading families. His grandfather had been counting on him to make a good impression, and Tomas would have bent over backward if it would have pleased that old man. He'd meant the world to him, a steady guiding force that juxtaposed so sharply with the strictness of his father.

As Tomas lowered his arm to look at Ciri, the lovely slope of her back, her golden skin, he remembered how everything else had ceased to matter the moment he'd met her. She had been *his*, every instinct inside him demanding that he claim his mate. It had been right, perfect, and they'd married as soon as humanly possible. The quiet tranquility of her personality had drawn him like a magnet, such a contrast to his high-energy, high-stress lifestyle. Being with her had centered him, grounded him in a way he'd never really felt before. He'd been excited with the prospect of introducing her to his family and Pride.

But his plans had gone awry before they'd even left Japan. Instead of a leisurely honeymoon to cement their bond, they'd been called back because of his grandfather's unexpected passing. Within days of that, his cousin Miguel had mated into the leading family of North America, and that had come with an offer to have Tomas serve as Second in command here in San Francisco. The show of support from another Pride was the best way to solidify his father's position as the new leader in Brazil.

Tomas and Ciri had been bounced from one continent to the next, with no regard for what they might need. The Pride came first. It always had, it always would. It was the one thing his conservative father and progressive grandfather had unequivocally agreed on. But his father was so concerned with Tomas doing a good job as Second, they had a daily phone call for a progress report. It was difficult to handle. He was thirty and still felt like an untried youth. He chafed under his father's constraint, but he also recognized that he had no experience in this area and his father did. In the end, it was his father who would have to deal with the possibly bloody consequences if Tomas failed. He had to earn his place as heir and prove that he was good enough to succeed his father.

He could do that. He *would* do that.

And none of those affirmations told him how to keep a grip on his marriage. He was trained as a politician, not as a husband. There, he was failing, and he didn't know how to prove himself. The violent, turbulent arena of Panther politics was often less daunting than dealing with his wife. Tomas felt himself pulled in too many different directions and he didn't know how to give everyone what they needed. Hell, there were days when he didn't even know *who* he was anymore. The heir, the husband . . . both were things he had no idea how to be, both had expectations he didn't know how to live up to.

Both were roles he didn't want to fail in, but he was barely keeping his head above water. He tried to do his best, tried to hide how fucking lost he was, but in the end, some part of him knew he was drowning.

There was no way he was sleeping now. His mind churned with disquiet, his belly coated with cold dread. Shoving to his feet, he grabbed a pair of pants out of the dresser and pulled them on.

"You're leaving?" Ciri's soft voice reached him in the dark, but she didn't turn to look at him. There was no inflection to her words, nothing to tell him if she even wanted him to stay.

"I was going to do some paperwork in the sitting room." Once, he would have asked her to join him. When they'd first arrived, there'd been many late nights where they'd sat together on the couch, shoulders brushing and thighs touching as they worked on their laptops. More often than not, those sessions had ended in lovemaking.

God, those had been the best moments of his life. Just *being* with her.

How had something so perfect crumbled so fast?

God, she hated these things. It was a daily ritual of awkwardness that bordered on painful.

Pulling in a slow, calming breath, Ciri straightened her shoulders and smoothed her simple sheath dress before she strode down the grand staircase. Her fingers trailed along the polished banister, and she admired the lovely curve of wood and the exquisitely appointed foyer. The gritty elegance of the antique furnishings was nothing like what would be found in

Japan, but the artist in her couldn't help but appreciate the aesthetics of the Pride's den.

Unfortunately, that was where her enjoyment of this place ended.

As she worked her way through the mansion, she passed Panthers in human and cat form, stretched out on the furniture, each watching her as she went by, staring in the way only cats could. Looking for weak points to exploit. She was the outsider here, and she had to restrain the predator inside her from baring her fangs in challenge. Controlling the Panther was something she'd been trained to do since she'd gained the ability to shift during the rush of hormones at puberty.

She sighed and tried not to let her shoulders droop. Showing weakness in front of any Pride was a dangerous gamble, especially the leading family. Her mate would feel the need to overcompensate for her, and he worked too much and too hard as it was. So much so that she spent more time alone now than she had when she was single.

Swallowing hard, she masked the hurt of that, the loneliness that ate at her soul. Some days she felt hollowed out from it. In the beginning, he'd made time for her, talking to her, asking for her opinions. They'd had quiet moments that were just for them. But in order to finish everything he needed to do in a day, more and more of his time had been eaten away by his duties. Which left her with no one to rely on.

Compressing her lips, she lifted her chin. Her life hadn't turned out the way she'd hoped, but no one wanted to hear her complain. It would only show weakness, and God forbid there was any weakness in a leading family member. She rolled her eyes and then quickly shielded that expression before anyone witnessed it.

"Hello, Mrs. Montoya." Eva, the Pride's newly acquired butler, held the door open to the dining room.

"Hello," Ciri replied, and the response was echoed from a woman coming down the hall from the other direction.

Andrea Cruz Montoya, sister of the North American Pride leader, and mate of Tomas's cousin Miguel. She was tall and lithe and as lovely as any former model could hope to appear.

"Good evening, ladies." Miguel turned the corner just a few steps behind his wife. Cool and collected as always, the man had an aura of quiet competence that should have been reassuring, but just intimidated Ciri.

That level of perfection she could never live up to. It simply reminded her how out of place she was in any leading family. They were the royalty of her kind; every move they made was scrutinized and shredded in a way that only felines could manage.

And because she'd mated to Tomas, she was one of them now.

"Good evening, Miguel. Andrea." She nodded to them both, allowing them to precede her into the empty dining room before she went to her accustomed place. Disquiet fluttered in her belly. The last thing she wanted was to eat, but she had no choice.

There were never any choices anymore. They'd been stripped from her one by one in the six months since she'd married. She stuffed that horrible thought down into the deepest, darkest corner of her heart. She loved Tomas and Tomas loved her. That was all that mattered. That was everything, wasn't it? Grabbing the glass of wine in front of her plate, she gulped down a drink.

Every Panther dreamed of having a mate, a person destined just for them. Not all Panthers had one, and hers was handsome, charming, and charismatic. He'd swept her off her feet from the first moment she'd met him. Asking for more would be selfish, wouldn't it? She had what every shifter wanted. She forced herself to relax and not give in to the dread that curdled in her belly. She hated these damn family dinners the Cruzes insisted on. She couldn't imagine ever being comfortable with them. She had nothing in common with these people.

In Japan, the Pride lived by tradition. It was valued there, important. Change was slow and carefully considered. They were very advanced in business and investments, but the Pride itself respected the past and learned from it before rushing into the future. America was different in every possible way. She liked some of the youthful enthusiasm in this Pride, but she didn't agree with their impatient drive to change the world.

"Man, you're insane!" Two identical men came barreling into the room, one of them colliding with the doorjamb. Both of them laughed, one a boisterous, booming guffaw while the other chuckled softly. The louder one was Diego, she reminded herself, and the other was Ric. Everyone in the Panther world knew the Cruz twins were half-wild. And they shared everything from their jobs as the Pride's legal counsel to their love of extreme sports to their mate, Isabel.

"I'm not crazy, I'm creative." Diego flashed a wicked smile and waved at the room before dropping into his seat. "Just ask my mate."

"She's my mate, too, idiot." Ric rolled his eyes and heaved a long-suffering sigh. "He's always been the slow one."

"You're the one who couldn't keep up when we were snowboarding in Tahoe last weekend." Diego thrust his fingers through his hair. "Dude, I love fresh powder. There's nothing better—except a fresh blowjob."

Ciri choked on the wine she'd sipped. The blunt way the Cruzes discussed sex never failed to startle her.

Andrea snorted. "So, what makes you creative and not crazy, baby brother? Because I'm only seeing the crazy side tonight."

12

Diego arched an eyebrow. "Just something I want Ric to help me do to Isabel tonight. She'll love it."

"Say no more." Miguel held up a staying hand. "Really. Say no more."

It had never happened that three Panthers were mated in a permanent ménage, and some didn't think it was possible, but Ciri had met the twins' mate and liked her immensely. She'd become the only person in San Francisco whom Ciri could even begin to call her friend.

Unfortunately, Isabel wasn't there yet. Neither was Tomas. So there was no one to cling to when Antonio and Solana Cruz walked into the room. Ciri fought the need to rise and bow to the leaders—the larger-than-life rulers of shifters on an entire continent. She'd found that such formality was unwelcome here, which would have been a sign of serious disrespect in Tokyo.

"What's for dinner tonight, does anyone know? I'm famished." Antonio's grin showed the kind of charisma that Americans would have attributed to John F. Kennedy. It invited the kind of intimacy that would never be acceptable to the Asian Pride leader. Antonio was known for his progressive politics, so much so that in more conservative circles, he was considered a bit extreme.

"Duck à l'orange, sir. Or so Isabel said at tea." Ciri quickly swallowed more wine when every eye in the room swung toward her. A blush rose to her cheeks. She hated being the center of attention. Give her a quiet corner and a computer to design her graphic artwork and she would be happy.

"Sounds delicious." Solana glided toward the table and let Antonio seat her beside him. She wore blue jeans, a tank top, and ropes of pearls. Somehow, she pulled it off.

Solana and Ciri had gotten off on the wrong foot, and little warmth had developed between them since. A few bumbles when Ciri first arrived had branded her as a conservative elitist, which wasn't true. What was right in Japan was always wrong here.

"Did I miss anything?" Tomas strode in, a man on a mission, with purpose. The sentiment reflected him perfectly. He bent to kiss her cheek before sliding his big body into the chair beside her. His shoulder and thigh brushed hers, crowding into her space, always touching her. Larger than life, just like the Cruzes. As she supposed any Pride leader or heir should be. How she matched him, she didn't know, but fate had decided it was so.

"The summit is coming together nicely. I talked to the European Pride and the African Pride today. The European leader is reluctant to come if Cesar Benhassi will be here." Antonio settled back in his chair, stroking his fingers down his chin.

Diego growled. "We're allied with Benhassi, and he's a good leader. The European Pride can kiss my ass—any issues between those Prides is Europe's fault."

Waving his wineglass in an expansive arc, Tomas jumped into the conversation. "The point of the summit is to have representatives from all Prides, to hash out issues, and to open up new avenues for trade in other continents."

Solana popped an appetizer into her mouth and chewed thoughtfully. "Europe may abstain from the summit altogether."

"That would be foolish of them. They'd be cutting their nose to spite their face." Tomas looked at Antonio. "It would also look bad for the summit if you couldn't get everyone to be here. You cannot allow this to happen."

And the conversation only got more opinionated from there. Isabel led a few Panthers in with serving trays, dinner was devoured, and the argument continued with each member of the family weighing in. Tomas's eyes sparkled, his hands slicing through the air as he made his points. He was truly in his element in these political discussions. Only Isabel and Ciri remained silent, focusing on their meals rather than the deliberations. It was part of why they got along so well. They were both quiet people who grew up as regular Pride members— neither of them was comfortable making decisions that affected their entire world.

Only Isabel wasn't mated to a future leader, so she could remain in the background to some extent. Ciri knew her time was running out. The moment they returned to South America, she'd be expected to take a hand in ruling, and she dreaded it. Her muscles tensed as the conversation grew louder, as opinions grew fiercer. This environment was not how business was conducted in Japan, where respect was paramount, and criticisms were voiced gently and indirectly. On every level, she didn't fit here.

"What do you think, Ciri?" Tomas's voice interrupted her musings, and she glanced up to meet his gaze. This was his way of trying to push her into participating in politics the way he did. She didn't mind discussing these kinds of topics with him in private, but this was as public as one could get. Silence engulfed the room as they waited for her response.

She felt every inch of color drain out of her face. The Panther in her wanted to snarl at being backed into a corner, but she'd spent her entire life having peacekeeping drilled into her. Confrontation wasn't in her nature. She liked tranquility in her life. Why was that so wrong?

Her mouth opened, but no sound emerged. The bottom dropped out of her stomach and bile rose in her throat. She feared the duck might come back up again. "I—I don't think you can have a global summit without every continent on the globe represented."

There, that was gentle enough, and it was a reiteration of

what Tomas had said, wasn't it? Or had he changed his mind when she wasn't paying attention? Her stomach pitched and she swallowed hard.

"You see?" Her mate whipped around to face Diego. "One more on my side."

Relief exploded inside her. She hadn't said the wrong thing this time. Surreptitiously, she wiped her clammy palms on her legs. Her claws scraped against the silk fabric, and she hadn't even realized they'd slid forward. She ran her tongue across her teeth to make sure she hadn't bared her fangs at anyone, but the sharp canines weren't in evidence. Thank goodness.

This was why she despised these family dinners. Everyone else engaged in a lively dialogue and debated matters in Panther politics, and she got to watch her mate's passionate nature in action. He thrived on these issues, advocating for his opinion, and everyone else seemed to feel the same way. But she'd found out quickly enough that her own more traditional understanding of Prides was not welcome at their liberal meeting of minds, so she kept her own counsel unless forced to speak.

Her first week here, they'd been arguing about whether they should take in a Panther who was mated to a human, much like another couple who currently lived in the Pride, and Ciri had reacted with horror. Humans and non-shifters were not allowed in Prides.

Except in this one.

When she'd said it, the sentiment had fallen into a horrible, awkward silence as Ciri realized that Solana had once been thought to be a non-shifter, a Panther unable to assume cat form, and thus unable to breed or form a full mate bond. Ciri had forgotten because the other woman had recently borne a child and therefore was *not* a non-shifter.

Non-shifters were considered a curse to most Prides and were destined to be outcasts. Except in this Pride. Panthers who were unfortunate enough to be mated to humans were expected to leave the Pride, but still maintain the secrets of their race, even to their mates. It was considered essential for the greater good of all Panthers. Except in this Pride. Anywhere else in the world, people would have agreed with her wholeheartedly. Except in this Pride. She'd tried to apologize for her rudeness to Solana, but the damage was done. After that Ciri never willingly spoke up again.

Worse, she'd embarrassed her mate and he'd had to explain to her that when she spoke before she considered all sides of the situation, she could cause problems for his entire Pride.

It was a responsibility she didn't want, and while she might learn to make peace with it someday, it was never something she would have asked for.

2

She was being stalked.

A shiver of awareness went up her spine. Ciri froze in place just outside the door of a small boutique, one predator sensing another. The fading sunlight made it more difficult to see, but her acute feline eyesight pierced the gloom. The last thing she wanted was to be caught unawares in foreign territory. In Tokyo she'd have the advantage over her hunter. San Francisco wasn't her city, and that meant she was in much graver danger.

Kuso!

Every curse word in all three of the languages she knew ran through her mind. Not that it would help her out of this situation. She inhaled slowly, trying to sort through the crowd of human smells, food, car exhaust, and the strange moist scent of eucalyptus that infused the city's air. She wanted his scent, wanted to know her stalker's essence. The Panther inside her clawed for the freedom to hunt, to kill, but she caged it as she must in the presence of humans. To reveal one's nature to the general population was to bring a death sentence down on one's head.

Bitterness shot through her. If she hadn't disliked this city before, she certainly did now. Her mate was supposed to be here with her, but instead she was alone, as she always seemed to be now that she was on the wrong continent. She'd thought mating meant she'd never feel alone again, but something had called Tomas away from this outing they were supposed to take together, which meant she was playing fetch for him as if she were his assistant rather than his wife. Then again, something always called him away.

And now it might get her killed.

Her heart leapt when she saw a flash of dark hair surfacing from the crowded street. That was *him.* She knew it—she felt it in her bones.

A Panther. Large and male. Her senses screamed at her to run, and she spun on her heel to dart into the throng of people shopping in Union Square.

She sincerely doubted that she'd outrun him, but the oppressive feel of his rage closed around her. He was getting closer.

Turning a corner, she broke into a swift trot, squeezing between people to try to get some distance from her pursuer. Her narrow skirt hampered her movements as she swept down the sidewalk, her hands shaking at her sides, a cold sweat beginning to bead her face. She'd have no fear of a human, but this was a shifter who wanted to hurt her. The tinge of his madness coated her tongue with its rancid flavor.

There was no one to help her, no one to ask for aid. Calling anyone on her cell phone would only slow her down . . . and anyone who answered would be far too late. Instead, she pushed herself harder, trying not to pour on so much speed that the people around her noticed she was moving far too quickly for a human woman. Reining in the need to *run* was the hardest instinct she'd ever had to fight.

Glancing back, she saw that same flash of dark hair and tanned skin before he disappeared into the crowd again. He was closer than he had been before, and bigger than she'd thought. Her stomach clenched, adrenaline flooding her veins. *Faster.* Oh, God. How much faster could she go without giving herself away?

Her breath rasped in her tortured throat, her lungs burning as she panted for air. Some distant part of her brain recognized that this was more from panic than exertion, but he was *gaining* on her. She would be caught in the horrible maelstrom of hate that poured from him. Her belly turned and it was all she could do not to gag, to bend over and vomit. Only the knowledge that it would slow her down stopped her from giving in to the overwhelming urge.

Whipping around another corner on an unfamiliar street in this godawful city, she slammed into a large Panther male. She hissed, struggling madly against his iron-hard grip.

"Ciri, what's wrong?" The big hands on her shoulders shook her almost gently. "Ciri?"

She fought against her own feral nature, barely kept her claws sheathed. A snarl ripped from her as she looked her captor in the face.

A wave of shock hit her as she realized it was the Pride's non-shifter. She recoiled automatically and he let her go, lifting his hands in a supplicating gesture. "Are you all right?"

His smell was different. Clean and sane. The stink of madness dissipated, leaving her standing there shaking and sweating. She sucked in a calm breath, trying to regain some modicum of her self-control. "I'm fine."

She might throw up on his hiking boots, but she was unharmed and that was all he really needed to know. It was odd to see him up close. She forced herself to focus on this man rather than the one who'd chased her. Anything to hold the horror at bay for a few minutes.

She stared up at the sandy-haired man. A non-shifter. A cursed cat. Until Antonio Cruz came to power, no self-respecting Pride would admit they'd fostered such a freak of nature. She cringed inwardly at the cruel thought, but the superstition was deeply ingrained in the shifter culture.

"Benedicto." His name finally came to her, and she winced after she'd blurted it out.

His smile was wry. "Just Ben."

She noted that he didn't offer his hand to shake. Guilt twisted through her that she was so uncomfortable around a young man whose timely appearance might have saved her life. A lifetime of training made her scuttle backward when he stepped toward her. She couldn't help it.

The glint in his bright blue eyes was more amused than offended and he moved to give her a wide berth. Stepping to the cement curb, he opened the door to a large Jeep. "Can I offer you a ride home?"

A flush of embarrassment heated her cheeks at his courtesy. It contrasted starkly with her own rudeness. Thrusting her arm toward him, she offered him a hand that trembled. "Thank you for your help."

Surprise reflected in his gaze and he stared down at her hand for a moment as if he were uncertain what to do with it. Then he reached out, squeezed her fingers for a split second, and withdrew. He cleared his throat and motioned for her to get in the vehicle. "Shall we?"

"Yes, please." Anything to get away from here. Hiking up her pencil skirt as best she could, she managed a graceless hop up into the passenger seat. Pulling on her seatbelt, she settled against the leather upholstery and laid her purse neatly on her lap. She fumbled for something to say to this non-shifter, something that had nothing to do with her stalker or the scent of terror that saturated her clothing in sweat. "This is Ricardo and Diego's Jeep, isn't it?"

"Yeah. Ric said I could borrow it." Ben wheeled the Jeep away from the curb and wended his way into traffic. "The twins are in meetings all night."

Like most cats, Panthers were nocturnal, their days beginning just before dusk. Ciri had been up early to get to the shop before it closed. The last of the sunshine disappeared, and streetlights began to wink on. The farther they went from Union Square, the more her shoulders relaxed. The feeling of being watched faded and she sighed in relief. "Meetings. I'm sure they'll love that."

Ben chuckled. "The twins don't like much that cages them, but their work is important."

"Of course." Ciri drew in a shaky breath and let it ease out. Her heart stopped pounding, and she finally got the shaking in her limbs under control. Exhaustion slammed into her as the adrenaline rush crashed. She sagged against the seat, wanting nothing more than to be back in Japan, in her own bed, and curled up in sleep. But that wasn't to be. She was stuck here in this strange country and this strange Pride, with a mate who became more a stranger every day. She stuffed away the sad thought, trying to accept her fate. It was an ongoing struggle, but it was for the best. Even her parents agreed when she called to talk to them every week. Acceptance, harmony, peace—that was paramount.

"May I ask why you were running?" The question was quiet and undemanding, which seemed to be characteristic of the man himself. Then again, a non-shifter would have learned young to keep his head down and try to blend in.

She glanced at him out of the corner of her eye to gauge his reaction. "Someone was following me."

Instead of brushing her off, he nodded. "I didn't sense anyone, but you seemed scared. I imagine my appearance changed their mind about your viability as a target."

"I suppose so." A sigh escaped her. He hadn't sensed anything. She had no idea how sharp a non-shifter's senses would be. As good as a full shifter's or not? Would anyone else believe her if no one could back up what she said? She hadn't managed to make friends with many Panthers here. There was no way the leaders would trust her word. Worry gnawed at her, and she just wanted to escape all of it and be somewhere safe. Somewhere thousands of miles from here.

"Did you see what they looked like?"

She shook her head. "He was tall with dark hair. Other than that, I just sensed him. He was . . . angry."

"Then I'm glad I happened along." Ben favored her with a kind smile. "Once we're home, Isabel will give you some of her famous pastries. Some food will settle you. It always helps me." One hand left the steering wheel to pat his lean belly, and Ciri had to wonder if food had always been plentiful for the non-shifter.

Guilt slithered through her once more. She was railing against being taken from her home, when this man may not have had enough to eat. At least she had always had an opulent Pride roof over her head and enough food to sustain an army within easy reach. She swallowed and focused on something besides herself. "What were you doing there?"

Ben pointed to a leather case in the backseat. "Taking pictures. That's what I do."

"You're a photographer?" That piqued her interest, drew her attention from her own troubles. As a graphic designer, Ciri was always intrigued by what other artists did with their work.

23

"Photojournalist, specifically." He gave her a glance that said he knew she was avoiding the topic of her stalker. "The shots I took are for a local newspaper. I'm heading out of town in a few weeks for a story in Bali."

"Who's that for?"

His broad shoulders shrugged, and she had to remind herself that he was a half-decade younger than her. He had turned twenty a month before—and Ciri only knew that much because she'd wandered into the kitchen when Isabel was making a cake for the occasion—but he seemed . . . older. The young man had ancient eyes. "A travel magazine. They want a big glossy spread."

"You also take pictures for Andrea's clothing line, don't you?" Ciri had spent an entertaining evening with the fashion designer when she'd come to Tokyo for a fashion show. That Andrea was the Pride leader's sister and was mated to Tomas's cousin played into the political closeness of the two Prides. When he was younger, Antonio Cruz had served as Second in South America the way Tomas served as Second in North America now. Ciri didn't pretend to understand the political intricacies and undertones that went along with leadership and heirs and Seconds. She was learning because she had to, but it wasn't natural for her like it was for her mate. It made her head spin, and seemed much too dangerous a game to play.

"Yeah, I shoot for Andrea occasionally. I take the jobs that pay." Ben made a sharp left turn and pulled up to the mansion's front gate. "Here we are."

Seeing the Pride's stronghold sent an enormous surge of relief coursing through her. She wanted to sink into that sense of safety, but could she really count on it here? She clenched her trembling fingers, took a breath, and fought the panic that had never abated since she'd come to San Francisco. Since she'd lost her husband's attention—his love—leaving her alone.

She glanced at Ben. "Thank you for helping me and thank you for the ride."

"Not a problem." He reached out the car window and typed in a code on the keypad, then set his palm against a scanner. Several video cameras swiveled around to zero in on the vehicle. After a moment, the gate swung wide to admit them. "I hope you're going to tell Antonio about what happened today. He'll need to know for security reasons."

"Okay, thank you. Good-bye." She didn't wait to finish the pleasantries with Ben, though she knew she was being rude again. Fumbling for the door handle, she shot out of the Jeep the second it rocked to a halt.

As wide as the distance seemed to be between her mate and her, she still wanted the protection of Tomas's arms around her right now. She wanted to feel not so isolated, she wanted . . . what they'd had before politics had interfered in their marriage.

She ran for the door of the sprawling mansion. The Pride's ever-competent butler, Eva, swung the door open just as Ciri reached it. "Thank you."

She tossed the comment over her shoulder at the other woman as she hurried by, making a beeline straight for Tomas's office. He was there; she could smell him. Every part of her soul ached for her mate. She needed him now. After a brief knock, she pushed the door open before he could respond.

He half-rose from his seat when he saw her, his brows arching. "Ciri. What a surprise. I thought you'd be out shopping longer than this."

The room looked like him. The rich furnishings were all leather and dark wood, with wild accents. One entire wall was blood red, and a pair of crossed *katanas* were mounted on it. Gifts from her Pride. A spear sat above them, from his visit to Africa. It emphasized how different they were—power and violence versus peace and serenity.

25

A small smile curled one corner of his mouth, and he looked happy to see her, which was so unusual these days, it was almost enough to make her burst into tears. She shoved away the storm of emotions that threatened to batter her into the ground. Peace and tranquility, she reminded herself. Her mouth opened, but no words came forth. When it came to her mate, she didn't know *how* to say what she needed to say. Not without creating strife between them, and she couldn't stand the conflict.

Hell, she didn't even know *what* to say to him anymore.

Ciri just stood there staring at him, and Tomas had no idea how to react to her sudden appearance. Normally, she avoided his office and anything that reminded her of his status in the Prides. The thought both worried and annoyed him, as it always did, but he dismissed it.

"Have a seat. I'll get us some coffee." He dropped a quick kiss on her cheek as he passed on his way to a large wooden sideboard his mother had sent from Brazil.

Ciri's essence overlaid the more masculine scents in the room, and it was all he could do not to drag her into the nearest dark corner and have his way with her. But there was work to do, and never enough time to do it. "Did you stop off at the calligrapher's to pick up everything we ordered for the dinner and ball?"

It was supposed to take place the night before the summit began, and would ease people into peaceful negotiations and good will. Tomas was in charge of planning it, as well as other parts of the summit. He'd also volunteered to be a neutral party and try to get the European Pride involved. A phone call with Spain was on his schedule for later this evening.

"No. I was about to go into the shop when I sensed I was being followed." Ciri shivered in the warm room, her arms wrapping around herself.

Tomas froze with his hand poised over the coffee carafe, a jolt of shock punching through him. His hackles rose, and the Panther within him snarled. "A human threatened you?"

Her eyes were wide when they met his, upset obvious in their dark depths. "A Panther hunted me."

"A Panther? Someone from this Pride?" His talons scored his palms when he fisted his fingers. If one of Antonio's people had gone after Ciri, Tomas would shred the offender to ribbons. "Who? I want his name."

She made a negative sound in her throat. "It wasn't anyone I've met before. He wasn't from this Pride."

Tomas blinked, shaking his head to push away the feral instincts and let the logical man rule the moment. A Panther in North American territory that wasn't in the Pride? The number of Panthers on the planet was incredibly limited, which was an ongoing problem for their race. For a cub to be conceived, both parents had to be in Panther form and claimed in a mate bond. Not all Panthers had mates, and their breeding rate was low. Extinction was an ugly possibility that always loomed over their people. The likelihood that an unknown Panther existed outside the purview of the Prides was little or none. "Are you sure it was a Panther?"

It was the wrong thing to say, and he knew it as soon as the words came out of his mouth. He tried to backpedal, but her hiss cut him off.

"I know what I sensed, Tomas. He was a Panther—one I've never met before. He was large, with dark hair and tanned skin. And he hunted me." Her words were stiff. There was something in her gaze that was almost reproachful. It was a look he'd become far too used to in the last few months.

"All right. He was a Panther." He tried to keep his voice as neutral as possible. The last thing he wanted was to make accusations. "Are you certain he wasn't someone you'd met before?"

"You think I'm lying about all of this?" Her chin lifted, her expression daring him to admit it.

"I never said anything of the kind. Don't put words in my mouth. I'm asking how certain you are about what you sensed, but I don't think you're lying." And he didn't. No matter what else might be wrong with their marriage, he knew Ciri wouldn't deliberately deceive him.

"But you think no one else will believe me." Her lips flattened into a line.

He sighed. "You've had some difficulty adjusting here, and people know that. It's not unfeasible for them to think this is an offshoot of that."

"You think they'll say this is some kind of excuse to get out of North America because I can't adjust?"

"I can't control what other people think, Ciri. But, yes, it is possible that Antonio and Solana will think that." If they did, it could be a serious problem for Tomas. He'd have to consider how best to deal with this before he approached them. It was no secret to anyone that Ciri's dislike of this Pride and her newly elevated rank among Panthers had been a sore spot since the moment they'd left Japan.

"I know what I sensed." Her eyes narrowed to dangerous slits and she hissed low in her throat, which was unusual for her. She usually avoided confrontation of any kind—and he thought it was unhealthy to let bad feelings fester. Something else they disagreed on. At the moment, the Panther was as evident as the woman, and cats were fearless. "I'm an adult, Tomas. I don't feel the need to make up imaginary friends *or* imaginary foes. If I wanted to leave here, I could buy a plane ticket to Tokyo right now."

Matching anger flashed inside him. He struggled to control

it. His father was always in command of himself, and expected the same of Tomas, but it wasn't in his nature to back down from a challenge. Ciri had the ability to push all his buttons in seconds. The mere mention that she could leave, that she might get on a plane and abandon him iced his anger down to chilly dread. No. He couldn't lose her. Not ever. He tried to muddle through the mess they were in as best he could, tried to show her by example that they could handle living here for a while.

The least she could do was make an attempt to fit in and get along with the people here. "You could *try*—"

"I *have* tried, Tomas." She rose from her seat, her hands planting on her hips. Her fangs bared. "I accept that this is where we live, but I don't like it here. I *don't* have to like it here."

He sighed and shoved a hand through his hair. How the hell had they gotten onto this topic anyway? Everything seemed to devolve into this same argument—when he could even get her to talk about it. "No one said you did, but you should try to make the best of it. It's not forever."

"Yes, because then you'll drag me down to Brazil for the rest of my life." She tossed her dark sheet of hair over her shoulder and crossed her arms. "Another foreign Pride that I didn't care for."

He threw his hands in the air. "We were only there for a few days, and the Pride was still in mourning for my grandfather. You didn't see everyone at their best. At least give it a chance."

She just stared at him, a mutinous jut to her chin. "It's not like I have a choice, do I? I haven't had a choice in any of this."

"Neither have I!"

"No, but we're with your old friends now, and your cousin is here. You get to talk endless politics, which you love, and then we get to go to your Pride forever." Her eyes went wide, her lips pursing. "That sounds terrible for you."

He tried to keep from her just how confused and jumbled up he felt most of the time, because he didn't want to add to her misery, but how could she not see they were equals in this? This wasn't exactly how he'd seen his life going either. He dragged in a breath and tried for some restraint. "You're being unreasonable."

A disgusted sound erupted from her, and she spun toward the door. "Then let's stop the conversation if it's so trying for you. I hate fighting with you anyway. Good-bye."

That spurred him into action. He grabbed her arm. "Ciri, wait. Don't do this."

"I haven't done anything. You're the one acting as though I'm a fool or a child because I don't care for this Pride, because I miss my own people, because *someone here hunted me.* I think it's perfectly reasonable to be upset about all of those things." A sheen of tears in her eyes belied the scorn in her voice. "Clearly, my mate doesn't want to hear what concerns me. How silly and childish of me to think so. Excuse me."

"Wait, please. I don't want us to fight right now either." He reeled her in, and set his hands on her shoulders, squeezing lightly. "I do want to hear what concerns you, and I do believe you were followed. I never said you were childish, and I *never* called you a liar. I'll ask Antonio to look into this."

"Thank you." The words were brittle, and her gaze told him she doubted that he'd do as he said. That stung, but he was fair enough to admit this fight hadn't made it sound like he had much faith in her, even though that hadn't been his intention. What a mess they'd made of things, and they only seemed to make it worse whenever they spoke.

He kissed her forehead because he couldn't resist the temptation to have his hands on her as often as he could. "Of course."

It was the way of Brazil, to touch, to kiss. Other Prides didn't share that local quirk, so he'd learned to curb it, but in his own land and among his own family, he felt free to reach out. With Ciri, he reveled in it when they were alone. He could never get enough of touching her, and it fed a need that ran far deeper than his culture. She was his mate, and he would crave her all the days of his life. It was that simple, and that complex, especially with the strain in their relationship.

She leaned closer to him when his lips brushed her forehead. She was almost in his arms, almost close enough to truly kiss him. He stopped himself, but he wanted her. *Dios,* how he wanted.

Ciri was suddenly desperate for the closeness, the contact. Anything to drive away the fear that had gripped her. Anything to hold it at bay, just for a little while.

Anything to avoid her entire life.

She wasn't doing very well at acceptance or harmony today. Shoving her fingers into his hair, she pulled him down for a kiss. She felt him startle, could taste the surprise on his lips.

He groaned, his breath emerging as a ragged gasp. "Are you sure this is what you want?"

"Don't I seem certain?" Cupping his cock through his pants, she pressed herself against him. "I don't want to think about what happened today. Help me forget."

A dark flush raced over his cheeks. When was the last time she'd initiated sex between them? Weeks, maybe longer. She'd followed his lead, allowing her feral side to dictate her actions. Now, she needed this connection so much it shredded her normal reserve. The last thing she could stand right now was to be alone, her mind trapped in an endless loop of the terror she'd felt. Her heart contracted at the thought, and as hard as she'd been trying to push it away, it wouldn't be ignored. Somehow, she had to burn off this feeling. This was as good a way as any.

Better than crying over things she couldn't change—she'd tried that in the last six months and it didn't help at all.

Her mate shuddered and groaned at her touch, and a rush of power filled her. Yes. This was what she needed. No longer helpless—right now, she was in control. Passion swamped her, and dampness gushed between her thighs. Yes, this was how it should be. Not just avoidance or anger, but desire.

Stroking her hand up and down the length of his shaft, she felt him grow thicker, harder. A little moisture seeped through his slacks and she grinned. His hips thrust forward, harsh sounds of lust spilling from his lips.

"Ciri, look at me."

Meeting his gaze, she was caught, drawn in by the need on his face. He was just as handsome as he had been the day she'd met him. His dark hair was brushed back in thick waves from his forehead and tapered to a neat point at the back of his neck. She used to love to thrust her fingers into those locks and muss them up, just to encourage him toward a little peaceful relaxation. When they were in private, he didn't need to be a Pride heir or an expert in politics and business or anything other than her mate.

He hadn't listened. They never seemed to get through to each other, and it made her heart ache.

"Ciri . . . please." The desperation on his face, the way his chest heaved for breath, the gold that swirled in his dark irises, the deadly points to his fangs, all told her exactly how much he craved her. That he was willing to beg only fed the power coursing through her veins. That he didn't try to take control from her told her he understood how much she needed this.

Good. For once, they were on the same page.

She reached for his belt, jerking the leather free from the buckle. In moments, she had it and his fly open. Her fingers slid into his slacks, and his hot flesh was in her hand. Pulling his cock from his pants, she stroked him with one hand and reached in with the other to cup the soft sacs at the base of his shaft. She rolled them between her fingers. He choked, his intense gaze locking on her, and she could feel the effort it took to restrain himself. His passionate Latin nature was never more in evidence than when he was aroused.

A bead of moisture pearled at the tip of his cock and she bent forward to lick it away.

"*Madras*, Ciri!"

She chuckled, released her grip on him, and stepped back until her ass hit the edge of his desk. Pulling her blouse over her head, she tossed it aside. Her hands were busy unfastening her skirt while he stared at her, so much lust in his eyes as he watched her strip that she felt scorched by the heat. Her nipples peaked tight, and she wanted his hands on them, his mouth. "Take your clothes off, Tomas. I want you."

Chin jerking down in a nod, he obeyed her. He wrenched his tie over his head, his fingers flying as he unbuttoned his shirt and pulled it off. His pants hit the floor and he stepped out of them as he strode toward her.

He swept an arm over the desk with a quick gesture, and most of the papers flew off. Then he scooped her off her feet and onto the hard wood surface. She fell back on her hands, arching herself to let him know exactly what she wanted. He didn't disappoint, dipping down to suck her nipple into his warm mouth. He laved the tight tip before switching to offer the same treatment to her other breast.

A hiss erupted from her throat, her back bowing to press herself deeper into his mouth. His lips shaped around her nipple and he suckled hard. Tingles exploded over her skin, and she barely contained a whimper. Her head fell back, her pussy clenching on nothing as the sensation rocketed through her. He bit her gently and she cried out.

It was so good, but not what she wanted.

Reaching between them, she circled her fingers around the base of his cock. The silky skin stretched taut over the steely shaft. It pulsed in her hand, and she pumped him between her fingers. He shuddered, hissing in animalistic yearning.

Leaning forward, she gave one of his flat brown nipples a delicate lick. His big body jerked in reaction, his fingers came up to grip her knees, pushing them apart until he could slip in to touch her as intimately as she was touching him.

"You're so wet." He gritted the words out between clenched fangs.

"Yes." Drawing him forward by the cock, she spread her thighs wider. "I want you inside me."

"*Dios, yesss,*" he hissed.

She rubbed the head of his dick over her slick lips, pressed it hard against her clit, and arched into the contact. His hands hit the desk on either side of her hips, his claws scraping the polished wood. She loved teasing him, loved having this big, strong male as hers to command. This was the only time she knew she had his undivided attention.

Guiding his cock to her opening, she eased the head into her pussy. He purred, shoving forward to work his length deeper into her channel. The stretch was divine. And she wanted more. She wanted the rest of the world to disappear until there was only her, only him, and only this.

She wrapped her legs tight around his muscular flanks, forcing him closer, deeper into her pussy. The thrust and recoil of his hips was fast, rough. Perfect. It drove her to the very edge of sanity, made her gasp for breath. Sweat made their flesh cling wherever they touched, and the scent of sex in the air was intoxicating. He ground himself against her clit, and she almost exploded. Her nails turned to claws on his back, and she knew she hurt him, but he only fucked her harder, gave her exactly what she craved.

He groaned. "I want to come."

So did she. "Not yet. Not yet!"

Choking, he snarled and held back his orgasm while she did the same. Her sex spasmed each time he entered her, tension twisting tighter until she thought she'd die before she gave in. Her body jolted when his pelvis slapped against her, when his cock filled her. The soft hair on his chest rubbed over her nipples, stimulating the sensitive points. All of it made her want to scream.

Her control broke.

"Now, Tomas! Make me come." She raked her claws down his flesh and bit his shoulder.

"Thank God," he rasped.

His hands grasped her ass and lifted her off the desk. He powered his cock into her over and over. Panther screams ripped from both of them as they reached orgasm together. She shoved her fingers into his hair and forced his mouth to hers. The kiss was a wild thing—they bit at each other, tongues twining, groaning into each other's mouths. Her pussy pulsed around his cock, squeezing him in waves that left her shaking and almost feral. His hot come filled her, and the Panther within her purred in satisfaction.

He groaned and set her back on the desk, his hands gliding up and down her back. "Are you all right?"

"Yes," she breathed. Relaxing, she rested her head on his strong shoulder and closed her eyes.

The phone blared loudly, a rude awakening from the euphoria that fuzzed her thoughts. They jolted at the sound, and he slid out of her. Their groans echoed in the office, but the phone hadn't stopped ringing. She felt Tomas's hesitation, knew he warred with his ever-present duties as Second.

She snorted. As if there was any real contest. She was simply grasping at straws to comfort herself. "Just answer it. You know you want to."

"It can wait." But he flinched toward it when it rang again.

"You're just going to be thinking about it until you call your father back." In other words, his mind would be on something besides her. As usual.

At least he didn't bother to deny it. "Are you sure?"

"I need a shower. I'm going to our room." Resignation shimmered through her, and her shoulders drooped. She was suddenly exhausted once more. Heaving a sigh, she picked up her clothes, shook out as many of the creases as she could, and put them back on. Her nose wrinkled as she caught a whiff of the cold sweat in the fabric. Her fear was a stink she'd have to get rid of as soon as possible.

"No, stay with me for a little while." He pulled on his own clothes, moving with a speed no human could match. The phone rang a third time, then a fourth. He grabbed her arm and reeled her in to sit on his lap, and then snagged the phone.

She settled her head against his shoulder, too wiped out to argue with him.

"Pai?" The Portuguese word for father rolled off his tongue, and as usual, he became an entirely different person in the blink of an eye. Gone was the warm lover and in his place was a zealous taskmaster. The younger version of his controlling sire. "Yes, of course I read through the documentation you sent me." He rifled through the paperwork on his desk and then leaned to the side to retrieve some of the scattered sheets on the floor. "I was just in the middle of an e-mail to you when I . . . when there was an interruption. No, I'm back on track now."

And even though she was in his lap, curled against the heat of his body, she was dismissed just that quickly for the more important aspects of his life. It was depressing, disheartening, and made her regret her impulsive need to find comfort in his arms. But he was her mate—wasn't she supposed to put him above all others?

Too bad he didn't feel the same.

A waft of hot sex mixed with the cold sweat hit her nose and her stomach heaved. The combination wasn't a welcome one. As much as she enjoyed sex with Tomas no matter how they weren't getting along, she didn't like the isolation she dealt with or the reminder that sex was all that earned her attention from her mate. She sighed, too spent for anger or tears. She forced her emotions to freeze into numbness—if she couldn't manage acceptance, then she could achieve nothingness. It was a habit she was unhappy to realize she'd developed.

Closing her eyes, she let the exhaustion take her. She simply couldn't deal with any more, so she retreated into sleep.

3

Dialing the phone before it could start ringing, Tomas tried to keep it from waking Ciri. She needed the sleep, needed the healing that rest would bring. The line connected, and a cool female voice answered. *"Hola?"*

"Teresa, it's Tomas." He'd sent the heir to the European Pride an e-mail saying he wanted to speak to her, but he thought this would be better finessed over the phone than in writing.

"It's good to hear from you again." They'd met for Tomas's visit to Spain during his mating tour. He'd liked her, thought she was intelligent with a keen understanding of Panther politics. If anyone could get through to—or go around—her father, it was her. "What can I do for you?"

The amusement in the question told him she knew exactly why he was calling. Of course she did. He decided bluntness would be the best approach for getting what he wanted. "You can get your father to send someone to this summit. Better yet, you can come yourself."

A long pause greeted that statement, and then she sighed. "I would love to, but Father is dead set against this. Trust me, I've tried. Every political benefit I can come up with isn't good enough."

"Hmm." He leaned back in his chair, cradling Ciri close to him. That Teresa was on his side helped, but he doubted he could bring something to the table she hadn't already considered. He stroked a hand down his mate's back, and then he froze as an idea struck him. "So give him an argument that's not political."

"I'm not sure what you're getting at."

A ferocious smile curved his lips. "How old are you? Twenty-eight? Twenty-nine?"

"My twenty-ninth birthday was three months ago." Her words were slow and drawn out, as if she wasn't certain she should tell him anything more.

"Perfect. That's close enough to thirty to justify a mating tour, isn't it? Give that benefit to your father, and see if he'll agree to let you leave Spain." He resettled the phone between his shoulder and his ear. "If your stop in San Francisco happens to coincide with the summit . . ."

"I can sell that."

There was a small hitch to her voice that made him sit up straighter. "But?"

Another long pause fuzzed the phone line. "It's nothing you need to worry about. I'll work this out, and I'll be there."

"I look forward to it, then." He stroked his hand down Ciri's hair when she stirred. "I'll let Antonio know you're tentatively on board until you confirm with your father."

"Do that."

"Good. Thank you, Teresa. I think this is an important event for every Pride to take part in."

"I couldn't agree more. I'll be in touch. Good-bye."

He said his farewells and hung up.

"That was well done." Ciri's head came up and she blinked sleepily.

Warmth flooded his chest at the unexpected compliment. When was the last time anyone had told him he was doing *well* at anything? "Thanks. I hope it works out."

"Then I hope that for you, too." She yawned and pushed to her feet. "I'm going to our room. I need a shower."

"Okay. I'll see you for dinner." He watched her shoulders stiffen at the mention of dinner, but she merely nodded and left the room.

It was the first time since she'd swept into his office that he'd had a moment of silence, where he'd had nothing pressing to occupy his thoughts. What to do about Ciri's possible stalker had nagged at the back of his mind, but now it was his sole focus.

He didn't know what to do.

He hadn't told his father what had happened to Ciri tonight. And letting Antonio know about it could turn into a sticky situation. Ciri was hunted in North American territory, and it was this Pride's responsibility to keep visitors safe. Tomas liked Antonio, respected him, and didn't want to cause trouble. Then again, if they proved Ciri's instincts were wrong, it would cause trouble for the South American Pride.

And knowing all of that did little to help Tomas decide how to move forward.

"*Mierda,*" he swore softly.

On reflex, he reached for the phone to call his grandfather. His hand paused as it hovered over the receiver and grief delivered a fresh blow.

He couldn't call his grandfather.

The man had died over six months ago. Tomas swallowed hard, his chest tightening until he could barely breathe as the pain of it hit him once more.

His fingers began to tremble and he dropped his hand to flatten it against the top of his desk. Pulling in slow, deep breaths, he blinked back the sudden moisture that burned his eyes. *Dios,* everything was in chaos. His life, his career, his marriage. One moment he'd had everything together and the next the world was spinning out of control.

Not for the first time, he wished he had someone to talk to. But there was no one. Telling Ciri how her being threatened was a political problem would be cruel, and would only add to her dislike of her position in the Prides. He couldn't do that to her. His father would want Ciri silenced or he'd use this against Antonio, depending on which he thought would offer the best advantage to the Brazilian Pride.

Sighing, Tomas pushed to his feet. He didn't know if it was the smartest thing to do, but the right thing to do was keep his word to Ciri. Antonio needed to know if there was a rogue Panther in his territory, for everyone's safety. Tomas would just have to deal with his father when it was done.

Leaving his office—the Second's office—he strode down the hall to see his cousin, Miguel. The man's metal and glass office was as cool and composed as he always looked. He glanced up the moment Tomas tapped on the open door. "Yes, *primo?*"

His cousin had been the Second in North America before he'd mated with Antonio's sister. And Antonio had been the Second in South America for almost fifteen years, relegated there until his tyrannical father's death. Most Seconds only stayed for a couple of years, and for Ciri's sake, Tomas was grateful they wouldn't be here for longer than that. The sooner she had to deal with her true position in their Pride, the better. She'd be unable to sidestep it in Brazil.

He cleared his throat. "I need to speak to Antonio, and I'd like you to be there, if you have a moment to spare."

"Sure." Miguel slid a hand down his long hair. He squinted. "Is this about someone chasing your mate?"

Tomas chuckled. "You always find out everything first."

"That's my job."

"So Antonio knows already?"

"Not yet. He's been in a conference call with the African Pride, but he's just finished." He unfolded his long body from his chair, moving to join Tomas at the door. "I was about to go talk to him myself. We can do it together."

"*Gracias, primo.*" He clapped his cousin on the shoulder. "I wish we were still in the same Pride."

Miguel slipped his hands into his pockets and began walking down the hall. "I'm happy with how things stand. My best friend is my leader, his sister is my mate." He shrugged. "Besides, I . . . I doubt Uncle Pedro and I would have agreed on how matters should be handled."

Tomas didn't agree with how his father handled things either, and they'd had more than one argument about it. He seemed to be at odds with everyone lately. However, he did agree with how Antonio handled matters, which was probably why he was far less eager than Ciri to leave San Francisco. He could see some of his grandfather's influence here. Antonio had learned a great deal as Second in South America. "I can see how you might feel that way. I'm glad I have the chance to be second in command here—to see how other Prides operate."

The Second system had been in place for centuries, a way to cement bonds between Prides. Humans once used arranged marriages in much the same way, to ensure alliances. But Panther matings were determined by destiny, and the Second system worked so well that even when arranged marriage went out of fashion in most cultures, Seconds were still sent to other Prides.

Seconds were usually members of a leading family, and most

typically the heir to the current Pride leader. The position lasted for a few years and then another Pride would negotiate to have a Second from among their members chosen. It was a constant struggle to stay in control, to form the strongest allegiances, to exert the most influence in other Prides.

He had no idea if what he was about to drop in Antonio's lap would gain him influence, or lose some of the influence he'd been trying to build. In the end, he was more worried about Ciri's safety than anything else, so he ignored the political consequences and did what he had to for his wife. The feline inside him still wanted to rip apart anyone who would frighten his mate, but the man was in control now, and logic would serve her better than bestial instinct.

It took only a few minutes to find Antonio in Solana's sitting room, their infant daughter cradled in his brawny arms. He nodded when they came in the room. "Gentlemen, how can I help you?"

"One moment." Miguel stepped back and held the door open as a lanky man strode in. "I asked Landon to join us. I think his input could be important to this conversation."

Toasting everyone with his ever-present cup of coffee, Landon smiled easily.

Solana's eyebrows arched. "Well, if we need our security advisor, then something is definitely going on. Start talking."

Crossing his arms over his chest, Tomas worked to hide his discomfort. Landon wasn't a Panther. He was mated to a Panther—or as mated as a human could be considering he couldn't assume cat form or bite and mark his mate. Antonio had allowed him to join his Pride along with his wife, and this was the one area that Tomas wasn't sure he supported the other man's decision. He knew Ciri disagreed with the idea vehemently. But no matter what they thought, Antonio could do what he pleased in his own Pride, and Landon was an expert in security. Even if he weren't a shifter, Tomas could count on his abilities in that area.

"Who wants to go first?" Antonio settled his hip against the arm of Solana's chair, jiggling the baby when she started to fuss.

There wasn't much to tell, but between Tomas and Miguel, the story was out in under a minute. Landon began pacing in front of the window, his brow furrowed in concentration as he absorbed every word. "Can she give you a description?"

"No, she just said it was a Panther." Tomas shrugged helplessly. "Other than 'tall with dark hair,' which describes the majority of Panther males, she only sensed him. But she was quite certain." His shoulders were tense as he waited for them to deny the possibility, to question his wife's sanity. *He* believed in her, but her unease in the United States hardly endeared her to these people. Still, he'd defend her with his last breath, make them listen. He wanted her to feel safe here.

"Huh." Landon sank into a chair, his coffee cup dangling from his fingertips.

"The Ruiz family." Miguel straightened away from the wall, his face suddenly alert. "I can't think of anyone else."

Solana went ghostly pale, her hand groping for Antonio's. "It's been almost two years, though. Why would they suddenly resurface now?"

"It seems unlikely." Antonio covered his wife's fingers with his own. The two reflected a loving, united front. Exactly how Tomas wanted to be with Ciri, exactly how they pretended to be, but weren't. Antonio's eyebrows drew together in a deep frown. "As far as we know, they weren't even in San Francisco anymore."

Landon unfolded his lanky body from his seat. He nodded to the Pride leader. "I'll look into it."

"Thank you. I look forward to your report."

It was then that it hit Tomas. As much as he trusted Ciri not

44

to lie, he'd had his doubts that her instincts hadn't played tricks on her. That she'd been stalked, he'd had no problems believing, but he hadn't been certain there could be a rogue Panther out there. It had seemed more likely that a human had hunted her. But Ciri's instincts *hadn't* been mistaken. A Panther had stalked his wife, threatened her, wanted to hurt her. The fury he'd been fighting since the moment she told him exploded within him. He balled his fingers into fists. He wanted to hunt the shifter down and rip his throat out. He wanted to kick his own ass for having any doubts. Guilt followed on the heels of his anger. He'd all but assured her she'd be called a liar, had sex with her, and then ignored her in favor of his work. He was glad he'd kept her with him, holding her close, but anyone would have needed more comfort than he'd offered, especially his *mate.*

He had no idea how—or even when—he could make this up to her, but he would try. At the very least, he owed her an apology.

Antonio's gaze landed on Tomas, and he cleared his throat. "I'm sorry that your mate was threatened in my territory. The situation will be rectified as soon as possible."

Reining in his anger and self-loathing, Tomas nodded formally to the older man. A calmer corner of his mind noted that what should have been a fool's errand had turned into the possible political quagmire he'd feared. He groaned inwardly at the thought of explaining this to his father. "My thanks. I trust that you'll do everything in your power to keep this Pride and its visitors safe."

"I appreciate your faith."

He nodded to Miguel. "My cousin has great faith in you, and we've known each other for many years, Antonio. Of course I trust that you'll honor your duty."

There was a hint of surprise in the Pride leader's gaze, and

Tomas wondered if he'd said too much. He was speaking for his Pride now and not simply for himself. With his father constantly checking up on him, he couldn't afford a misstep.

Antonio returned the formal nod. "Thank you, Tomas."

The reserved gesture just emphasized what was always bombarding him of late—everything had changed.

It was difficult to deal with just how *much* things had changed. He could no longer view Antonio as an older friend he looked up to. He could no longer view Miguel as simply his cousin.

Both of these men whom he'd had simple, straightforward relationships with now gave their first allegiance to another Pride. A wide gulf had opened between them.

"Please keep me up to date on anything Landon discovers about these Ruiz men. Or anything else pertinent to what happened with my mate." Tomas glanced between Antonio, Solana, and Miguel.

"Of course. Please inform *Tio* Pedro that we're doing everything in our power to see this resolved." His cousin held the door open, offering the same courteous nod.

Tomas exited, wandering back to his office, his mind latching onto the interaction with the two older Panthers in order to avoid thinking about his mate. In some ways, it was interesting to have them treat him with more . . . respect wasn't the right word, because neither man was the type to look down on others, but perhaps it was that they now viewed him as someone whose word carried more weight, who acted as though he had authority.

He supposed they were right. As the heir apparent to the South American Pride, he had to be aware that what he said and did reflected on his people, on his father. His opinions could no longer simply be given lightly. Or passionately, as was his nature. He had to stop and think first.

It was difficult, because he'd once been able to discuss anything with both men, and they'd help form his opinions on many issues. There had been many a night when he'd listened to them debate Panther politics with his grandfather, and many more when he'd been old enough to join in the debates himself. His grandfather had been good about listening to everyone's point of view and understanding that everyone's experience could be used to benefit the Pride.

Antonio now used that same philosophy to rule his people, which was refreshing to see, because Tomas knew that the openness would be slowly strangled out of his Pride by his more authoritarian father. There was nothing wrong with how his father ruled, it just wasn't the approach Tomas would take when he took over. His father operated under the assumption that if the responsibility for the Pride was his, so should the power be his. He wasn't one to delegate authority. Tomas pressed for more flexibility from his father, though he had doubts about his success.

He had hope in seeing how well Antonio had done with the North American Pride. Esteban Cruz had been far worse than Tomas's father, but Tomas didn't have Miguel as his right hand, nor did he have boisterous younger brothers who would help him change the culture of the Pride.

He was totally alone in his political agenda.

His younger sister was quiet and shy, not the type to help enforce his rule. She would do as she was told by their father and she would do the same when Tomas took over. Their mother supported his father in everything, using her charming smile and sharp claws to see that his will was done. But, like Tomas's sister, his mother did as she was told.

Ciri wasn't the type to do that. She hated everything to do with power and political strategy—he had a feeling she'd hate every second of being the Pride leader's mate. It worried him.

Something else he had no idea how to deal with. Something else he would have asked his grandfather about. Something else he desperately wished he could consult with Antonio and Miguel about, but the distance between them seemed to widen by the day.

Much like the distance between his mate and himself.

The thought made his gut clench, but he couldn't hide from it. What had started out so beautifully was quickly devolving into nothing more than a sexual liaison where they lived their lives, ignored each other most of the time, and slept together whenever the urge struck them.

He knew matings weren't guaranteed to be happy, knew couples who had marriages exactly like that and were perfectly content with it. Perhaps he should be also. Perhaps that was another role he needed to learn how to fit. Antonio and Miguel's matings seemed more . . . open and caring, but they weren't Tomas and they weren't married to Ciri.

He sighed, exhausted by the endless round of concerns that never seemed to have a solution. What more could he do? He tried to set a good example for his people, serve them well, do everything Ciri needed him to do, and it never seemed to be enough.

Perhaps that was the truth. He wasn't enough. He couldn't have what he craved because he wasn't enough to hold on to it. He'd never live up to his grandfather or Antonio as Pride leaders or as husbands.

It was thoughts like this that made him want to give up, to throw up his hands and walk away. Why did he beat his head against the wall? It would be easier to simply stand aside as heir. Doubtless his sister would be the perfect heir for his father. She'd never disagree with him, do exactly as he wanted.

But then what would happen when she became leader herself? Would it be fair to do that to her, to his Pride? Would she know how to maneuver amid the treacherous dealings of the Panther Prides? No. Because *he* had been raised to do this. *He* was the one who loved this. The strategizing, the guessing games, the challenge. He just wished he wasn't so damn alone in all of this.

And none of it helped him deal with Ciri's stalker and his boorish behavior this evening.

4

_____

God, he was tired. He could sleep for a month and still not feel rested.

Tomas carried a tray of food up the main staircase and down the hall to his suite. He didn't feel like dealing with other people right now, and he hoped Ciri felt the same. Then again, if she had her way most of the time, she'd eat in the kitchens with the regular Pride members rather than the formal dining room with the leading family.

Tonight, the food was a peace offering. He usually wanted to hash things out between them, get the disagreement out in the open and deal with it, but that wasn't her way. If she were like him, she'd have yelled at him for picking up the phone instead of being there for her. The problem was, he had too many priorities pulling at him, and all of them demanded first place. That was no excuse for his behavior toward her tonight, and he needed to apologize for not protecting her, for doubting her. That was hardly the way to encourage open communication between them.

He nudged the door open with his shoulder and paused to

watch her. It struck him how much she'd made the suite *hers* since they'd moved here. The energy of the place was always soothing to him. The walls were a pale green, and he thought the wallpaper was silk, but she'd added touches of art, of Asia, to the place. A painting of stark, bare branches transitioned to budding pink cherry blossoms. A set of woodblock prints. A small tray held a rock garden, with sand raked in patterns around smooth black stones. She sat on a large leather sofa that reflected his taste more than hers. Hunched over her laptop, her brow furrowed in concentration as she worked. After a few moments, she started, her gaze flying to meet his. "Is something wrong?"

"Why would anything be wrong?" He arched an eyebrow.

She pressed a few buttons on her computer and set it aside. "You've been standing there for a while, haven't you?"

"Your instincts didn't warn you?" He asked it even though he knew the answer. He was her mate, so her instincts wouldn't alert her to any danger with him. He would never harm her. She shrugged and looked away. He sighed, stepped into the room, and kicked the door closed behind him. "I spoke to them."

"You did?" Her eyes went wide, and he could see the momentary shock before a shy smile curved her lips. "You told them what happened today?"

Dios, the smile hit him like nothing else could. It was the same smile she'd given him the first time he'd seen her, curled up with her laptop, creating one of her designs.

He'd never seen anything lovelier.

Her hair parted simply in the middle, falling in an inky sheet just past her shoulders that framed her heart-shaped face. Her small nose and full lips did nothing to distract from the exotic beauty of her dark eyes. They'd captured him immediately, drawn him in and never let go.

He cleared his throat. "Yes, I did. They've had some troubles with an outcast family in the past, but those people had left the city. They're looking into when and why the outcasts might have returned."

"I hope they can find out." Her grin bloomed into the most open expression that he'd seen in weeks. "I'm glad you told them."

"I'm sorry I thought anyone would doubt you. I should have given more care to your needs. I'll try to do better in the future."

"Thank you." She tilted her head to the side, but her smile remained in place.

He wanted to hold on to this so badly, and he was sure he'd do something else that might push her away. "I—I brought dinner, if you'd like to join me."

"No family dinner tonight?" The hopeful tinge to her voice sent a reflexive shaft of impatience through him. Was she never going to accept her place as a member of the leading families? That wouldn't change, no matter how she avoided it.

Suppressing the urge to start one of their endless arguments, he decided to ignore her stubbornness for the time being. *That* would definitely kill this receptive mood she was in, and after the day she'd had and the way he'd treated her, she deserved to have her way. He set the tray on the low coffee table and sat in the middle of the couch. "I thought we could eat in here, unless you're working on a commission."

"I am, but it can wait." She straightened her legs from where she had them tucked beneath her, but didn't move closer. "I'm ahead of schedule."

"Oh. Good." When had it become so awkward to have a simple conversation? Could they sound more stilted? She was friendlier with complete strangers.

He lifted the lids from the two plates and set them aside. From the corner of his eye, he saw her hesitate, then tentatively scoot over to sit next to him. "Isabel made Beef Wellington tonight."

"She's an amazing chef." Ciri reached for her plate and began to eat with delicate feline movements.

He pushed aside a bowl of fresh strawberries and picked up a bottle of wine. Pouring a generous portion for both of them, he handed her a glass. They could definitely use it. He took a deep swallow of his, let the mellow flavor of the red wine settle on his palate. It combined well with the meal. A sigh of contentment filtered out of him and he relaxed back into the soft leather sofa. "This is delicious."

"Mmmhmm." Ciri sniffed the wine, gave it an experimental taste. Her actions were so catlike, he had to grin.

"You're so beautiful." The words were out before he could stop them.

She stilled and stared at him for a moment, her expression quizzical. "Um . . . thank you?"

Was it really so strange for him to compliment her? He thought about it and winced inwardly. Yes, it was. Just as her complimenting his work with the summit had been unusual. Anymore, they argued, they had sex, or they ignored each other to avoid the other two options. Moments like this were rare, but moments like this had always been rare in his family. He didn't remember spending much time with his father—he was always working for the betterment of the Pride. His mother saw to the children's needs, and she made everyone's lives comfortable.

As usual, he had no idea what the hell he was doing. He was just throwing himself into it, and falling flat on his face. He thought he knew what he wanted, he just didn't know if he and Ciri could get to that. They were more like his parents than his cousin and Andrea.

"You're welcome." He reached for the wine, realizing his silence had made the moment even more awkward. "I think we need more of this."

"Yes, please." Handing him her glass, she let him fill it to the brim.

Throughout dinner, they managed to kill the bottle, and chatted in spurts about inconsequential things. It was nice. He enjoyed spending time with her—there just never seemed to be enough of it to spare for things he *enjoyed* doing. It was always spent on whatever his duties dictated, but he liked his work too, so it had never bothered him before his marriage.

"Will you be going back down to the office after this?" She shifted her head on the sofa to look at him.

He plucked a strawberry from the bowl they'd situated between them. Taking a bite, he let the juices, sweet pulp, and seeds roll over his tongue. "Probably. I have some more paperwork to handle before I can call it a day."

"You need an assistant."

"My father doesn't have one." No, his father managed to take care of everything on his own. He expected Tomas to be able to do the same. So did Tomas. If he couldn't equal his father in work ethic and productivity, how could he consider himself fit to be the next leader? He had as much to prove to himself as he did to anyone else.

Her gaze went from his hand to the bowl between them. "Oh, you took the last strawberry. I love them."

"You can have the rest." He proffered what remained of the fruit.

Leaning toward him, she licked his lower lip. "Perhaps we can share."

His body reacted before his mind did, his cock hardening until it ached.

Dios, this was twice in one day that she'd come to him instead of him reaching for her. A tiny part of his mind warned him that earlier had been about her fear and right now was about the amount of wine they'd both consumed, but his instincts cared nothing for the man's rationality. His mate wanted him, and he craved her as he would nothing else in his life.

Taking the last bite of strawberry between his teeth, he offered her the fruit. She melded her lips to his, and the fruit dissolved in their mouths. He didn't know which was sweeter—the strawberry or her. He knew which he wanted more. Her. Always her. He all but inhaled her, sliding his tongue between her lips and taking her taste into his mouth. She wrapped her arms around his neck, and he pulled her into his lap, arranging her legs until she straddled his thighs.

The soft feel of her sex against his made him feel as though he'd explode out of his skin. He loved touching her; he could never get enough of it.

His claws shredded the cotton of her shirt. He wanted his hands on her skin. Now. Retracting his talons, he caressed her back, flicked open her bra, and ripped the garments away.

Then her breasts were free and he buried his face between them to inhale the scent of her. So lush and exotic and uniquely Ciri. His mate.

Turning his head, he licked one nipple, teased it until it puckered to a tight point. Little moans spilled from her, and she slid her hands into his hair to try to guide his lips to her breast. He chuckled and pulled the nipple into his mouth, sucking strongly. Her back bowed and she cried out. "Tomas!"

He purred, loving the sound of his name on her lips, the sharp passion that edged her voice. It was moments like this that made him recognize why they were mates—when there was nothing but the raw connection between them, the Panthers shedding the trappings of civility, the synergy was perfect. They fit each other.

Her claws scraped against his scalp when he released the

nipple and blew a cool stream of air on the tight tip. She twisted in his arms, her sex grinding down on his. He turned his head to take in her other nipple and she made a frantic noise that drove him to the edge of madness.

Sweat broke out on his forehead, and he wanted her pants *gone.* He wanted her naked in his arms. Shoving her to her feet, he had her stripped out of the rest of her clothing in a few seconds. The firm feel of her ass in his hands when he skimmed her panties off made him shake with lust. Yes, he wanted her this way. He ripped open his pants to free his dick. Spinning her around, he brought her back down on his lap so that she straddled him again, but faced away from him.

"Wh-what are you doing, Tomas?" She gasped and braced her hands on his knees.

But he could smell her increased moisture, could sense the intensity of her arousal. This new position excited her. She flexed her thighs, opening herself to rub her slick flesh against his cock. He hissed, his fangs punching through his gums. The Panther within him clawed for the freedom to rut with its mate. To claim her again and again until there was no distance between them and never would be.

Wrapping her tight in his arms, he coasted one hand down her belly to tease her clit. The wetness he found made him snarl with the need to be inside her. She made a choked sound, her hips arching to meet his stroking fingers. "Do you like this, Ciri?"

"Of course I do." She wriggled her ass, her dampness gliding against his cock. "You can't tell?"

It was his turn to choke at the sensual movement, the pleasure. She purred, casting a wicked glance over her shoulder at him. He slipped his other hand up to fondle her breast, and he watched her eyes close in ecstasy. "I can tell. I just had to hear you say you want my hands on you."

"I love . . ." She shivered, her fingers locking around his wrist to hold his hand tighter to her clit. "I love your hands on my skin."

His heart had tripped at the word *love.* When was the last time she'd said she loved him? When had he last said it to her? A long time. Far too long, but it didn't feel right to voice the sentiment anymore. He knew what he felt for her, but did she still feel the same? He had no idea, and he didn't have the guts to ask. It was the one fight he couldn't face. He didn't want to hear the truth, because he was terrified of what she might say. It might bring an irrevocable end to what he needed more than he needed his next breath.

"Tomas, please. I want you inside of me." Her talons pierced the fabric of his pants, digging into his knees.

He bent forward and licked a path up her delicate spine. She shivered, and he watched goose bumps break out across her skin. He nipped at the edge of one shoulder blade, let her feel the sharpness of his fangs. "Oh, you'll have me inside you, my mate."

She stilled at the tone in his voice, no doubt sensing that he had something interesting in mind. The she-cat would be too curious to resist. He chuckled. Slipping his hand farther between her thighs, he thrust two fingers deep into her pussy. She moaned, the sound loud in their sitting room. He liked that, the feline within him fascinated by every detail of her. Her skin, the smell of her, the feel of her, her every reaction.

Twisting her nipples one at a time, he kept them hard little points that made her squirm the longer he played with them, the more sensitive they became. At the same time, he continued to shove his fingers into her wet sex. Every cry of his name, every one of her little movements, made fire burn in his veins. It took every ounce of his control to keep a grip on the wildness inside. Her body moved with his fingers, grinding down on his hand to increase friction. He pushed her hard and fast, felt the clench and release of her inner muscles, sensed when she was close to orgasm.

And then he stilled his movements.

The feline screech of a Panther ripped out of her. "Don't stop!"

"I'm not stopping." He drew his fingers from her pussy and trailed them to her ass. Teasing that tight pucker, he slipped one finger in, using her own slickness to ease his path. He moved back and forth between her two channels until he could slide three digits into her. "I'm just getting started."

"Yes, yes, please, *yes.*" She shoved her hips back to take him, her pussy growing even wetter for him, her excitement a heady aphrodisiac that drove him to the edge of sanity.

He needed her. Now. Right now. He couldn't wait. Jerking his hands from her body, he clasped her hips and guided her backward until his cock pressed to her anus. With inexorable pressure, he forced the head of his dick into her ass.

"*Tomas.*" The sound was little more than a guttural hiss, and he could sense how close the Panther was to the surface, how she struggled to control it. He liked that she grappled with the same instincts he did.

Working his cock deeper into her anus, he groaned at the tightness of her channel closing around his shaft. It was almost too narrow for him, but it felt fucking amazing. He brought both hands up to circle her nipples, and she choked on a sob. He could feel her muscles shaking, and he decided to increase her torment.

Gliding one palm down, he rubbed a finger over her hardened clitoris. She jerked against his hold each time he swept over the bundle of nerves. "Why aren't you moving?"

"You move, Ciri. Ride me." He eased away from touching her clit, just teasing her unless she arched forward to increase the contact. She did, of course, and they both cried out at the sensation.

She followed his lead, pressing into his stroking fingers, working herself faster and faster on his cock. Sweat slid down his skin, and he lifted his hips to drive himself deeper into her ass. The leather couch creaked under their weight, adding to the carnal symphony they created together. The sounds she made each time she forced herself down on his cock made him shudder, barely able to hold on to control.

"I'm going to . . ."

"Come," he ordered, pressing down directly on her clit and shoving his dick inside her. She screamed and her inner muscles closed around him. He kept stroking her, kept thrusting into her ass. Her body heaved each time he flicked a finger over her clit. "Don't stop moving until I tell you to. Come for me again."

Her hair fell forward as she bowed her back to work herself harder on his cock. The movement revealed the mate mark on her nape—the only scar that a Panther could keep. Sleep healed them of all other wounds. The magic of their race didn't grant them longer life than a regular human, but it did guarantee them extraordinarily good health for the years they had. Ciri's back arched, and possession swamped him. *His.* She wore his mark. She was his in the most fundamental claiming of their kind.

The thought made him explode. His body locked in a tight line and he jetted come into her ass. He pinched her clit hard, and she sobbed, shaking as another orgasm thrummed through her. The clench of her muscles around his cock just dragging the sensations out for him. It was perfect. Being with her like this was the only time in his life when everything felt right, when he didn't have to fight to prove himself.

Unfortunately, it didn't last beyond the time it took reality to return and all the problems to resurface and begin nagging at the back of his mind. He sighed as his high crashed. Wrapping his arms around her, he rested his forehead between her shoulder blades. "Are you okay?"

"Yes, that was good."

He chuckled, kissed her soft skin. "I'm glad you liked it."

"Didn't you?"

Purring softly, he repeated her own words to her. "You can't tell?"

Whatever she might have said was drowned out when the cell phone in his pocket blasted out a loud samba. He released her and dropped his head back against the couch. It was a repeat of earlier. "Shit."

"Don't pick up the phone." The soft plea in her voice broke his heart.

"I won't." He sighed, stroking a hand down her naked back. "But you know Father will just call back."

"I know. Just forget I said anything. I'm sure whatever he wants is more important than this." She lifted herself off of his lap as the phone stopped ringing. The silence would only be temporary. He pushed to his feet, tossing aside what remained of his clothes.

Twirling her into a dance as the phone began the samba again, he spun her into the bedroom. "I'm not going to forget about it. We're going to talk. After we have a shower."

"Argue, you mean." She clutched at his shoulders when he dipped her backward over his arm.

"If that's what it takes." Better than her being upset and hiding it behind a wall of insufferable calm. He rolled his hips in a dance move, then swung them both around until they reached the bathroom. The tiles were a cold shock against his feet. "Let's get cleaned up first, then we'll worry about other things."

* * *

She didn't want to fight.

They stood under the hot spray of water, washing away reminders of the sex they'd had on the couch. What she wouldn't give to go back to that uncomplicated moment. That seemed to be all she wanted—less complication. She didn't see why that was so wrong.

The water ran down her body, and she couldn't help but recall this was her third shower of the day. After she'd left Tomas in his office, she had run into Isabel, who noticed something was wrong and dragged her into the kitchens to have tea. Isabel's domain was always a comforting place to be, and the other woman had a quietness that Ciri liked. While they were sipping tea together, Ben had joined them. Neither of them mentioned that she smelled of sex and fear. Instead, Isabel filled them with tea and sweets while Ben pulled out his laptop to show them the pictures he'd taken. It wasn't as odd as she would have expected to have a non-shifter spend time with her. Gradually, she'd felt herself relax. While she was inside the mansion, at least, she was safe.

An hour later, she'd felt ready to take her shower and get some design work done. That always helped her feel calm and centered. But first, she'd had to have that bath. Her own stink had been driving her nuts.

At least this shower was for more pleasurable reasons, but that sense of serenity she'd sunk into had evaporated like steam. Because Tomas wanted to argue again.

Dropping her head back, she let the water rush through her hair and run down her face.

A low growl sounded from Tomas. "You look so sexy when you do that."

She couldn't help her laugh, pushing away a few locks of

hair that clung to her cheeks and jaw. "You always look sexy. Especially wet and naked."

A flush rose to her cheeks at her own bold words, but she'd found that he liked it when she spoke of her desire for him. She preferred to show him rather than tell him, so she stopped talking and started doing. If it kept the sweetness of their dinner together going a little longer, she wanted that. She wanted it badly. As badly as the Panther inside her wanted its mate. For once, she and the cat were in agreement.

Reaching forward, she set her hands on his muscular chest. Water matted the dark curls there, and she danced her fingers over them until she touched his flat nipples. They puckered for her and she grinned. He groaned. "Your fangs are showing, Ciri."

"Are they?" Her smile widened and she ran her tongue down a sharp tooth. "Well, I will have to be very careful, won't I?"

"Madras." His hands shot out to brace himself on the slick tile walls when she bent forward to lick his nipples. She twirled her tongue around them one at a time, shaping her lips around them. The taste of his skin, the smell of him, was something she'd never get enough of. She closed her eyes, savoring him, and made certain he felt the scrape of her fangs on his flesh.

His hips jerked, and she groped blindly for his cock, knowing she'd find him hard and more than ready to take her. Moisture gathered between her thighs, and the shower spray running down their bodies only accentuated the anticipation thrumming through her.

"My turn," he rasped. His hands closed over her shoulders, jerking her upright. "I couldn't take any more."

Burying his face into the crook of her neck, he bit her hard. She jolted in shock, tingles exploding down her skin as her entire body reacted to the pleasured pain. His fingers slid down to cup her hips, pulling her up until she had to wrap her legs around his waist. Every inch of her was plastered against him, the water sealing them together.

Her nipples rubbed his chest, the hair there stimulating her sensitive flesh. He turned to press her back to the slippery wall, lifting her higher until his cock nudged the lips of her pussy. Her sex fisted, her desire ratcheting up.

"Fuck me, Tomas." She moaned, her head rolling against the wall. "Now."

He laughed, the sound strained. "As you wish."

Gravity would have impaled her on him, but that wasn't good enough for them. She tightened her legs on him as he thrust upward. Crying out as he filled her to the limit, she felt her muscles clamp down on his thick length. So right. So perfect. Her flesh was already swollen from his use earlier, and if she hadn't been so wet for him, it might have hurt.

Slipping her fingers into the silk of his hair, she used her superhuman strength to jerk his head up for a kiss. He snarled, gold flickering in his eyes, shimmering beneath his skin, the Panther showing through on his handsome face. She sucked his lower lip into her mouth, grazed it with her fangs. His movements inside her carried the same amount of ferocity as her kiss. She shoved her tongue into his mouth, and he hammered his cock into her pussy. The feel of his claws digging into her hips sent shivers racing over her skin.

The shower's steam wrapped around them, caressed them, and beads of hot water cascaded down their writhing bodies. It turned her on more, drove her ever closer to the edge. Tomas filled her again and again, the angle making him hit her G-spot every time. She hissed into his mouth, the Panther struggling for freedom. She knew her eyes would have burned to the same gold as his, both of them just short of feral.

She tilted her hips up, letting his thrusts grind his pelvis against her clit. The increased stimulation was enough to spin her into oblivion. Her pussy spasmed around his cock, one huge pulse that made her scream at the intensity of it. The sound was more cat than woman. Her orgasm continued, each convulsive wave dragging her toward the most animalistic side of her nature.

Hilting his cock inside of her, he rotated his hips and came hard. A growl ripped from him, his talons scoring her hips as his grip turned painful. "Ciri!"

They were shaking when it was over, the water still pouring over them. He reached out and turned off the shower. She let her forehead rest on his broad shoulder and panted, her heart pounding in her ears. The power of their coupling always took her breath away, stunned her with its force. She had never truly believed that sex was better with a mate until the first time Tomas had touched her.

Cradling her close, he carried her out of the shower and set her on the end of their long marble vanity. The cool stone made her shiver, but it also felt good. She leaned against him as he used a soft towel to dry them both. It was wonderful to have his tender ministrations, his sweet attention. Something that was so rare, but had typified the first weeks of their courtship. Hot tears welled in her eyes at the thought, pain spilling into her heart. She swallowed hard and pressed her face to his chest so he wouldn't notice. She wanted nothing to interrupt this moment.

As if on cue, the sound of his cell phone carried through the bathroom door. A human might not have picked up on the noise, but she was a shifter, and the ringing scraped across her nerves. Was it so much to ask that everyone *leave them in peace* for the night? Just one night! But, no, members of a leading family were always on duty.

She hissed at the second ring. "God, I hate that you can't have a life outside of being the heir."

She regretted the words the moment they fell from her lips. It would only start the fight she'd wanted to avoid.

Stiffening away from her, he met her gaze. "I can't change who and what I am, Ciri."

"But you expect me to!" Her temper flared and for once she couldn't squelch it, couldn't hide it. The upheaval of the day had broken through her carefully constructed sense of serenity.

His jaw tightened, a muscle beginning to tick there. "We've both had to deal with a lot of changes."

Squelching the urge to scratch his eyes out for managing to remain calm when she could not, she spat at him, "And still, *you're* not the one who has to change who and what they are."

"What do you want me to do, Ciri?" Gold flickered in his eyes, belying his restrained tone.

She sniffed disdainfully, hopped down from the counter, grabbed the towel from his hand to wrap around herself, and spun away. "Nothing. Forget it."

"Don't do this." He wrapped his fingers around her bicep, his grip almost painful. "Don't turn away from me."

Jerking at his hold, she gave a futile attempt at escape. He was a male feline, much stronger than her. She snarled at him, frustration shredding her control with Panther's claws. "I haven't done anything. Except mate with you."

"And you regret that?" His question was flat, his expression going carefully blank. He released her, his hand wilting to his side. She hated that, hated herself even more for doing this to him. This was why she usually resisted arguing with him. He wanted the bad feelings out in the open, but what use was hurting each other more? It didn't solve anything.

She swallowed hard and tried to pull herself back together,

but her tone still had a bite. "I regret that I had to give up my whole life for a man who can't spare an hour for me unless it's in bed."

He flinched, and she knew she'd hit her mark. "You know my work is important."

The ugly bitterness that festered in her soul poured forth. "Yes, I do. The most important thing in your life."

"The Prides *are* the most important thing." He thrust his fingers through his wet hair, droplets flying through the air. "Without them for protection, we'd all be lost—scattered to the wind with no defense against humans discovering us and turning us into lab rats."

She sighed and rested a hand against the bathroom door-jamb. "Right now, I feel like I'm lost even with them."

"Ciri . . ."

"Don't worry about it." She shook her head, closing her eyes as the purest truth came out. "I just . . . didn't realize before we were married how very different we are."

His voice softened, but she could still sense his aggravation. "I had a lot less responsibility to deal with at the time. I wasn't yet the Brazilian Pride heir, or Second in another Pride."

"I know." She compressed her lips, and just felt . . . sad. Meeting his gaze, she blinked back tears. "I know."

A hint of desperation filled his voice, and his usual ardor animated his face. "We have a lot in common."

Disbelief zinged through her. "Name something. Anything."

"We love each other."

She snorted, and she could tell that stung him. "What else? We value none of the same things. You love politics, and I want nothing to do with it. I love art, and you couldn't tell a Monet from a Picasso if your life depended on it. You were born to power, and I was born as no one special. You're Brazilian, and I'm Japanese. You're progressive, and I'm a traditionalist."

He shook his head. "We're both driven by our work, defined by it, even. We value our families and want the best for them, for all Panthers. We just go about it in different ways."

"That's not a lot of common ground."

"We can find more." He threw his hands in the air.

"When are you going to make time for that?" She shrugged helplessly. "Do you plan to give up the three hours of sleep you get each day?"

He growled. "It would be easier if you could find some way to care for Pride politics."

That foreign, terrifying rage stabbed through her again, and she flared back at him. "It would be easier if you weren't a Pride heir, but it's unlikely either of us will get what we want, is it?"

"This is important." He gestured at the Pride den around them, his hands moving in sharp, jerky motions. "What I'm doing here affects so many people. It's vital that I do well. *This is important.*"

The wilder his manner became, the more she withdrew behind her reserve. She just couldn't relate to this fervent side of him. "I understand that, but that doesn't mean I want to be the one to do it. There are other things that are important too, Tomas. Like our marriage, for example."

"I'm not saying that's not important." He jammed his fists down on his hips, magnificent in his nakedness and anger.

She arched an eyebrow. "But it's not worthy of your time or attention."

"I won't be Second forever."

Dropping her forehead against the doorjamb, she sighed. "I know . . . but you said it would get better after you got used to being Second, it would get better after the first state visit, it would get better after, after, after." She rolled her head so she could look at him. "It's never going to get better, Tomas. There's always going to be something. I know those some-things are important, but why isn't what other people value important, too?"

"The Prides are the most important thing."

"Okay." She turned around and walked away, as she did from all their arguments. In the end, what else could she do? They were mated, but they really didn't understand each other. They knew what was fundamental to the other, but many of those things were at odds. If they changed the very foundations of themselves, they would no longer be who and what they were. If they gave in to the other's needs, would they still be mates?

5

Tomas was still stewing over their argument three days later. It frustrated him and terrified him at the same time. His mate wasn't happy. Not with him, not with their marriage, and not with their fate to rule the South American Pride.

Until now, he'd told himself that she would come to accept her place, that she just needed to adjust, that she just needed to learn about what it meant to lead. After what she'd said, he was no longer so certain. What could he do about it? He was drowning in his own problems, and he just wanted this to *work*. Was that so much to ask? That one thing go right? Just *one*?

Landon poked his head into the office. "I have an update on the Ruizes, if you have a minute."

"Yes. Please, come in." Tomas motioned the lanky human to the couch against one wall.

Antonio stepped in behind Landon. "I'd like to hear this as well, if you don't mind."

"Of course." Tomas rose to get them all a glass of whiskey.

Passing snifters over to the other men, he settled into a chair next to the couch. Landon took a sip of the alcohol and sighed. "That is good stuff."

"Twenty-five-year-old Glenlivet." Tomas lifted the glass to admire the deep amber liquid. "A wedding gift from the European Pride."

"Nice." The human took another swallow, then looked between Antonio and Tomas. "I put my contacts on trying to find out what's going on with the Ruiz family. I've kept light tabs on them as a potential, but unlikely, threat to the Pride. Or so I thought."

"Right. I agreed with that policy at the time." Antonio waved a hand. "What have you found?"

"The mother, Lucia, recently passed away." The human grimaced. "She was buried in a pauper's grave."

Leaning forward to rest his forearms on his knees, Tomas asked, "And that sent the sons over the edge?"

Landon nodded. "That's the assumption I'm working with at this point, yes."

"Thank you, Landon." Antonio settled back in his seat, sighing. "The Ruizes were an influential family in my father's reign. Lucia was his lover in the last years of his life. When I came into power, they thought they'd get away with defying me. They also decided it was acceptable to harass Solana when she was an outcast and presumed non-shifter. I forbade mistreating her; they disobeyed me and tried to kill her. Roberto Ruiz, specifically, but the younger brothers, Juan and Marcos, had some involvement." He ran a hand through his hair. "The entire family supported Roberto's actions, so I cast them all out. We haven't heard from them since. Until now."

"There's more, sir." Landon gulped down the last of his scotch.

"Tell us." Tomas made a short motion with his hand. Everything these men were saying got worse and worse, and coldness fisted in his belly.

"My contacts have traced all three Ruiz sons to San Francisco. They'd been living in Chicago since they were outcast."

The knot in his gut expanded. If the Ruizes would try to murder a Pride leader's mate, then everyone was in grave danger. And Ciri had been stalked by one of them. "How big a threat would you call them now?"

"It's difficult to say. I think it's safe to assume they blame this Pride—specifically the Cruz family—for their fall from affluence and for the death of their mother." Landon paused for a moment, his long fingers cupping the glass in his hands. "It's possible they have a specific goal in mind, a single target. But considering their hunting of a woman they'd had no known association with, my guess is they want to make trouble for the entire Pride and any Panther who associates with the Pride."

Tomas set his scotch down, the fiery liquid churning in his belly. "Ciri said she sensed only one man."

"It could be one of them working alone, but all three are in the city." Landon shrugged, his gaze hardening. "In all likelihood, they're working together."

Antonio nodded slowly, his expression both concerned and considering. "So, what do we do now?"

"We wait. We stay alert." The human set his empty glass on a side table and stood. "I'm going to keep my people looking for them, see if we can beat the bushes and get them out in the open. It would be better if they left, but I've yet to meet a Panther that wasn't tenacious. And dangerous, when provoked."

Tomas snorted. Truer words had never been spoken. Panthers were predators. "Thank you."

Landon slid his hands in his pockets, his gaze meeting Antonio's. "I'm going to recommend that no one be allowed off the property alone, especially the women and children."

Protect the most vulnerable Pride members. Tomas and Antonio spoke at the same time. "Agreed."

The human left the room, but the Pride leader stayed where he was, sipping his alcohol. "I've known you for a lot of years, Tomas, and it may not be politic considering our positions, but . . ."

"But what?" Tomas wouldn't have thought the knot in his stomach could get tighter, but it did. Whatever the leader wanted to say, he was pretty sure he didn't want to hear it. He really didn't think he could handle one more thing falling apart.

"It's your mate. I hadn't said anything before now, but even without the Ruiz incident . . ." One of Antonio's broad shoulders dipped in a shrug. "She's not happy here."

"She'll adjust." The words were reflexive. He'd thought the same thing himself, but the last six months had been a lesson in pretending nothing was wrong, when in reality, nothing was right.

"I'm not so certain about that."

Neither was Tomas, and it made every last pressure that weighed down on him feel even heavier. It seemed no matter what he did, it made things worse. If he pushed Ciri into the very public arena of politics, it made him and his father happy, but made his mate miserable. There was no way to please everyone, no compromise to be found. The breath eased out of his lungs. "Well, she doesn't have to live here forever. I'm sure South America will be more to her liking."

The older man arched an eyebrow. "You're that sure?"

A bitter little smile curved Tomas's lips. "It's her destiny to be there, isn't it?"

"Only if you're the Pride leader."

That sent a jolt of shock through him, and everything in him rebelled at the thought. It was one thing for him to consider it at his darkest moments, but quite another for someone to voice it aloud. "That's my destiny, isn't it? It would be foolish to give that up. My people need me."

Antonio hitched his ankle onto the opposite knee. "Do they need you more than Ciri does?"

"That's beside the point."

The leader opened his mouth, closed it. "You know that I mated with Solana before we were certain she could shift forms."

Surprised by the non sequitur, Tomas tilted his head. "I didn't know that. I assumed her non-shifter status was cleared up by then."

"No."

"That was quite a risk." An enormous one, in fact. If Solana had been a non-shifter, it was possible that Antonio would have been forced to relinquish his leadership. If there'd been no clear line of succession, it could have resulted in a struggle for power . . . it could have caused a civil war in this Pride. Before Cesar Benhassi had taken over in Africa, there *had* been civil war there, so it wasn't unheard of even in the last century.

"Not to me, it wasn't." Antonio spread his hands. "The Pride might not have accepted her, but I needed her more than they needed me."

Tomas tapped his fingers on his thigh. "Andrea would have been a good candidate for a leader, especially with Miguel by her side. My sister is not of the same independent spirit."

"You're missing my point." Antonio sat forward. "Sometimes, Tomas, you *do* have to put yourself before your Pride. You're not just a leader, you're a man."

Disquiet mixed with the cold dread twisting within him. The sentiment went against everything Tomas had ever believed. "The Pride always comes first."

The older man sighed. "It's not as simple as that, not when you have a mate. It's your destiny to always have two first priorities."

"Shouldn't a mate help you with those, so they don't conflict?" Or was that simply wishful thinking? Tomas didn't know anymore.

"In other words, shouldn't a leader's mate be like your mother, and sacrifice everything she loves—including her mate—for the good of the Pride?"

He shifted uncomfortably in his seat. "My mother is happy with her life."

"I believe she is as content as she could be under the circumstances, but according to your grandfather, it wasn't that way in the beginning. She had to be broken first, like a young horse." Antonio met his gaze. "Is that what you want for Ciri?"

"It wouldn't be like that." But the protest sounded weak even to his own ears. "We both have a lot of adjustments to make. Change is always inevitable."

"Perhaps she's not the only one who needs to change."

"I'm doing my best."

"For the Pride, yeah." Antonio stood and headed for the door. He paused to glance back before he exited. "But not for your mate, and not for yourself. Think about that."

Ciri threw herself into her work, shutting out everything and everyone else to immerse herself in the intricacies of her design. Sketches lay in scattered piles around her as she sat cross-legged in the middle of the bed, hunching over her laptop.

It was her biggest commission yet. This was for a multinational company's new logo that would be incorporated into websites, letterheads, business cards, promotional material.

Her work would be out there for anyone to see, so it needed to be perfect.

She loved the challenge of making each new piece her best ever. It was almost like she became one with her computer, an entity with a single purpose—to create something unique and beautiful. At the moment, that meant adding a black swirl here, *just* the right shade of red there. She was close to finishing, and this time, she'd almost achieved her original vision. Almost.

Her client would be pleased, which was the most important thing, in the end, but for once *she* was truly pleased.

It would be a good way to end her burgeoning career.

Her breathing hitched as that unwelcome thought intruded on her concentration. She blinked rapidly, trying to clear sudden tears from her eyes. A runny nose and burning, blurry eyes would not help her make the deadline on this project. And if she was going to be forced to quit, she was going out with her professionalism intact. Damn it.

She sniffled, swiping a renegade tear away impatiently.

Why did she have to be mated to a Pride heir? Why did her life have to consist of supporting everything he wanted to do? That's what he wanted, what his family would expect. One meeting with his parents and she had known nothing less would be acceptable to them. The moment she returned to South America, the last part of her life that was *hers* would be gone. In fact, the moment her father-in-law found out that she was still working, it would be over. And with his arrival for the summit, that was it. Done. Over. Gone.

She gritted her teeth against the wave of pain, and forced herself to focus on the task at hand. This was the most important thing right now. Everything else would have to wait. That was how she'd learned to survive since she'd left Japan. Focus on one thing, one breath, one heartbeat, and she wouldn't be overwhelmed by the storms ripping through her life.

"Hey." A soft knock sounded on the door as Tomas announced his presence.

Her instincts had already recognized him, singing that her mate was near. She slapped her instincts away, still too hurt and angry about everything to want to acknowledge them.

"Yes?" She didn't even look up from her screen. He'd see the pain and demand to know what was wrong, which would only start a fight. Or, even worse, he'd decide he didn't want to deal with her feelings and just ignore them. He'd done both in the last few months and she didn't think she could handle either reaction, so she didn't give him the chance to react at all. It was the only way to stop herself from coming apart at the seams.

"Dinner will be served soon." He hesitated for a moment at the edge of the bed before he sighed and moved toward the walk-in closet to change.

Her shoulder twitched in a shrug. "I'll be ready in time. I'm still working now."

His deep voice floated out of the closet door. "We need to go down soon."

"You go ahead without me," she called. "I can find the dining room."

"Fine. I'll see you at dinner." His tone turned curt and rough, and she couldn't tell if it was from hurt or just annoyance that she hadn't leaped to do his bidding. It was her duty to make them look like the perfect couple, to support his every agenda. She fought down a hiss, struggling with the angry Panther within who hated being caged. Calm, serenity, acceptance.

The Panther didn't want to listen to the woman's reasoning.

Tomas came out in a polo shirt and a pair of jeans that hugged his muscular legs to perfection. It was all she could do not to drool, and her body reacted whether she wanted it to or not. Damn her hormones and her instincts.

He glanced in the mirror above the dresser, pushing a hand through his hair to tidy it. She loved the way he looked in his usual business suit, but the Cruz family, being as American as they were, tended to dress more casually for their family dinners. Which Tomas and she were required to attend.

It was odd, as was everything else about this country and Pride. In her Pride, dinners had been formal, and the leader's family hadn't had informal meals together. She sighed. Something else for her to adjust to. Normally, it wouldn't bother her, but it was just one more thing on top of *everything else* that had changed. *Nothing* in her life was the same.

Except her work, and she wasn't even going to get to keep that. She groaned in disgust and shoved away the self-pity. Her life wasn't that bad, and no one had a perfect life, did they? Tomas certainly didn't. It was clear that he'd have preferred a mate who loved his politics, which wasn't her. She might learn to deal with it, but it wasn't in her to love it.

It was too bad for Tomas, and too bad for her.

When she glanced up, she saw him still staring at her in the mirror. She looked away, put her laptop aside, gathered up her sketches, and set all of it on the bedside table. When Tomas threw himself back into work after dinner, she'd finish her design in the sitting room. Stretching her kinked muscles, she sighed at how good it felt.

"Landon came to talk to me today."

That got her attention. "Oh?"

"The family of outcasts they were worried about have been tracked to San Francisco. Antonio's decided no one goes out alone until the outcasts have been located."

"There's more than one of them?"

He nodded. "Three brothers—Roberto, Juan, and Marcos. Landon believes they may be working together to cause trouble for the Pride that cast them out, so just because you know one of their scents doesn't mean you're safe. Be careful."

"I will, I promise. You promise too." The concern on his face warmed her and she held out a hand to him. He came to her, engulfing her fingers with his larger ones.

That he enjoyed touching her was something he'd never hidden. He ran his thumb over the backs of her knuckles, lifting them to his mouth for a kiss. "You have my word."

"Good." She started to pull back. It was time to dress for dinner. She resisted the urge to wrinkle her nose.

He squeezed her hand. "I was thinking we could . . . do something together soon. Something you'd like."

Tilting her head, she arched her eyebrows. "Like what?"

"There's a new exhibit opening at the modern art museum here." A smile that was almost bashful curled his lips. "You could teach me a little about art, so I could tell the difference between a Monet and a Picasso."

It was the first time since he'd become heir that he'd offered to try something that interested her. Could they really find more common ground, as he'd suggested? What might have been hope began to unfurl in her chest. She tried to crush the feeling before it grew, but knew she failed. Hope was a dangerous thing—it could flay you alive if it was dashed. "I'd like that. Just us, together?"

"Just us." He bent forward to brush his mouth over hers, the touch gentle.

The Panther within her purred at its mate's touch. She suckled his lower lip, letting herself savor the flavor of him. Groaning softly, he swept his tongue into her mouth, deepening the kiss. She brought her hands up to clutch his shoulders, squeezing her thighs together to stop the ache between them. It was no use. She wanted him, she was wet for him, just that quickly. Her breathing sped, her pulse leaping.

He pulled back slightly, his lips swollen, his pupils expanding, his lungs bellowing. Lust flushed his high cheekbones, his hands closed over her bare legs, and he pushed the hem of her skirt higher. "I can smell your desire."

"We'll be late for dinner," she taunted. "You're shirking your responsibilities, Pride heir."

He growled and shoved her skirt up to her waist, his talons shredding her panties. She laughed when he pushed her flat against the mattress. It was moments like this that made everything worth it. If they could make it happen more often, she might be more willing to accept her fate.

He dropped to his knees beside the bed and hauled her hips to the very edge of the mattress. Excitement writhed like a live thing within her. She gasped when she felt his hot breath brush over her naked sex. More moisture flooded her pussy, and she pressed her thighs wider for him. "Please. I want your mouth on me."

A low purr answered her, and the vibrations hit her flesh as his lips closed over her hard clit. Shock passed through her and she arched off the bed. The purr intensified, and he held her down, forcing her to feel everything he wanted her to feel. Reaching down, she pushed her fingers into his hair and held him closer. His tongue slid down to stab into her sex, fucking her with his mouth.

The effect was electric, and a scream burst from her throat. Orgasm caught her by surprise, her pussy clenching on his thrusting tongue as his rumbling purr drove her beyond ecstasy. Starbursts exploded behind her lids and her fingers tightened in his hair, her inner muscles contracting. She twisted on the soft sheets, her nipples beading and goose bumps breaking down her flesh. She'd never come so fast in her life, the intensity enough to leave her shaking and sobbing.

"I want you inside me," she choked. Tugging on his hair, she tried to pull him toward her.

With a sound like a human volcano erupting, he was on the bed beside her in under a second, moving far faster than any mortal could. He simply ripped their clothing away and threw the garments aside. Then he dragged her underneath him.

His naked flesh against her made her back bow at the feel of him. Big and hot and perfect. Taking his cock in hand, he guided himself to her opening and thrust deep into her pussy. She moaned and wrapped her arms and legs around him, holding him close. Just where she wanted him.

Dark gaze locking with hers, he let her see how she affected him. His need for her was there, and it made her heart trip. He slid his dick into her, his speed almost too fast, too rough. It only excited her more, made her burn for him. She could feel another orgasm building deep within. Her muscles tightened around his thrusting cock. Close, so close. Climax beckoned, an unstoppable, irresistible force that was more powerful than either of them.

"Come for me," he breathed, and she couldn't refuse him.

She imploded, her sex fisting on him in rhythmic pulses, and every time he shoved into her set off another wave. The feel of it was so good, she couldn't help but laugh. "*Y tú, Tomas.* Come for me."

He froze over her, his head thrown back, his fangs baring as he hissed. Pumping hot fluids into her pussy, his eyes burned to gold, the Panther so close to the surface, she could see both of them in his face.

When it was done, he crashed down on top of her, and she

cradled him close. She stroked her fingers up and down his sweat-dampened back, smiling when he broke into a rough purr. Her eyes drifted shut, and a matching purr soughed from her throat.

If only it could always be like this.

6

The next day, Ciri popped into Tomas's office, slinging her purse over her shoulder. "If we hurry, we can get a good two hours in before the museum closes. Do you want to stop for something to eat afterward?"

Tomas's eyebrows rose, his palm rising to cover the phone receiver. "Today isn't going to work for me, sweetheart. I'm going to be in conference calls all night putting the final touches on which Pride representatives are coming to the ball versus those who are staying for the summit."

"Of course. Some other day." A flush of shame raced up her cheeks at how eager she'd been, how hopeful.

His voice dropped to a low, reassuring rumble. "I will go with you, Ciri. Just not today."

"You know, I set aside my work because I was excited to be with you *outside* the bedroom. I'm sorry you can't say the same." Her chin bobbed in a short nod, and she backed out of the room, shutting the door quietly behind her. If she had to fight with him to spend time with her, it didn't really mean anything, did it? She forced herself to be calm, to be fair. He *hadn't* said he'd go with her today, that was her assumption.

"Idiot," she whispered.

Tears welled in her eyes, and the hope she'd warned herself not to feel shattered around her like glass. This would be her life, alone. Raising children alone, taking care of everything. Alone.

He would handle the Pride, and she would handle whatever he delegated to her, much as he did now. She'd give up her career to be his political and social helpmeet, just the way his parents had told her the one time she'd met them, and he would never find time to do anything other than screw her.

At the moment, it felt more like she'd been screwed over by fate in this little mating game.

She was angry at him and at herself. She knew it wasn't fair, but that was how she felt. To hell with being serene. She was just tired of being disappointed, tired of not being good enough. There was *nothing* wrong with her. Her Pride leader had been well pleased with her in Japan. Her politics hadn't been wrong, her career had been considered a productive money-producer for the Pride. Her quietness, dislike of arguments, and artistic nature had been an asset, not a detraction.

Spinning on her heel, she stomped down the long hallways to the kitchen, where she found Isabel finishing her shift. "Feel like going for a drive?"

The blond woman hesitated while pulling off a chef's coat. "Well, I was going to have coffee with my mates, but if you need something . . ."

She ground her teeth together, felt her fangs press against the inside of her lips. "I want to go to a new museum exhibit, but no one is allowed to go out alone and Tomas doesn't have time to go with me."

As usual. Her flash of anger crumpled under the sting of rejection. Why had she believed him *again?* Why had she put faith in him ever having time for her? He never would.

It was hopeless.

Depression crashed through her, and she pressed her lips together to keep from crying. She blinked rapidly, holding back the salty moisture. Focusing on the wall behind Isabel's shoulder, she fought the suffocating feeling that the room was closing in around her. "I need to get out of here for a little while and no one is allowed to go out alone. Will you come with me?"

"Sure. Let me grab a sweater and tell my mates where we're going and why. They have a meeting in an hour, but they'll have one of Landon's security guards go with us." Of course they would. Because her mates gave a damn.

Unlike Ciri's mate.

The look on Ciri's face haunted Tomas after she'd left, and her words haunted him even more. He hadn't meant for her to think he would go out with her immediately. He hated that he'd disappointed her, but he didn't know what to do about it. It was another no-win situation. He'd have to talk to her later, apologize and get this settled between them. He'd meant what he'd said about going with her. He wanted to, he was looking forward to it. A few hours with nothing to worry about but relaxing with his mate would be heaven. It had been so long since he'd truly relaxed that he'd almost forgotten what it felt like.

He'd make time for it when this ball and the subsequent peace summit were over. Sighing, he tried to focus on his work. His success was only limited, but he forced himself to sit and continue. This was his duty and no one else could do it.

A brief knock sounded on his door, breaking his somewhat

dubious concentration. He glanced up to see the butler come in carrying a tray. "Hello, Eva."

"Tomas." She nodded, gracing him with a contained smile. There was a wariness in her eyes every time she was around him that he didn't like, but that he could unfortunately understand.

Eva had joined the North American Pride shortly after Tomas had arrived. She'd been raised in Brazil, like he had. She was about six or seven years younger than he was, so they'd never been close, but his grandfather had found it charming to have a female butler and had allowed her to follow in her uncle's footsteps in that position. Tomas had found her excellent at her work, despite her relatively young age.

He doubted his father had been as amused at having a young woman in the traditionally male role. It hadn't surprised Tomas at all to find that she'd decided to abandon her post in South America and to make a place for herself somewhere else. It had surprised him even less that she'd chosen the most liberal of all the Prides. Antonio rarely put fetters on his people, limiting them in what they were inclined toward, so long as it didn't endanger the Pride.

Tomas agreed with that philosophy. Then again, they'd both been schooled under his grandfather, so it wasn't unexpected that they shared some of the same views. His parents' outlook was much more conservative, and Tomas hoped that didn't drive away all the members who might be less traditional.

It worried him, but it worried him more that he'd have to live under his father's rule for decades. He'd never do anything to drive a wedge into the Pride, and that meant biding his time on all things political, lobbying for that which he was passionate about, and swallowing the bitter pill if he couldn't convince his father to agree with him. He knew that wasn't entirely fair.

His father wasn't a bad man, he was just a Pride leader whose viewpoint was different than Tomas's. It was difficult, but hardly impossible.

"How are you settling in here, Eva?"

Her body tightened and her gaze sharpened to alertness. "Fine, sir. Thank you for asking." She set the tray on the side of his desk. It was piled with sandwiches and a traditional gourd filled with tea called *mate.* "You worked through lunch, so you probably needed a more substantial tea."

"My thanks." His stomach rumbled loudly, and he plucked up the hollowed gourd, drawing on the polished metal straw. The strong herbal flavor burst over his tongue, and the calming, pleasant taste that he'd grown up with had a relaxing effect. He motioned Eva into a chair and offered her the gourd.

It was customary to share *mate,* so she perched on the edge of the seat and accepted the offering, taking a drink of the tea. "I had Isabel order *mate* from a shop I know in Rio Grande do Sul. Miguel seemed happy to have some in the house."

"As he should be. Thank you for taking care of us."

She tilted her head, the corners of her eyes crinkling. "That's my job."

"You are excellent at it."

A startled look crossed her pretty features. "I . . . *muito obrigado.*"

He grinned when she broke into Portuguese. It was rare to see her discomfited. "It's only the truth."

Rising to her feet, she handed the *mate* gourd back to him. Sadness reflected in her gaze before she glanced away. "I wish your father had agreed. He didn't care to have someone so young in charge of the household staff. I couldn't stay in Brazil."

Not to mention that she was a woman. Tomas didn't bring it up, but his heart squeezed in sympathy. He knew exactly what it was like to have his father think him inadequate for a job.

"I'm sorry." He wished he could offer some assurance to the woman that she wouldn't always be estranged from her homeland, but he couldn't. To do so would invite a rift in the Pride that he wouldn't stand for. Gathering followers to himself to undermine his father could lead to the kind of disaster that had decimated the African Pride a few decades before. No. They would all have to live with his father's rule, and it wasn't as if there was no one who agreed with him. His mother and her family had always been a powerful conservative force within the Pride, and they would appreciate the freer rein they now had. Politics went in waves, whether one was dealing with a human situation or the more feline version of things.

Tomas wanted a strong Pride when he became the leader, so he had to cultivate a healthy environment of communication and compromise. He might have to duke it out with his father to make that happen, but that was a private matter between them, not one that he would ever allow Pride members to become involved in. It was what his people needed, and he had always told himself that he would do what he had to, even if it meant working day and night as he had been. He'd thought he owed nothing less than his best to his grandfather's memory.

But if Eva still wanted to return to Brazil when he came to power, he'd welcome her with open arms. Her family had been with his Pride for generations, and it made his soul ache that she felt she was unwelcome in her own home.

However, if he gave in to what Antonio thought, if he gave Ciri what she seemed to need, he'd never be able to help people in South America. People like Eva. He'd never come to power.

Instead, his sister would. But the idea hadn't stopped nagging at him since the older man had brought it up. If he never saw that disappointed look on his mate's face again, it would be too soon.

The door closed silently behind Eva as she strode out. She didn't say good-bye, but there really wasn't anything to say, was there?

7

By the time Ciri sensed him, it was too late.

They'd left the museum and were walking toward a small café, passing by an alley, when he reached out and rammed his fist into the back of their guard's skull. The rogue Panther had already grabbed Isabel before the guard went down in a silent heap. A scream locked in Ciri's throat, terror freezing her in place. He slammed Isabel against the brick wall, and her head made a sickening thud when it contacted with the side of the building. Blood turned her golden hair a rusty red. She was down, unconscious like their guard, and Ciri faced their attacker alone.

He was on her before she could react, and she knew death had come for her.

The reek of insanity swamped her, clogging her nose until she thought she'd gag on the stink. His claws shredded her, ripping through cloth and flesh. There was pain, so much pain, so much blood.

She felt something deep inside her snap, some inner wall giving way. The Panther came to the fore, and all of her predatory instincts kicked in. Every sense she had intensified, scent and sight locking on the man before her. She had never let the feline have so much control, but it was that or die. Her heart hammered, lungs bellowing. She snarled a warning as he came at her. She fought hard, fangs and claws bared, slashing at his eyes, his throat. Deadly blows if he didn't block them quickly enough. She gave no mercy—it was kill or be killed. But he was too big, too fast. There was no way she'd win against a full-grown Panther male.

His fist slammed into her face, and she felt the reverberation through her skull, her head snapping to the side, the tendons in her neck screaming in protest. Blood gushed from her mouth and nose, so much that she couldn't breathe through the flood of it. She coughed, vomiting up the crimson fluid.

Then she was falling, slamming against the pavement. It was over now, she was lost. He'd kill her, this man she didn't know.

But death never came.

Instead, the sounds of fists on flesh continued, but she couldn't feel anything. A Panther's scream rent the air, sending chills down her spine. Heaving herself onto her side, she tried to see what was happening.

One eye was too swollen to blink, but she tried. She lifted a hand to swipe the blood and tears from her vision. Two of the fingers were bent at odd angles. Broken.

She wavered where she propped herself up when she saw the two tall males fighting. The madman hissed. "She's mine. My prey. You cannot have her."

"I won't let you do this, Roberto."

Roberto. That was his name. Her mind clung to that detail as if it were the most important thing in the world.

"How will you stop me, little brother?"

Her rescuer didn't answer. He simply drew his fist back and slammed it into his brother's face. Roberto went down, unconscious before he hit the ground next to her.

She felt herself lifted from the cold pavement and into strong arms, cradled against a warm chest. For a moment, she thought it was her mate, but his scent was wrong. Her instincts told her he was safe, and that was all she required.

"Tell . . . Tomas . . ."

"Oh, no." His voice was as warm as his body. "You can tell Tomas yourself. Hold on and I'll take you to him. You and your friends are going to be all right."

"Promise?"

"You have my word."

She slid in and out of awareness on the way home. They were in a car, she knew that. Agony wracked her when she coughed up blood. The guard was awake, snapping out questions that Ciri didn't understand. Isabel was with her, but the other woman remained still and silent. That should have concerned her, but her mind couldn't quite grasp why.

She heard shouting, knew people were upset, scared. One of the twins had Isabel in his arms. The Pride's doctor arrived, his gaze sweeping their guard and her before he focused on her friend. Ciri tried to push herself to her feet. Strong hands grasped her arms, helping her out of the car. It was the man who'd saved them. She focused the one eye she could open on him. "Who are you?"

"My name is Marcos." His grip was gentle, and he held his hands out to catch her when she pulled away to stand on her own.

Tomas's voice drew her attention. "Are you all right? Ciri!"

"Fine. I'm fine." She swayed in place, held out her hand to ward him off. "Don't touch me."

No, she didn't want him to touch her. If he'd made time for her, this might not have happened. Isabel wouldn't be hurt and Ciri wouldn't be in more pain than she knew was possible to feel. Every part of her stung or ached, sharp agony stabbing from her worst injuries straight to her brain. Would Roberto have attacked their guard and Tomas? Two large Panther males might have given Roberto pause, or at least a more even fight. Tomas hadn't cared to come with her, and she'd been hurt. That was all she could process through the pain. She was done pretending everything was all right. Nothing was. Nothing ever would be again.

It was over.

Tomas froze with his hands outstretched toward her. He hovered before her, desperation and fear ripe in the air. Too late for him to care. Far too late.

"Don't . . . Just don't touch me." A deep shudder wracked her, followed by another and another. Wrapping her arms around herself, she stumbled away from her mate. She couldn't control the shaking no matter how tightly she hugged herself.

"Come on, Ciri. You need some rest." The doctor stepped forward, his warm steadiness a balm to her battered soul. His touch was lighter than a butterfly's wing as he supported her elbow. She leaned against him gratefully.

"Rest. That would be good." She'd like to sleep forever. Maybe then the world would make sense when she woke up. Now things were broken in ways she didn't think would ever be fixed. And she was so tired, so hurt.

She just wanted it all to be over.

Tomas watched her stand at the window to their sitting room, her arms wrapped around herself. The doctor had banned Tomas from their room so that she could rest undisturbed. He wanted nothing to wake her. Sleep had healed all her injuries. Her physical injuries, anyway.

"I can't do this anymore, Tomas. I can't spend my life waiting for you to find time for me. Our mating isn't working, and I don't think it ever will. I just . . . can't do this."

The words fell in the silence between them. He took two more steps toward her before they hit him, the blow so painful he staggered and almost fell to his knees.

"No." Panic fisted in his chest. "Don't do this, Ciri. Why can't we just talk about this? Let's have it out and be done with it!" He gestured wildly, and she flinched.

He saw her arms tighten around herself. "We're just too different."

"We balance each other! There's nothing wrong with that. We don't have to be the same."

She laughed, and it was an ugly sound. "You want us to be the same. You want me to be like you, but I'm not."

"Just talk to me!"

"I *am* talking to you." Her chin lifted, and he wanted to shake her out of her detachment. "I'm just not fighting with you, and that's what you want. We can discuss this calmly."

He thrust his hands through his hair, gripping the strands tight. "You're saying our mating is wrong and you want me to be *calm?* Have you lost your mind?"

"I'm saying that maybe we rushed into things. Perhaps we should consider that." She tried to say it as gently as possible, tried not to accuse or criticize. He'd learned when he was in Japan that it was the way of her people not to confront, to maintain harmony and respect. At the moment, he hated that part of her personality.

"This is insane! We're mated. There's nothing to explore about being mated. You are or you aren't, and we *are.*"

"It's more complicated than that."

"It's as simple as that, Ciri."

She shook her head, her jaw set in a stubborn line. "I've asked Eva to find a new room for me. It's done, Tomas. My decision is final."

"A new room?" His tone sounded blank even to his own ears. A part of him couldn't believe this was happening. Not any of it. Another part of him felt like this was inevitable. They'd been heading for this point for months. This was just what had pushed them over the edge.

"I think the suite next door is free." Her voice rose and shook and he wanted to pull her into his arms and tell her everything would be all right, but he couldn't because it would be a lie. It wasn't all right. It never would be again. She cleared her throat. "M-mates don't do well when separated, so I won't be so far that we'll go insane, but . . . I can't stay."

"I understand." Numbness spread through him, a mortal wound that went so deep he couldn't even fathom the extent of the damage.

She nodded, the movement jerky. "Good. I'll go, then."

"Good," he echoed. Turning on his heel, he left. He just put one foot in front of the other and walked. His heart thudded in his chest, the beats unnatural and slow. Reaching the top of the stairs, he glanced around, uncertain where to go. There was no safe place. He couldn't go back to his room and watch his wife leave him. He just couldn't do it. He wasn't strong enough for that. The last place he wanted to be was in the Second's office. He felt like a sham in the position, and if he got another call from his father, he might lose control in a way he never had before.

Eva started up the stairs, a stack of linens in her hands, and he knew they were for his mate's new bed. A bed he would never share. His stomach heaved and he moved down the steps, away from Ciri, away from everything.

He was in Panther form before he'd even passed Eva, his clothes abandoned in a heap on the stairs. The butler would have it taken care of, and he refused to think about the sympathy he could see in her normally impassive gaze. By the time he reached the bottom of the stairs, he was at a full run. One of the housekeeping staff jerked the front door wide for him and he pelted through the opening.

Claws digging into the soft, green grass, he raced for the farthest edge of the property, knowing it wouldn't be far enough to run off the agony poisoning his soul. The landscaping blurred as he sped by, but there was no way to escape himself. Everything had fallen apart, and worse, he'd failed his mate. Failed to protect her, failed to give her everything she needed. Failed.

He was as unworthy of her as he was of the Pride leadership. He'd been pretending all along, but he didn't know who he was or what he was doing. And he'd failed in the attempt to find out.

He skidded to a stop before he hit the huge wall that ringed the property. Head down, he panted for breath. His lungs burned, but that was the least of his pain. If there were a way to rip his heart out, at that moment, he would have.

Turning slowly, he made his way back to the mansion. He didn't know what he'd do when he got there, but for once he didn't give a damn. His paws crunched when he reached the gravel path that circled the house. The window outside of Antonio's office stood open, and he paused when he heard Ciri's name mentioned.

A voice spoke that he couldn't place at first, and then he remembered. The man who'd saved Ciri. Brother of the madman who'd tried to kill her. Outcast.

He didn't stop to think. One nimble leap and he stood on the windowsill. The tableau froze before him; every adult member of the Cruz family except Isabel was present. They turned to stare at him. He ignored them, his gaze locked on the young man who'd played a part in the evening's horror.

He paled under the scrutiny, but his chin lifted. "You're Tomas Montoya."

Tomas nodded, stepping down to the window seat and then to the floor. His tail lashed through the air behind him, and he drew the man's scent to him, locking it in for all time.

"I'm Marcos Ruiz." The boy's clothes hadn't fared well in the fight with his brother, but they'd clearly been threadbare before that. Life hadn't been kind to the young man since he'd been cast out, an unnatural thinness hollowing out his cheeks. "I—I'm sorry your mate was harmed."

Marcos met Solana and Antonio's emotionless gazes. "I'm also sorry for how I behaved toward you. My brothers will never apologize, so I'll do so on their behalf. I—" His voice faltered. "I never understood what it was like to have nothing, to be nothing. I didn't know life outside the protection of the Pride. I had no idea what you'd gone through. I do now." He snorted, the sound full of self-derision. "My family hasn't done as well as you did, and we had each other." He shook his head, looking straight into Solana's eyes. "I'm never going to have the opportunity to say this again, so I want to get it out before I leave. We were bullies, arrogant and wrong. We should have offered you empathy, not scorn. We deserved everything that's happened to us, and you deserved none of what happened to you. I'm sorry for my part in hurting you, and even more ashamed that I thought I had the right to do so."

Solana's mouth opened and closed, but no sound emerged. Antonio reached over and took her hand, their fingers lacing tight as they looked at each other.

Marcos rose to his feet. "I hope Ciri and Isabel recover quickly, and this leaves no lasting damage."

Psychologically, he meant. Both women had awakened physically fine. He didn't know Isabel well enough to guess, but how this affected Ciri's mind and her emotions was less clear. Panthers had no magic to cure the emotional pains. If they did, Tomas would be taking advantage of it now, but there was no easy way out of the chaos his life was in. And, unlike the man before him, he still had his Pride.

Returning the younger man's nod, he watched while he turned for the door. He felt as if he should do something, but his mind couldn't grasp what that might be. The man had saved his wife's life, after all. But the thought of Ciri made pain shaft through Tomas, and he wanted to howl with the agony of it. If he thought for even a second it would help, he'd do it, but there was no end in sight, nothing that would give him back what was so precious to him.

"Wait." Solana half-rose from her seat, and Marcos paused, his hand gripping the doorknob.

"Yes, ma'am?" Wary surprise reflected in the man's eyes, and he tensed as if ready to flee.

It was in that moment that Tomas understood the courage it must have taken to walk into this mansion. Marcos was outcast, one who'd threatened the Pride leader's mate. Free game for anyone who wanted a target. He must have known that there was always the possibility his brother's actions would be revenged upon him; he must have thought there was at least a chance that he might not get out of this den alive.

If his brother had been there, there would have been bloodshed. Given even the slightest opportunity, Tomas would have torn the man open with his claws. He saw the sidelong glances his cousin kept throwing him, and suddenly he saw that they expected him to hunt down his wife's attacker. He wanted to.

God, how he'd love to unleash some of this pain on a man who so richly deserved it, but it would solve nothing. It wouldn't bring Ciri back to him; it wouldn't heal the breach in his mating.

The chair creaked when Solana sank back down. She seemed to have lost the ability to speak after that one word. Swallowing, her throat worked for a second. "I forgive you," she croaked.

Antonio's hand came down on her shoulder, squeezing in support. "I think . . . we might consider revisiting your outcast status, Marcos."

Stunned silence greeted that announcement, and no one looked more dumbfounded than the man in question. Marcos shook his head a bit. "I don't . . . I don't know what to say."

"We'll find a room for you for the night. Get cleaned up, and we'll discuss it tomorrow."

Marcos's gaze roved the plush surroundings, then looked down at his filthy wardrobe. It wasn't hard to grasp that he was thinking of how far he'd fallen in the time he'd been away. "I don't know if I can live here again, not with the memories of my family, but I'd like to no longer be outcast. At least I could leave the continent if I wanted to, and not be considered a dangerous trespasser in another leader's territory."

Antonio tilted his head. "I understand. We'll review your situation and find a solution that works for everyone."

"Thank you, sir." Some relief showed on Marcos's face. No doubt his brother—perhaps both of his brothers—would have been hunting him to exact the same kind of vengeance they'd hoped to visit upon the Cruzes.

"I appreciate that you stood against your brothers and saved innocent women who are under my protection. That can't go unacknowledged."

"Thank you again." Marcos pulled the door open. "Until tomorrow, then."

"Yes."

Solana sighed when he left the room. "That was the right thing to do, but I'm not sure I want him to live here either."

"We'll find a solution that works for everyone," Antonio repeated. "We might find another Pride to take him."

Diego crossed his arms where he slouched against the mantel. "Africa is looking for new members."

"But taking in a former outcast wouldn't be the impression that Benhassi wants to give to the other Prides. He wants to show his Pride as unified, upstanding, and trustworthy." Miguel lifted his hands in a helpless gesture. "A man who attacked a woman, a Pride leader's wife, wouldn't be considered trustworthy. Even if he regrets his youthful stupidity."

Antonio glanced at Tomas, and he straightened, understanding the question in the older man's gaze. South America. He could bring him into the Brazilian Pride. Marcos had saved the heir's mate, so even if he was viewed as untrustworthy, no one would question the debt of honor that bound the Pride leader to admit him as a member. Tomas met Antonio's eyes, nodding decisively.

He might not be able to do anything about his situation with Ciri, but this he could do. He would have to convince his father of it, which would be more than a little difficult, but it could be done.

Dragging in a deep breath, he felt a small sense of calm center him—the eye in the terrifying storm his life had dissolved into. He had a purpose, something to do, some good that he could make come of this disaster.

He needed to call his father.

* * *

Ciri stood in the new room, which felt even less like hers than the one she'd shared with Tomas. The furnishings were the finest money could buy, lovely and bright in shades of cream and gold.

It was the night of the ball—the one Tomas had worked so hard to put together, the one where she would pretend that they were still happily mated. She couldn't bring herself to shame either of them by admitting the truth publicly. It was no one else's concern. For tonight, she would do what duty dictated. After that, she didn't know. Could she refuse to play the political game? What could they do to her if she did?

Her long sheath gown sparkled as she walked over to the window. She didn't want to sit down, didn't want to touch anything, didn't want to acknowledge that this was her room, her space, her life now.

Fog blurred the edges of the city's skyline, making it look like an Impressionist's painting. Beautiful, like the room, and just as ill-fitting. It was nothing like Tokyo, and her destiny was nothing like she'd dreamed. This was supposed to be an adventure with her mate; instead it had shown just how different, how ill-suited, they were for each other.

It seemed cruel that fate should do this to them. Neither of them were bad people, were they? They both did the best they could, tried to live the most honorable life they could, but those lives didn't fit together, not without one giving up all of who they were for the other, and that wasn't fair. Not to either of them. They would spend their days as Ciri had spent the last few months—resentful, hurting, lost, and alone. Separated from everything that was *her.*

Antonio had asked her to meet the Japanese representative when he arrived at the Pride den, and it was almost time. A storm over Tokyo had almost canceled his flight, but he'd made it out just in time. It would be nice to see someone from home, to reconnect with that part of herself. Gathering her long skirt, she turned and swept out the door, along the hall, down the main stairs. The scents of Panthers reached her, the representatives who had come for the ball and summit. Each smell locked into her memory, distinct and individual. She'd found since her attack that her senses were keener, the wildness unleashing in a way she had never allowed except in the bedroom with Tomas. She hadn't bothered trying to cage it again. The feline side was one of the reasons she—and Isabel—were still alive.

The feel of life and activity hummed around her. It was odd to have so many in one place, filling the mansion with people and music. A small orchestra of musicians had been assembled from different Panther Prides, and Ciri was curious to see how well they played together. As usual, she was more interested in the art than the politics. The thought made a sad smile curl her lips. It had been more than a week since she'd spoken to Tomas, and a small part of her wondered how he was doing. No doubt better than she was.

As she reached the foot of the stairs, she tilted her head to listen to the musicians playing. Because she was straining her sensitive ears, they picked up the sound of voices coming from the Pride leader's office.

"Juan Ruiz was arrested earlier today," Landon said.

Ciri's heart slammed into her ribs. *Ruiz.* One of the two rogue brothers who still posed a threat to Panthers in North America. Without thinking, she picked up her skirts and strode into the leader's office. She didn't knock, she just pushed her way in.

"What about the Ruizes? What happened?" Her cheeks heated as the people in the room turned to stare at her. Normally, she'd have run from being the center of attention, especially when that attention came from leaders of a Pride. Antonio and Solana, Miguel, and Diego and Ric all turned to stare at her.

Landon cleared his throat, tugging at his tie as if it were strangling him. "I'll . . . I'll start at the beginning. Juan Ruiz was arrested for petty theft this afternoon. He subsequently escaped while they were transferring him to county lockup."

Everyone in the room drew a sharp, collective breath. Miguel gave voice to all their fears. "Did he reveal—"

"No. He overpowered a guard and escaped while being transported, but there was nothing in the attack to indicate he was anything other than human. The Pride's secrets are still safe." Landon let out a breath, but his gaze kept straying to Ciri as if he thought she might explode.

She folded her arms. "For now."

He nodded. "Yes, for now."

"What do we do?"

"I'm not certain." Antonio answered her rather than the human. "Panthers aren't above the laws of humans. In fact, we try to obey the laws in order to go unnoticed. Normally, I would try to arrange for this to be taken care of quietly, but he's no longer a member of this Pride."

Ric swirled the liquid around in his champagne glass. He, like every other man in the room, wore a tuxedo in honor of the ball. "He could expose us."

"Any one of us could expose our race," Miguel replied. "He knows what would happen to him if he tried."

"He's outcast, imprisoned, and grief-maddened. What does he have to lose?" Ric shrugged. "He'd definitely screw over the Cruzes if he exposed himself."

Diego growled, "He'd screw over every Panther on Earth."

Straightening the floaty layers of skirt on her gown, Solana groaned. "Every other Panther on Earth refused to take his family in after he was cast out of this Pride. No one wanted a disloyal family sullying their name."

Antonio pinched the bridge of his nose. "That thought hadn't escaped me."

Throwing up her hands in exasperation, Ciri said what no one else would. "You know what you should do, what every other Pride leader would already have done. As long as there's a rebel loose, this is a risk that will plague you. If your Pride is the one to leak our secret, you'll be held responsible. It won't matter that he's an outcast, and you know it. They'll say you should have killed him then, and hold you liable anyway."

"I know."

Though Antonio's jaw clenched and she knew she should shut her mouth, Ciri pressed her point. If this had been taken care of when these men were cast out, she and Isabel wouldn't have been mauled. There would be no threat. Maybe she wasn't the most powerful person in the room, but she was the most conservative, and they needed to hear the other side of this argument. She amazed herself with her boldness, but being attacked had shown her there were a lot more important things than worrying about making everyone happy. "You cannot afford to have the other Prides turn against you. One outcast's life is not worth your entire Pride's safety."

A muscle in the Pride leader's jaw began to twitch. "I know this, and I'll think about it. You're not an impartial judge of this situation considering what Roberto Ruiz did to you."

"No, I'm not impartial, but that doesn't mean I'm wrong." She nodded and swept out of the room, closing the door firmly behind her.

Her pulse pounded and she felt a little lightheaded, but it wasn't bad. She swiped her damp palms down her gown as reaction set in. It was good to stand up for herself and give voice to her opinion. She snorted, remembering the stunned looks on everyone's faces while she'd faced down a Pride leader.

"Ahem." Eva cleared her throat to get Ciri's attention. "The Asian Pride's ambassador just arrived."

Goito Fukuda was an unassuming man. He walked into the mansion, bowed politely to Eva and offered a deeper, longer bow to Ciri. It took her a moment to remember why a man so much older than her, who'd known her her entire life, would give her so respectful a gesture. Just in time, she caught herself from bowing too deeply in return. Socially, she outranked Mr. Fukuda now. She was in a leading family, and while he was head of a very influential family in the Asian Pride, he was not in line for leadership.

"*Konnichiwa*, Mr. Fukuda. Welcome to North America."

"Many thanks, Mrs. Montoya." He bowed again. "*Konnichiwa.*"

"Shall we?" She gestured toward the ballroom, where light and laughter spilled out into the foyer. No one had come out of Antonio's office yet, and she forced herself not to worry about what they might be discussing. She'd said what she needed to say. The final decision wasn't hers.

Goito nodded and they fell into step beside each other. "Your parents send their regards."

A pang of longing went through her that they weren't here to give those regards themselves. She'd avoided their calls for the last week—there was no way they would understand what had happened with Roberto Ruiz. Or with Tomas. Her mother had sent a package to help spice up her marriage with Tomas, and thinking about the contents still made Ciri blush. Sadly, that part of their mating had needed no help. It was everything else that was wrong. "Thank you for passing the message along. I miss them very much. And home."

Goito made a sympathetic noise. "I can imagine that this Pride den would be a very different place than ours. Too loose with the rules we all live by, too liberal. Our leader is not pleased."

She stiffened a little at the criticism. It wasn't like her people to be so blunt, but Antonio had ruffled more than a few feathers with some of his policies. "It's been a challenging transition."

They paused just inside the doors of the ballroom. Goito's gaze narrowed on something to their left, his nostrils flaring a bit. His face flattened in disapproval. "Is that the human or the non-shifter?"

She followed his gaze to see who he was looking at. Well, at least one person had left Antonio's office. "The human, Landon. He's in charge of the security here."

Goito sniffed, his voice lowering to an irate hiss. "It goes against all laws of the Prides. Humans. Non-shifters. It upsets the balance of things. It causes problems when there is no need. We have our rules in place for a reason. Cruz has no right to endanger us all."

A spurt of anger blasted through her, and the heat of her reaction surprised her. "Please do not upset yourself, Mr. Fukuda. You know Antonio may do what he wishes in his territory. The human and non-shifter have not caused harm."

"Yet." A muscle ticked in his jaw.

She tried to think of all the sides to the argument, scrambled to consider how Tomas would want her to deal with this. In the end, she just gave her true reaction. As upset as she was about Antonio's nonaction with regard to the Ruizes, there were many areas where she could find no fault in his leadership. "I've found Antonio to be a good man. He is very different, yes, but he is beloved by his people."

Goito looked at her as if she'd sprouted horns and a forked tail. "You seem unwell, Mrs. Montoya. This place is not good for you." He bowed to her. "Please excuse me."

She bowed automatically in return but found that her hands were shaking in rage. She didn't bother pushing aside the reaction. She was tired of pretending she didn't feel what she felt. Her confrontation with Antonio and her unexpected anger at Goito's comments made it finally hit her exactly how much she had changed since she'd come here. A few months ago she would have agreed with Goito wholeheartedly, but now . . . she knew these people better. They were *people* now, not just concepts, abstracts. It wasn't as simple as that.

Her focus was no longer on remaining harmonious and maintaining the status quo.

Roberto's unprovoked attack, her fight for her life, her terror for Isabel, all made her see that she should be more interested in doing the right thing than doing the peaceful thing. It was a new dichotomy for her—considering the greater good for all Panthers, but also accounting for the needs of individuals. There had to be a balance between those two things. Japan was too concerned with the greater good, America too focused on individual comforts. Somewhere in between was where she thought the right line should be drawn.

She snorted at herself. Here she was, involving herself in politics not once, but twice in the same night. But she couldn't stand aside and pretend none of it involved her. It would never be her interest or passion, but it definitely impacted her life when a leader acted or chose not to act. The change in attitude would please her father-in-law, but she wasn't so sure about

Tomas. She doubted that she could be the kind of wife he wanted, and perhaps it was best to leave things as they were. It hurt to acknowledge that, but they were still so very different, and she couldn't live her life as he wanted her to—devoid of her art and her career, waiting for him to notice he had a mate.

No, it was best to let things lie. No matter how much it pained her.

8

She was slowly going mad.

After he'd entered the ballroom, Tomas had claimed her for a dance and then didn't leave her side, his hand on her shoulder, sliding down to the small of her back. She'd once loved how much he touched her, but now? It would drive her insane if she had to take much more. She hadn't had him in more than a week, and Panthers didn't do well without their mates. It wasn't until now that she'd understood exactly how true that was.

Her body was more than ready for what her mind and heart knew she'd be better off without. She sensed him in the suite beside her every day, which kept her from truly losing her grip on reality, but even that slight distance was starting to wear on her.

It hurt. It hurt so much, she didn't know how she'd stand it.

And her hormones didn't care about her feelings, about logic or right or wrong. All her instincts told her was that her mate was beside her, touching her, and she should reach out and take what she craved. The internal demand clamored louder and louder as the evening wore on, as her nerves tattered and frayed.

"I've heard your parents brought your niece with them." Cesar Benhassi smiled at Tomas.

He nodded. "Yes, they did. Marisol wanted to visit with Miguel and Andrea, and my mother decided to indulge her. No one can resist my niece."

"She's a sweet girl," Ciri added. It was the most coherent thought she could manage. Marisol was a little tornado, a charming, vibrant force of nature that left everyone reeling in her wake. She was the one member of Tomas's family that Ciri had liked on sight.

Tomas's arm settled around her waist, drawing her close until their sides pressed together. She could feel the heat and hardness of him, and she nearly crawled out of her skin with the desire pounding through her. Every inch of her felt sensitized, readying itself for his claiming. Her skin felt flushed, her sex dampening, her nipples tightening to points that she didn't even have to glance down to know were plainly visible in this dress.

She squeezed her thighs together to quell the ache that built there, but the movement only increased her agony. A tremor passed through her body when his long fingers began to stroke her waist. Her sex clenched hard, so needy, so ready to be filled by him. It had been so long, *days* since she'd had her mate. The Panther within clawed for dominance, and her breathing hitched as she struggled for some semblance of control. It was so much harder now than it had been.

His fingers drifted in slow, warm circles up her ribs, and she broke. She flashed a brilliant smile at the people they were talking to. "Will you all excuse me for a moment?"

A few of the Panthers cast her knowing looks. No doubt

they could smell how turned on she was, but that would only play toward them thinking everything was fine between Ciri and Tomas. It wasn't.

Turning on her heel, she picked up her long skirt and fled to one of the bathrooms off the ballroom. She shoved her way inside and braced her shaking hands on the edge of the vanity, dropping her chin to her chest. Sucking in deep, slow breaths, she wrestled her hormones before they forced her to seek out her mate.

She couldn't go on like this. She just couldn't. His scent called to her like a Lorelei, undeniably the most erotic thing she'd ever smelled. One whiff and she was shaking like an addict in need of a fix. Her claws scraped against the marble vanity as she struggled to stay where she was and not give in to the heat ripping through her.

"Ciri."

When she glanced up in the mirror, she could see him behind her. He was here. God, he was here and she was lost. She couldn't fight it anymore. "I forgot to lock the door."

"I know." His nostrils flared and she knew he'd caught the scent of her lust. His eyes glowed a shimmering gold, the Panther in him as apparent as the cat in her. He'd been as unable to resist following her as she was unable to resist him now. "I've tried to stay away from you the way you asked, I really have, but I want you. You're my mate. I can't help it. I'm sorry."

The heartbreak on his face wrenched at her soul. A sob caught in her throat even as she reached for him. She shouldn't do this. It wasn't fair to either of them, but the Panther in her ruled the woman just then. Instincts weren't fair, they just were.

He groaned and dragged her into his arms. His lips met hers and the taste of him was so wonderful she thought she'd die. She hated herself for how much she craved him, how she'd never rid herself of this addiction, but the cat writhed in mating heat, uncaring of the woman's emotions.

The dichotomy would break her, the war within herself too fundamental for her to survive the internal battle.

Tears welled in her eyes, even as she clutched at him, her body screeching in bone-deep recognition. Her fingers slid into the rich silk of his hair, holding him close as their tongues dueled. Her fangs nipped at his flesh, and she tasted blood. It only called to the feral cat, ripping away what was left of the woman's hesitation.

Too late. Too late for doubts, for hesitation. All she could do was turn herself over to pure, driving instinct. His big body pressed to hers, the heat of him searing through her thin dress. She twisted to get closer, to gain the contact she needed. His hands gathered her skirt up and he wrenched his mouth from hers long enough to pull her gown over her head and toss it across the end of the vanity.

Then he turned her around, leaned her forward, and set her hands where they'd been when he found her. The marble had cooled and the chill of the stone on her flesh sent shivers racing through her.

"Tomas," she gasped.

She heard the jingle of his belt and the rasp of his zipper, then she felt the hot press of his cock between her thighs.

"Spread," he ordered, his tone guttural and barely human. Exhilaration twisting through her, she obeyed. His hand roughly bent her farther forward and the head of his cock pushed for entrance within her.

She hissed, her fangs punching through her gums when he shoved deep in one stroke. It hurt. A lot. But it also felt so good after so long, that hot connection with her mate. The cat inside her purred with satisfaction, and Ciri choked on a cry of utter need as Tomas began thrusting within her.

Setting his hands over hers, he held her in place for his possession. There was no escaping, not from him and not from herself. Her hair fell into her face as she bowed her head forward, taking his thrusts and pushing her hips back to give him more access.

"Faster." It was little more than a snarl, and she teetered right on the edge of shifting, a loss of control that she'd never faced as an adult. But this was her mate, a man who called to every part of her animalistic soul.

His mouth open over the back of her neck, his fangs digging in to the exact spot he had marked her all those months ago. He had taken her from behind then, too, and she'd known it was the most perfect moment of her life. A sob caught in her throat, her breathing hitching as the woman's pain burst through the Panther's craving.

Flicking his tongue over the sensitive mate mark made her legs shake and threaten to give out from under her. He sucked the flesh hard. It was as if electricity shot through her body, making her arch in shocked reflex. Her sex clenched tight on his pounding cock, and they both groaned. Her claws scraped against the vanity top as she twisted in his arms. But he held her tight, his arms imprisoning her, his hands pinning her down.

"Make me come. I need to come. Please, please, please," she begged shamelessly. She couldn't take much more without imploding with the conflict that tore her apart inside.

A low, rumbling growl told her how close he was to losing his grip on the Panther. The thought excited her far more than it should. He bucked his hips, driving deep inside her. Her pussy flexed around his cock each time he entered her, and she could feel orgasm building and building. Her anticipation made her pant for breath.

His scent filled her lungs, and beads of sweat gathered at her temples. The carnal sound of their skin slapping together, his heavy breath rushing against the damp skin at her nape made the sensations intensify. The heightened senses of her feline side caught every detail, from the smells and sounds to the taste of sex on the air.

Shoving deep, he ground his pelvis against her and the angle was just right. It was too much for her to handle. She exploded, her sex fisting on his cock, milking him in waves that made her fight against his hold on her. His arms tightened around her, forcing her to feel it, to endure the overwhelming pleasure that pounded through her.

She glanced up, seeing the feral cat more than the woman in the reflection before her. Her eyes burned to pure gold, and as her mouth opened in a silent scream, her fangs gleamed in the overhead light.

Releasing her hands, he shoved his fingers between her thighs and rubbed her clit in sharp, rhythmic motions that sent her flying over into oblivion. Stars burst behind her eyes, and it was all she could do to hold back the Panther's chilling shriek. His cock continued to fill her, to push her into yet another wave of orgasm. He rocked against her, his belly spanking her ass with each hard, fast stroke. A harsh growl broke from him, and he froze behind her, his come pumping deep within her pussy.

When her vision cleared, she found that her fingers were laced with his again. He purred soothingly, his arms cradling her with such tenderness it made tears prick her eyes. It felt so right and so wrong all at the same time. It was all she could do not to scream in agony. She hated the separation, but she didn't know how to change things. She was who she was, and he was who he was. Except in bed, they seemed to have no way to reach each other. They each wished the other was a different kind of person.

She swallowed hard. "This changes nothing."

"I know." The purring stopped and he sighed; he slid out of her, reached out to pick up her dress and handed it to her. He looked down, swallowing hard. "I'm sorry, Ciri. I . . . I've been so busy trying to prove I could live up to my father's expectations and my grandfather's reputation that I never told you how hard the last six months have been for me, how much difficulty *I* was having adjusting to the changes in my life. I thought I was protecting you. I thought if I dumped my problems all over you, it would just make you more miserable to be here, to be mated with me. Instead, I just made you feel more isolated."

"Thank you." She clutched her gown to her chest, feeling more naked and vulnerable than she ever had in her life. "I haven't exactly been easy to live with either, refusing to communicate with you."

He drew in a breath and then let it out. "But I pushed you to be open with me when I wasn't open with you, and I'm sorry. For more than I can say. For . . . everything. You deserve to know that."

The finality in his voice made her insides twist, and she knew this was his good-bye. She cleared her throat, her entire body beginning to tremble. "I'm sorry, too. I've realized that I was punishing you for being who you are, being a Pride heir and for all the strings that are attached to that position, and that's not fair either."

"So where does that leave us?"

"Nowhere." It hurt to say it, but being sorry didn't change anything. It didn't help them fix anything; it didn't allow them to move forward. There was nowhere for them to go.

He snorted out a short laugh. "That's what I thought."

"I wish . . ." She couldn't even finish the thought. There were so many things she wished for—she just couldn't have them. She just had to accept, as her parents had told her all along. She simply hadn't realized that in her case, acceptance meant accepting there would never be a close relationship between her mate and herself.

What was left of her battered, broken heart shattered as that truth finally hit her.

"There's trouble with your mate."

"She was attacked, Father." Tomas tensed, reflexively leaping to Ciri's defense. "That's hardly her fault."

"No, that's Antonio's fault. It's his job to protect Panthers in North America." Pedro sniffed in disdain as though nothing of the sort had ever happened in South America, which was hardly the case. Accidents had occurred, assassinations, murders, coups of former Pride leaders. Panther politics were nothing if not deadly.

His mother stepped in smoothly, her hand curving into his father's arm. "What we meant was that . . . we've noticed an obvious strain between your mate and you, *despite* your little tête-à-tête in the bathroom an hour ago. You need to cover these things better, dear. It's not for the world to know when tiffs occur."

"We're doing our best." The words were stiff, and Tomas wanted to snap at his parents for pressing on a sore point. This was no one's business but his, and it was embarrassing that anyone had noticed, least of all his parents.

"Do better." His father's gaze was like black ice. "Don't shame us."

Dios, how many times had he heard that sentence from his father? More than he cared to count. He stared at the colorful couples swirling around on the marble dance floor, yearning to be anywhere but here. "Disagreements happen in any relationship, Father."

"Of course they do," his mother replied, and he reluctantly

refocused his attention on the conversation at hand. Her eyebrows rose, her face still unlined and lovely despite her age. "I hate to be blunt, my dear, but when is the last time you coupled in Panther form? Are you both doing your duty to continue our line?"

Tomas felt a humiliated flush heat the back of his neck. Partially because his mother was right—they hadn't tried to breed in months. He took a large swallow of his champagne and wished it were something a hell of a lot stronger. "We've had some difficulty settling in to our new positions in the Pride."

"That's natural, especially as she learns her place. She needs to adapt to her duties as your wife. There's much change for her to make still. Your mother and I would like to see her take a more active role in the Pride, and not hide in that computer of hers." His father smiled and it wasn't pleasant.

His mother's gaze hardened. "Doubtless you thought we didn't know about her little job, but this isn't how she should be spending her days, and you know it."

On reflex, Tomas opened his mouth to agree. He'd had those same thoughts a hundred times, but then he stopped. Suddenly, it hit him so clearly exactly what his parents had planned for Ciri. It wasn't just an adjustment to a new life, it was total change in her character, it was forcing her to become someone else entirely.

"Like you gave up your little job?" The words fell unheeded from his lips. His mother had been in medical school, with the promise of becoming a Pride physician, when Pedro had claimed her as his mate.

His mother flattened her lips. "Yes. It's necessary for leaders' mates to make themselves fit into the proper role, the correct lifestyle."

The implacable expression on her face made him want to

growl. Because his mother had sacrificed all her personal ambitions, Ciri had to as well? He'd known that some adjusting needed to take place, some bending, but this? No. He didn't want Ciri to become someone else. He loved her just as she was, *because* she was perfect for him. It would be so easy for him to lose himself in Pride politics, to forget the rest of the world existed. He needed her to remind him, to hold him back from becoming . . . his father.

As much as he admired his father, Tomas couldn't help but recall the underlying strain that had always existed in his parents' relationship. His mother did as she was told, just as his sister did, but in every way that mattered, they had separate lives, separate activities. She had her duties and he had his. For his father, his family always came second or third or last on his list of priorities.

"No. You're wrong. I think Ciri can spend her days any way that she sees fit. Her work is important to her, just as my work is important to me." Internally, he staggered a bit. It was the first time he'd ever admitted that there didn't have to be an all or nothing change for either of them. They balanced each other, as he'd told her, and that was a *good* thing. Before now, he'd always agreed with his sire on this issue, but where would getting what he wanted leave him? Exactly where he was. Without Ciri. Which was the last thing he wanted.

Pedro's face mottled an ugly red. "Nothing is more important than the Prides. Everything else must be sacrificed if we are to remain strong."

"That's my job. I am the heir. I will be the Pride leader. That's my destiny, not hers." And unless he made some drastic changes, all he was going to have was his parents' mating—one where Ciri was only on the periphery of his life, and her resentment for him grew until there was no love left between them.

No. A thousand times, no. Everything in him rejected the very idea.

"Let me make myself clear." He glanced back and forth between his parents. "You are not welcome to comment on my marriage or how my wife and I conduct our affairs. If she wishes to work, I have no problem with that. She'll provide the appropriate portion of her income to Pride upkeep as everyone else does. She's my wife, not my secretary. She's also not you, Mother, and I don't expect her to conduct her affairs as if she were. Her life is her own." His father opened his mouth to speak, but Tomas cut him off. "Also, I'm taking on an assistant. I'm going to be spending more time with my mate and less time chained to my desk. If you want those grandchildren, I have to have time to beget them."

Pedro's mouth flapped, a gurgle bubbling out of him.

Patting his sire's shoulder, Tomas smiled. "Some people need to make changes, Father, but Ciri's not one of them. Try to force her and I'll step down as heir, and if you think your other offspring is strong enough to be a leader, you're wrong. Think about what would happen to the Pride if I left."

The breath whooshed out of Pedro's lungs, but he made no response. It was the first time in his life that Tomas had ever seen the man speechless. His mother's face was flushed and the hand that gripped Pedro's arm was now tipped in deadly talons. Tomas thought about what the consequences of this confrontation might be. His father might be angry enough to disinherit him, but there were worse things.

Losing Ciri would be the worst thing that could ever happen to him—far worse than shaming his family, than disappointing his parents, than letting down his Pride. Antonio was right—a good man, a good mate, would have to balance having two first priorities. Tomas had had to confront so many changes in his life lately that he often thought he didn't know who he was anymore. But whoever he was going to be, whatever kind of Pride leader, of *man*, he was going to grow into, he needed Ciri with him.

Which was exactly what he should have been assuring her of all along.

9

Ciri avoided Tomas for the rest of the ball. It was bad enough that the extra senses of the Panthers meant they could smell him all over her, but she didn't want to tempt herself again. She didn't trust the wildness inside her not to jump him. Anytime she sensed him coming near, she moved somewhere else. She knew he was looking for her, could *feel* it, but she managed to skirt him.

She was less successful at avoiding Solana, who caught her as she was sneaking out onto the terrace for some fresh air. Several other guests were out there, so it didn't look conspicuous, but it didn't smell like Tomas out there. Solana passed her a glass of champagne and looked out over the large hedge maze they had on the property. "What do you think of Australia's bid to provide our next Second?"

Ciri's belly clenched for so many reasons. Isabel had mentioned earlier that week that Ciri being attacked in North American territory meant Tomas was being recalled to South America and his father would expect reparations from Antonio for not keeping her safe. That couldn't have been good news for this Pride, and after Ciri's confrontation with Antonio, it made her wary that Solana would ask her opinion for anything. It had been obvious since that disastrous dinner her first week that they agreed on nothing. Her mind scrambled for an answer that would get her out of actually answering. "I'm sure my mate believes it would be an interesting move to make."

Solana flipped a lock of hair over her shoulder, the style deliberately mussed and somehow perfect for her. "I didn't ask what your mate thought, I asked what you thought."

"I leave the politics to Tomas. Unless it really matters to me, I avoid playing those petty little games." The words were out of her mouth before she could stop them, undeniably harsh and likely to embarrass Tomas and his family. She wished she could make herself not care, but knowing she shouldn't be with Tomas didn't mean she didn't love him.

Solana shrugged. "It was never a deep interest of mine, either, but you can't help but pick it up if you're around this crowd long enough."

That was true enough. Ciri knew far more about the interworkings of the different Prides than she'd ever thought possible. She opened her mouth to make a polite reply, and then decided against it. If she was going to embarrass her mate, she might as well make the most of it. She was already on a roll with interfering bluntness this evening. "I think you'd do better to take a Second from the African Pride."

The older woman blinked. "Oh? Why is that?"

"Because you have more to gain that way. Australia already has a firmly established power base, but Africa is still new and they'd be willing to make a lot more concessions to get a Second in another Pride so soon." She sipped her champagne and wished she had strawberries to go with it. The thought sent a pang through her as she recalled the last time she'd had the fruit. "Tomas said you recognized the Benhassis claim to the leadership first, but this would solidify your alliances much more."

"Your father-in-law would never risk it. He's still waiting for them to have a civil war again."

She shrugged. "I know. But Antonio *would* risk it, so take advantage and strike while the iron is hot. It's of the most potential benefit to your Pride."

Solana snorted. "You know, after tonight, you're not going to be able to claim you don't care about Pride politics. And, in this case at least, I agree with you. I'll talk to my mate."

She was right. Ciri swirled the bubbly liquid around in her glass. "I've changed my mind about non-shifters. They aren't a curse, and they can provide income for a Pride, if not children." She took a breath. "But I still disagree about *any* humans knowing about us."

Tilting her head sent her chocolate-colored curls cascading over her shoulder, and Solana narrowed her gaze. "You want to throw out a person just because they happen to be *destined* to mate with a human."

"Yes." Ciri nodded decisively. "I know it sounds cruel, but one person's comfort isn't worth *everyone's* safety. Every human who knows puts all of us at risk. One word, one leak to a reporter and that's a secret we can't take back. It's a danger to all of us. I'm sorry for those Panthers, I truly am, but they can't bring their humans to the Prides and they can never tell our secrets. Ever."

"I understand your point of view. I don't agree, but I understand."

"I feel the same about your stance on this issue."

"God, we sound like our husbands." Solana rolled her eyes.

"True." Ciri burst into laughter. It felt good, as if she hadn't laughed in the entire time she'd been here. She'd been through so much, but it had made her grow in ways that perhaps she needed. Repressing everything she'd felt hadn't been healthy.

Solana's expression sobered. "I know you haven't enjoyed your time here, and some of that was my fault. I wasn't as understanding or welcoming as I should have been—no, really." She held up her hand when Ciri tried to speak. "I just don't want you to think that you won't make a good leader's mate because this Pride didn't suit you. You wouldn't do well ruling *this* Pride, but South America is different, and I think Tomas and you will be fine there." She waved her champagne flute. "You also don't have to buy into the bullshit that you have to give up your work and live for the Pride if you're in a leading family. Andrea has her fashion design business, and I still run the bar I owned when I married Antonio. There are examples in other Prides too."

"I'm not going to give up my graphic art." It was the first time Ciri had said it out loud, and it felt good. She could bend in certain areas, help with political things sometimes, but she wouldn't give up *herself* for anyone, and her work was a large part of who she was. Which was something Tomas had said they had in common. He was right.

"Tomas is looking for you." Solana's gaze went to the open French doors that led back to the ballroom. "He knows you're avoiding him."

"I know."

"Did you know he'd decided to get an assistant so he can spend more time with you?" She waited a beat, a cat aware that her prey was now hanging on her every word. "Did you know he threatened to resign as heir if Pedro tried to make you stop taking graphic design commissions?" Her dark gaze sparkled mischievously. "And that if he interfered in your marriage or tried to change you in any way, you'd both leave the Pride entirely?"

Ciri's heart stopped in her chest. "Are . . . are you sure?"

"That's what he told Miguel. Of course, Miguel told Tomas about your run-in with Antonio." Shrugging delicately, the other woman grinned. "You know how gossip is, it spreads like wildfire. I just thought you might like to know."

"Thank you," Ciri croaked.

Her head spun as Solana walked away. Could this mean what she thought it meant? Tomas didn't want her to change everything? He was willing to fight for her to keep her art? She stumbled over to a stone bench and plopped down. He wanted to spend more time on their marriage. He wasn't just *saying* he would, but actually *doing* something that would make more time for them to be together.

There was so much she needed to talk to him about, and she couldn't even stop herself reeling enough to get up from the bench. Hope exploded inside her, so white-hot and fierce that it rocked her. She wanted their mating to work so much, and she knew Tomas would never have said such things to his father if he didn't mean them. He wouldn't have repeated them to Miguel if he intended to back down.

If he was willing to meet halfway, so was she. If they tried, if they worked with each other instead of pulling against each other and insisting their way was best, they could do this.

She loved him too much, needed him too much, not to risk it. If she'd learned anything from all of this, it was to fight for what she believed in.

And she believed in them. She wouldn't have held on so long if she didn't. She'd have given up and stopped struggling for acceptance months ago.

She needed to find Tomas.

* * *

Tomas woke up and tried to roll over, but found he couldn't move.

Panic exploded through him, and he lunged against his bindings, the animal in him wild to escape any cage.

"Shh. Don't fight it, my mate."

He caught Ciri's scent the moment before his gaze found the slim shadow of her in the dark room. "Untie me."

"No." She reached out and flipped on the bedside lamp, and he blinked against the sudden glare.

He hissed and turned his face away. "What are you doing here? I thought you didn't want to be in this room anymore."

"And I thought you wanted me here." Her hands cupped his jaw, urging him to face her.

"You were avoiding me tonight after we had sex." He gave her a pointed glance, daring her to refute him.

She nodded, not running from the argument, which made something loosen inside him. If they couldn't talk honestly about their problems, then they would never get better, and he admitted to himself that if he couldn't listen when she did tell him what was wrong, then he wasn't doing much to help improve their relationship either.

That she was here, that she'd come to him now, and what Miguel had told him about standing her ground against a Pride leader, made more hope than he'd felt in months spread through him. It had hurt to have her run from him tonight, but so much had hurt lately. And he'd hurt her too. They had a lot of ground to make up.

Her fingers stroked along his jaw. "I . . . I heard about what you said to your father. About me. About us."

"I meant every word." He met her gaze, let everything show in his. "I swear I'll work harder."

Her nose wrinkled. "You work too hard as it is."

"On our *marriage*." He tugged at his bindings, but they held fast. He ignored them. Talking this out with her had all his focus. "I'm going to delegate more work in the Pride. I don't want to be like my father. I don't want you to be like my mother, where you give up everything for me and hate me for it in the end."

"I won't be like your mother. I'm not going to give up my career for you. It fulfills me, and I refuse to believe that I have to sacrifice that just to facilitate you keeping what fulfills you. Solana still has her business and I'm going to keep mine. I have to. I need my art."

He nodded, feeling the soft pillowcase rub against his cheek. "Father's not going to like it, but I'm with you in this fight."

"Good." A little smile curled her lips, and she dropped her chin to her chest, her dark hair falling around her shoulders. "That's good."

"Yes, it is." He tried to sit up, to reach for her, and remembered he was bound. He growled and subsided back to the mattress. "We have to support each other, Ciri, or we'll lose the most important thing, and that's *us*. I refuse to have my parents' marriage."

"I refuse to have your parents' marriage, too." Her fingers tightened on the thin rope she clutched in one hand. "I refuse to become your mother."

He snorted. "I refuse to become my father."

"Okay, then." Her grin widened and she met his gaze. "I can live with that."

"So can I. We've changed a lot and we'll change a lot more in the future. I don't know who we'll be, but I know I want to find out *together*." He searched her face as he said it, hoping she felt the same. "I don't want to be separated."

"I don't either." Her eyes were wide, and her expression was open. "I want us both to have what we need to be happy."

"I want that too."

Shaking her head, she sighed. "We should have had this conversation a long time ago."

He shrugged and the ropes tying his wrists to the headboard went taut. "Maybe we didn't know how. Maybe we weren't ready. Maybe the last few weeks have shown us just how much we have to lose if we don't hold on to each other."

"I don't want to lose you. I really don't, but I don't want to lose *me* either." She pressed the hand holding the rope to her chest.

"I know exactly what you mean." He couldn't have said it better himself, how he felt about all of this. He wanted them both to be themselves and still have each other.

She smiled at him. "I knew you would, my mate."

He'd never loved her more than in this moment. He'd opened his mouth to tell her when her lips closed over his, her tongue sliding in to tease his. His reaction was immediate and powerful, as it always was with his mate. He suckled her lower lip, pulling it between his teeth to bite down softly. She moaned into his mouth and his cock went hard. He pulled away, but his movements were hampered by the bindings.

He rolled his head on the pillow to look at the ropes. Slim and paler than cream, they smelled of something natural. Hemp, maybe. They were twisted in intricate patterns up his arms. His eyebrows arched and surprised sparked within him. "You know *shibari?*"

She chuckled. "That word just means 'to bind' in Japanese. We call this *kinbaru.*"

"I didn't know." He didn't know if he meant the new vocabulary or the new information about his wife.

Grinning, she bent forward to lick one of his nipples, and he jerked against the bindings in reflex. "As you said, we're constantly changing, but there is also much we don't know about each other, much we have yet to learn."

"Why didn't you ever do this to me before?"

A flush rose to her cheeks. "My mother sent the ropes to me. They arrived yesterday."

He tugged at the thin ties again, truly testing his strength against theirs. A human man would have been trapped, but he was no mortal. "I could escape from these."

"Do you want to escape me?"

He met her gaze, saw a warmth and affection there that he hadn't seen in months. There was no way he was going to do anything to discourage that. "No. I trust you."

"Good." She leaned forward and kissed the mate mark that scored his left pec. "That's very good."

A shudder passed through him at the contact with the mark. Lightning forked through his body, and his cock jerked. Her fingers drifted along the ropes on his arms, and suddenly they loosened and he was free.

"Would you kneel on the bed for me? I want to do this right." Her gaze met his, and he saw the questions there. Would he really trust her with this? Would a man born to lead be willing to give her *all* the power?

He pushed himself upright, shifting around until they were on their knees facing each other. "What should I do now?"

"Just stay there." She stretched up to kiss the side of his neck, to nip his flesh with her fangs. He shuddered, but didn't grab her and roll her under him as he wanted to. Whatever game she had in mind, he was going to play.

She draped the rope around the back of his neck, letting the ends dangle down his chest. Moving around him and behind him, she formed a variety of knots that made the rope crisscross over his chest, between his shoulder blades, around his waist, and between his legs. She drew his wrists behind him and tied them at the small of his back. It felt odd, but the scent of her, the feel of her hands on his flesh made him purr.

There were times when she brushed against his cock, and he knew it was deliberate. He was so hard, so ready, he felt beads of pre-cum rolling down the length of his shaft, but every second that passed cranked his anticipation up a notch.

She let one finger trail after a drop of fluid. "You're very hard, my mate."

"You're touching me." His chuckle was a rusty sound. "Of course I'm hard."

Humming in her throat, she swirled that fingertip around the head of his cock. "I like that. And I hope you'll like this."

And then she began tightening the ropes.

He hissed as the bindings began to rub over his skin, exerting pressure on his cock, the bindings biting in to separate his balls and pull his buttocks apart. The blood was effectively trapped in his dick, which flushed a deep red the tighter she drew the ropes.

Every movement of the bindings pushed him closer to the edge, and he feared he'd come before this game was anywhere near done. God, he'd never been so hot in his life. The ropes slid over the mate mark on his chest and he choked on a breath.

Sweat broke out on his forehead and every thought fled his mind. There was nothing in the world except his mate, the ropes, and the lust that consumed his body in living flames. The binding grew so taut he could barely breathe, and the pressure on his cock made groans wrench from his throat.

She pushed him onto his side, and his shoulder bounced hard against the mattress as he landed. Her fingers curled in the ropes on his chest, holding him close as she wrapped her thigh over his hip. He thrust forward as best he could, and she met him halfway, seating herself on his cock.

Dios.

Her gaze met his and never left. They were together in this, just as they promised. Connected. Mates. It was the most amazing thing he'd ever known.

The feel of her silky flesh sliding against his, the utter perfection of her heat squeezing tight around his cock, made the Panther within snarl and claw for freedom. His fangs bared and he groaned each time she sealed her pussy to the base of his cock. Every second sharpened to a clarity that would be seared into his memory for the rest of his days—her dark eyes flickering to gold, her fangs as deadly as his, moans spilling from her throat.

"Tomas." She gasped his name, the sound a rush of air in his ear.

"Ciri." He had to grit his teeth to keep from coming. All he could smell, feel, and taste was her. "God, you feel good."

She gripped the ropes tighter, pulled him closer. Her slim body arched, took him deep—deeper than he'd been before. "Yes."

And still they held each other's gazes, neither willing to release this precious link.

His hands fisted behind him and he struggled to move his body in the harsh bindings. He ground his hips against her, angling himself in the way he knew made her scream.

"Tomas, *Tomas!*" Her fangs scored his flesh as she bit down on his shoulder. The pain sharpened his pleasure until he thought he might die.

Her inner muscles clenched on his cock, milking him. He gave up on any hope of control, slamming into a wave of orgasm and letting it drag him under. The bite of the ropes only accentuated his pleasure; that he could barely move, barely breathe, just made it more intense. His come exploded out of him, jetting into her lovely body. The only word he could form was the one that meant the most to him. "Ciri!"

Just her name. That was all. That was everything.

They lay together, gasping, shuddering as they came down from the high. Her gaze never left his, and he saw every emotion on her face. She hid nothing from him, there was no pretense, no reserve. Just his Ciri. Sweet woman and ferocious predator all in one package that balanced his own nature to perfection.

After the sweat had cooled on their bodies, their breathing and heart rates had returned to normal, he winced as his muscles began to cramp in their bound position.

He chuckled again at the rare gift that was his wife, the unexpected fire beneath the cool exterior. "What other secrets have you been keeping from me? I hope they're all this good."

"I can only think of one." She leaned back, cupped his face between her palms, and met his gaze. "I love you."

He could see it in her eyes, could feel it in her touch, and it was heart-stopping in its intensity. "I love you, too."

Tears welled in her eyes, but she smiled the smile that had stolen his soul the very first day. "Good."

"Good." He leaned his forehead against hers. "Can you untie me now?"

She purred, her midnight eyes sparkling with joy. She ran a finger down one of the ropes. "Perhaps I should do this to you every time I want to get your undivided attention."

"I like that idea." He watched her eyes flash with feral gold light, and sensed how much she enjoyed his ready acceptance. Her talons sliced through the bindings, and gooseflesh broke down his limbs as his muscles relaxed in one great rush. He grinned at her. "Perhaps you should teach me the knotting techniques so I can return the favor."

Her breath caught, her nipples peaked tight where they pressed against his chest, and the smell of her damp arousal flooded his nose. "I . . . could be convinced."

"Convincing people is what I do." He grinned at her, but the expression faded. There were still things he hadn't said to her. Things he needed to ask her, so he just let the biggest question out. "Do you want me to step down as heir?"

He didn't know who he'd be if he wasn't a politician, but he'd figure it out. If he didn't have Ciri, he had nothing of real value. He would be half-dead, his soul ripped in two. For the first time since his *avô* died, he felt like he had his priorities straight.

A wry smile curved his lips. "Though it may not matter, since my father could be asking for my resignation after our conversation tonight."

"No, you will *not* resign. You love this; you're good at it. I wouldn't ask you to give up a part of yourself for me, and I won't give up myself for you." She pressed her hands to his chest. "We're in this together, remember?"

"But you hate this. You'd hate the life you'd live with me as a Pride leader's mate."

She pulled in a slow breath, her brows drawing together in consideration. "I'd hate living your mother's life, yes. But I'm not her and I never will be. I'd also hate living in a Pride as liberal as this one. I won't do things the way your mother does, or Solana does, or the way any other leader's mate does. I'll do them my way. Just as you'll do things your way. You don't intend to lead the same way that Pedro or Antonio leads, do you?"

"No. I won't. I don't agree with either of them on everything."

"Well, then." Her shoulder lifted in a shrug. "We'll make our own way. You're going to have a fight on your hands with your father, but I'll be by your side the whole way. Just like you'll be by my side. It's going to be rough, but we can do this. I know we can."

"I love you." More honest words had never come from his lips. It was the most fundamental truth of his life.

"I love you, too, Tomas. I always have. I always will. We'll work the rest out."

"Yes, we will." No one would ever fit him as well as she did, in and out of the bedroom. She was his balance, and he was grateful, so very grateful, that he had realized it before he'd lost her entirely. It staggered him that she'd been willing to give him another chance, that she had enough faith in him to come to him tonight. Her quiet courage and simple strength were traits he would never take for granted again.

As she'd said, they had so much to learn about themselves and each other, and now they had the time to do that. To savor each other, to build their relationship as they should have from the very beginning. He would always regret the time they'd lost, but they had now, they had today. They had every day for as long as they lived.

It was more than enough, no matter what other changes the future might hold for them.

They had each other.

Want Me

I

He had blood on his boots.

Exhaustion threatened to crush Rafe under its weight. He hadn't even noticed the rusty stains splattering over his shoes and up the legs of his pants until he'd gotten up to shuffle off the flight from Cairo.

Then again, he'd damn near missed his connection in New York, so he'd been sprinting through the airport to make it. Or running as fast as a human could. Even dead on his feet, a Panther could go a lot faster than any mortal. He'd passed out in his seat before they'd even backed away from the JFK terminal, which might be why he hadn't seen the gore on his clothes.

Luckily, the guys he was meeting wouldn't care. In fact, Ric and Diego would think it was awesome and want details of his latest adventure. A wry smile twisted his lips. If anyone was up for an adventure, it was the Cruz twins.

"Excuse me," an older man said politely as he elbowed Rafe in the gut.

"Don't worry about it." It was all he could do not to snarl at him.

This assignment had been grueling. One of those times when nothing went right. It happened, but this time it had grated on Rafe's nerves so much that he'd come close to losing his cool with a panhandling teen the day before. Normally, he was more amused than anything else with the ploys the kids used, but not lately. He was just . . . tired. Tired of not having roots, tired of not having family, tired of going from one place to the next and never having any permanency at all.

Sure, he was a member of the North American Panther Pride. He could stay there forever and never leave again if that was what he wanted, but it wasn't. As a travel journalist, he'd been everywhere at least once and lived to write about it. He'd gotten caught in riots, pinned down in war zones, stranded in the desert, and lost at sea. He'd seen all Seven Wonders of the World, hiked through rainforests with pygmies, ridden camels with Bedouin tribes, and seen sunrises on mountaintops that would make God Himself weep from the beauty of it.

It had been one hell of a life so far, and he'd loved every minute of it, but something had been riding him lately. A restlessness he couldn't understand. It used to be he got antsy staying in one place too long, and now the constant travel frayed his nerves. He'd cut his last trip short to come back to the Pride for a while. Some instinct told him he needed to be there, though he couldn't put his finger on why. Maybe staying put for a month or two would do him good. It couldn't hurt, and might let him shake whatever it was that was eating at him. He could catch up with old friends, get some writing done and thus make his editors happy at the same time.

He wove his way through the crowded airport, leaving the old man far behind. The smell and sound of so many people were an assault to keen Panther senses. The overhead speaker blared security warnings, and it was something he'd seen and experienced so many times it battered at his fatigued mind.

Hitching his backpack higher on his shoulder, he rode the escalator down to the luggage claim where he would meet the twins.

"Rafael!" Ric's voice caught his lagging attention, and he turned to shake the man's hand. A wide smile crossed both their faces and Ric slapped his shoulder.

Diego wrapped him up in an exuberant bear hug. "Hey, Rafe! How've you been, man? What happened to your clothes?"

"Not bad, and I'll tell you about it later." The weariness that had ridden him for so long hit him again. "I'm ready to get home and catch some Zs, though."

The twins glanced at each other and Ric's mouth tightened. Diego met Rafe's gaze. "That's going to have to wait for a few minutes. We have another pickup."

"Oh? Who?" The terse reaction—so unlike the energetic man—made curiosity rear its head.

After a long moment, Ric answered. "We have a Panther coming in on a flight from Tokyo."

Rafe waited a beat, expecting more information. The twins' uncharacteristic reticence definitely had his attention. "Someone from Ciri's family, perhaps?"

"No. The heir to the Spanish Pride." A muscle in Diego's jaw ticked. "Fernando Garcia's daughter. Enrique Garcia's sister. Teresa."

"Shit." There was no other word he could put to the concept. There was bad blood between the European and North American Prides. Hell, there wasn't a lot of love lost between the European and African Prides either, and it all came down to one man.

Enrique Garcia.

The madman was the Pride leader's son, and he'd become obsessed with Isabel, insisted she was his mate, and assaulted her, biting her to mark her as his. She'd fled Barcelona and sought asylum in San Francisco, where her childhood friend was now the leader's wife. When Isabel had arrived, she'd found not one, but both of the leader's younger twin brothers were her mates.

Rafe shook his head. "I mean . . . uh . . . shit."

Diego snorted. "Yeah, exactly."

"Are you sure you're the right ones to be dealing with this woman?" As far as Rafe knew, none of the mated trio had had any contact with the Garcias since they'd gone to Africa to represent the Pride for Cesar Benhassi's recognition ceremony when he'd come to power.

"We wanted to meet her before Isabel has to see her." Diego's gaze hardened, and the pure protective instinct of a mated Panther male was evident in his expression.

Enrique had also been in Africa for the ceremony, and in his madness had tried to attack Isabel again, demanding she return to his side as his mate. The twins had laid him out flat, and Benhassi had publicly rebuked Fernando for keeping a crazed man as his heir, forcing him to denounce his son and make his daughter his heir.

Such reckless idiocy could have led to civil war, to the exposure of Panthers to humans, to the end of their race as they knew it. Civil war had decimated the Pride in Africa a few decades before, so if anyone knew what he was talking about, it was Benhassi. The altercation had soured relations between Spain and the other two Prides.

And now the Pride leader's new heir, Teresa, was coming *here*. It sounded like a recipe for disaster.

Clearing his throat, Rafe hitched his pack higher on his back. "What's she coming to North America for, anyway?"

"She's attending Antonio's peace summit. She missed the opening ball last night because a storm over the Pacific delayed her flight, but she'll be here for the actual summit." Ric crossed his arms. "But let's be real, she's doing a tour of the Prides to find a mate. They're saying it's a dignitary tour to meet all the other leaders, heirs, and Seconds, and this summit is just the cap on the tour, but she's unmated and around thirty, so . . . you do the math."

"No doubt Garcia wants to get her mated up and breeding since his *loco* son isn't churning out potential heirs for his line anytime soon." Ric slid his hands into his pockets, a muscle flexing in his jaw.

Rafe sighed. This did not look promising. Ric was usually the rational one of the two, while Diego had a gilded tongue. If both of them were defensive and pissed off, they had a good chance of offending this woman and making relations between the two Prides even worse. Great. Just great. This was not what Rafe wanted to be dealing with right now. A hot shower and a bed were what he had in mind, in that order.

"How long until her flight lands?"

Diego checked his watch. "Any minute now."

"I'm getting a cup of coffee. You guys want anything?" The two were strung so tight, Rafe didn't think they needed caffeine.

"Nope, we're good, thanks." They spoke at once, their attention focused on the arrivals area.

If he hurried, he might be able to get back in time to save the woman from a possible mauling. But without some coffee, he might not last long enough to help anyone. He was about ready to drop where he stood.

Swinging around, he headed straight for the scent of coffee. Of all the overwhelming scents in the terminal, that one was the most welcome. The line was long, of course, but the bored-looking baristas shuffled people through with practiced precision. Within ten minutes, he had a steaming cup of pitch-black sludge. He burned his tongue when he guzzled it, but it was exactly what he needed.

"Damn," he groaned. He'd missed the woman's arrival. Her chin was lifted and she met the twins' gazes coolly. Whatever greeting they'd given her had been less than welcoming.

Even from a distance, he could see she was an attractive female, with a smooth sweep of inky hair that brushed her shoulders. Her business suit was tailored to her curves. Not too slender, like most women were these days. Her eyes were a startling pale gray, and her lips were a little too generous for her face, but she was lovely in a reserved kind of way.

"I thought Tomas was going to be the one picking me up. He *is* the one I've been dealing with to make arrangements for this trip." Her voice was as frosty as the look in her eyes.

Diego shrugged. "He and his mate took the day off. I'm afraid you'll have to make do with us."

"I see."

Not good. Not good at all. Rafe tossed the remainder of his cup in the nearest trash bin and pasted a smile on his face before he approached the trio. "Hello, Ms. Garcia. I'm Rafael Santiago. It's nice to meet you."

The moment she turned to meet his gaze, some instinct rang in his head, reverberating like a clarion bell until it almost ached. He blinked, struggling to fight through the exhaustion to decipher what his senses were telling him. Then it pierced his sleep-deprived mind, and he jolted in shock.

Mate.

He froze, every muscle in his body locking tight.

"Hello." She held out a slim, elegant hand for him to shake.

He could only stare at her, gaping like a fool. She let her hand hang there for a second, her expression growing stiffer. Her arm began to wilt to her side. Losing the chance to touch her finally spurred him into action. Thrusting his hand out, he wrapped his fingers around hers. The fine bones and soft skin absorbed his senses, and he drew in her scent, the heady aroma like a hit of opiates.

When their flesh met, her eyes widened. Yes, she felt it too, this incredible connection that snapped between them. Triumph bloomed within him, the need to claim a bone-jarring recognition of mating fever. A flash of utter horror sparked in her pale gaze and she dropped his hand as though he were diseased.

Stunned pain rocked through him at her sudden, unexpected rejection. His heart squeezed at this stranger's reaction, this woman who was supposed to be a perfect match for him.

She looked at the twins. "I need to collect my luggage."

Not waiting for them to respond, she spun on a heel and marched away. The three men glowered at each other before following her. Rafe had no idea why his mate would be so upset about having found what she was apparently looking for, but it didn't stop the protective instincts that flared to life within him.

The tiredness fell away as energy and alertness pumped through his system. He'd crash again later, but for the moment, every fiber of his being was focused on the female who was walking away from him. He made his living observing people, finding out what made them tick, and then writing about it, but this time he wanted to know everything without the need to put pen to paper. Curiosity ate at him.

Who was she, really? Being an heir was only one piece of a person. Why was she unhappy to find a mate? What had put the shadows in her eyes, the sadness that seemed just below the surface?

He had to know.

She studiously avoided his gaze while they got her suitcases out to the car. Of course they'd picked her up in the Jeep, instead of the Pride's limousine. It was one more way to make sure she knew her Pride wasn't favored here, and that sent a punch of anger through Rafe. Her face was composed when she gracefully climbed into the backseat. The space was too tight when Rafe settled beside her, his shoulders wide enough to touch hers, his legs cramped enough to be bent and crowding into her.

"Sorry," he said, but he didn't mean it. His body reacted as if lit by a live wire every time he brushed up against her. His cock stiffened uncomfortably, but there was no room to adjust his position.

"De nada." Her voice was a bit breathless, and he heard her swallow.

After that the car fell into silence. Even the exuberant Diego stared out the window and said nothing. Rafe ended up pressed to Teresa's side when the car turned a corner, and he drew back immediately, but not before he got a whiff of her arousal. It surprised him, and he looked over her calm features. The woman knew how to hide her emotions from the world, but a closer look revealed that her fingers twisted together in her lap, a fine trembling in her limbs.

She glanced at him from the corner of her eye, and he felt that bone-deep connection again. For whatever reason, she didn't *want* to want him, but she did. And, God, but he wanted her too. The need was clawing at his insides. Resisting it was almost painful. He dropped his hand to the seat between them and subtly rubbed his knuckles against her thigh.

Her breath caught, and her body grew even tauter. The tension all but hummed from her, but the scent of her passion increased as well. His cock went rock hard, chafing against his fly. It was all he could do not to groan aloud.

This was a stupid idea, with the twins close enough to smell the pheromones wafting off of them, but at the moment, the Panther in him refused to give a damn. This was far too primal an urge to fight.

A shudder passed through her and he could see her breasts lift as her breathing sped. Her tongue flicked out to lick her lips, and he damn near jerked her into his lap. He wanted to be inside her, the scent of their combined arousal permeating the air around them while they rutted in a big bed.

Soon. God, soon. How long before he could drag her away from the Cruz family and have his hands on her naked flesh? Would she resist or be as animalistic in her need as he would?

He had no idea, but he wanted to find out.

Madre de Dios.

Teresa was going to lose her mind if she didn't get out of this cramped Jeep. Now.

This was a nightmare. It was a complete and utter nightmare. After what had happened with her brother, she'd been hoping she didn't *have* a mate, and if she did, it could at least not be a man from America. Or Africa. But no, she had to deal with both problems at once.

And it would be a lot easier if she weren't also being driven insane by that American man as he stroked slow circles against her thigh while she tried not to come right then and there.

She had never truly understood until this moment that sex could be better with a mate, but now she did. *Dios,* she did. She clenched her fingers together in her lap, trying not to reach for him.

He was hard. She could see the clear outline of his erection in his khaki pants, and her sex clenched with want. Her nipples stood out in similar flagrant fashion under her silk blouse.

What would it feel like to have him inside her? A rush of heat flooded her, and she could feel her skin sensitize as though preparing for his touch.

Maybe it was. If the single point of contact was enough to indicate how good it would be, she didn't know how long she could resist. It had been a long time since she'd taken a lover—not since Enrique's fall from grace and her elevation to the intense responsibilities of heir.

Her body clamored for her to make up for lost time. She squeezed her legs together and tried to ignore the ache between them, but she knew it was a fruitless effort before she did it. Every sense she had was focused on him. His scent, the way his brown hair ruffled in the breeze from the open passenger side window, the feel of his knuckles rubbing against her leg. She wanted to try all her other senses on him. What would he taste like? What would his bare skin feel like on hers? *All* of hers? What would he look like naked? The question was enough to make her even wetter, her sex fisting on emptiness.

The Jeep pulled to an abrupt stop and she rocked in her seat, barely bringing her palm up to catch herself before her nose hit the back of Ric's seat. At least she thought it was Ric. The men looked exactly alike and she hadn't entirely sorted out their scent differences yet. She'd been too distracted by Rafe.

She blinked and looked around. They were in front of a huge mansion, and from the smell of it, there were dozens of Panthers in the vicinity. The Pride den. Her belly executed a slow flip and she swallowed sudden nausea. This visit was so important. Her father might be willing to cut ties with leaders who'd insulted him, who'd insulted Enrique, but Teresa knew they couldn't afford that. There were too few Panthers in the world, and their politics were too rocky to isolate their people. She'd used the excuse of a mate search and tour of the Pride just to get to this peace summit.

She hadn't really wanted a mate, but her father wanted grandchildren, wanted to prove that the European Pride's leading family was as strong as ever. Stronger.

If only it were true, but she'd do what she could in the coming days to strengthen their ties and keep Europe a force to be reckoned with. She pulled in a deep breath and pushed down her trepidation. There was no time for hesitation or fear.

Rafe's hand closed over her shoulder, and lust ripped through her so fast she almost snarled with the ferocity of her inner Panther's reaction to his touch. "We're here, Teresa."

"So I see." She tried to keep her tone even, but doubted she succeeded. Turning to look up at him, she found him closer than she'd realized, his lips only a hairbreadth from hers.

They froze, their gazes locked together. His eyes were like dark chocolate with flecks of gold in them. Rich and provocative. That hot spark of recognition sizzled through her again. *Mate*. Her mouth dried and she licked her lips. His gaze followed the movement, and her body turned to living flame.

At that moment, if he had reached for her, she wouldn't have protested. A smile kicked up the corner of his lips, the gold in his eyes glowing with feline intensity. "We have to go inside."

Yes, they did. Coupling in the backseat of a car was a bad idea, but she couldn't quite recall why. In a daze, she climbed out of the Jeep, took one of her suitcases from Diego—or was it Ric?—while Rafe commandeered her other two bags, and they walked up the front steps. A pretty young woman opened the door for them, nodding as they passed her and entered the foyer.

"What room is she in, Eva?" Rafe gave the woman a charming grin, and Teresa fought an unexpected wave of jealous possession.

Eva linked her hands in front of her and returned the smile with a small one of her own. "The blue suite."

"I'll show her up." Rafe hefted Teresa's bags higher. "I know you're busy. The visiting politicos are probably running your staff ragged."

"That's about right, yes. Thank you, Rafe." A flash of relief showed in the woman's gaze. "Please let me know if there's anything I can do to make your stay here more comfortable, Ms. Garcia."

"I will. Thank you." Her mind spun when he pressed his chest to her back, urging her forward. The full-body contact made her lungs seize. Her heart pounded so loudly in her ears, it drowned out every other sound. She felt her claws dig into her palm where her fingers were wrapped around the handle of her suitcase.

"Go left at the top of the stairs, third door on the right." His voice was rough with lust, and she could sense that he burned with the same fire that consumed her.

A feeling of unreality flooded her. She couldn't believe she was going to do this. There was no doubt in her mind what would happen when they reached her suite. But she couldn't *not* do it. *Mate.* It rang in her mind, in her soul, in every inch of her hypersensitized body. She obeyed his direction, turning blindly for the room he indicated.

The door swung open on silent hinges and she stepped through, her eyes adjusting to the mellow lighting. The suite was decorated in pale blue with bronze accents, and a huge four-poster bed was visible through a set of open double doors. The bedroom was much too far away. She dropped her suitcase to the carpet and heard the thuds of him doing the same with her other bags. He shrugged out of his backpack and swatted the door closed behind them.

When he turned to face her, his hands were already busy on his belt and fly. "Come here."

Her legs shook as they carried her the few feet to him. He

kicked his boots aside and stripped out of the rest of his clothes in short order. She just stared at him as all that male flesh was revealed. He was beautiful, tall with wide shoulders and a muscular torso that tapered down into narrow hips. She wanted to touch him, slide her hands over his skin, the crisp hair on his chest, and the long cock that stood in a hard arc to just below his navel.

Her nose twitched when she drew near him, and she stopped in her tracks. "It smells like . . . blood."

"Uh, yeah. About that . . ."

Glancing around, she spotted his shoes and pants. She sniffed the air and made a face. "That isn't human blood."

"Probably goat or cow." A flush rose to his cheeks, and he rubbed the back of his neck. "I was in Cairo for Eid al-Adha, and they still sacrifice animals for the holiday celebrations."

She blinked up at him, intrigued despite the grotesque mental picture his statement provided. "You're serious?"

"Yeah." His broad shoulder dipped in a shrug, and he took her arm to lead her away from the malodorous garments. "I'll tell you about it later, if you're curious."

"I'm a cat. Of course I'm curious." It felt as if a brand had been laid to her skin everywhere his skin touched her, and just that quickly, her mind dismissed everything that wasn't her mate and his large, naked body. Then again, he'd apparently had gore on his clothing since she'd met him and she hadn't noticed it because she was so intent on the rest of him. It wasn't like her to miss that kind of thing, but today was no ordinary day.

"I want you to be curious about other things right now." His lids dropped to half-mast and he purred as he looked her over. "I'm curious about what you look like with no clothes on. I'm curious about what color your nipples are and how they'll taste when I suck on them."

Her mouth opened, but no words came out. Her hormones rioted at his vivid description. She wanted what he wanted. "Yes."

A laugh burst out of him. "Well, all right, then."

Reaching for her pants, he unfastened them while she worked open the buttons on her blouse. She stepped out of her flats and kicked them aside as he worked her slacks, panties, and hosiery down in one motion. She unhooked her bra and let it fall. His eyes flickered to Panther gold when he saw all of her. The blood rushed through her veins so fast she felt lightheaded. Her nipples were tight enough to ache, and her pussy slickened with juices.

He backed her up against a wall, and she gasped when every inch of him came into mind-blowing contact with her. Rising on tiptoe, she tried to align their sexes, tried to rub her breasts against the rough silk of his chest hair. Her pussy clenched, so ready for him to be inside her she was almost panting with need. The Panther within writhed in mating heat. "Now, please."

"Shh." His mouth touched hers and she froze. They were naked, about to rut, and his lips brushed hers with the lightest of touches. His body was hard and demanding, pressing hers into the wall, but his mouth was a soft request, a slow seduction.

The contrast was stunning, made her knees buckle, and she sagged against him. He purred, his hands dropping to cup her hips, his length pinning her to the wall to keep her upright. He licked his way into her mouth, his tongue twining with hers.

He lifted her, and her back scraped against the texture of the wall. She arched in reflex, and his fingers bit into her flesh, holding her tight. Still he kissed her sweetly, while his touch was rough. It excited her. She wrapped her arms around his neck and her legs around his hips. The head of his cock probed at her wet opening and she shuddered at the anticipation screaming through her. She nipped at his lip, felt her claws dig in to his shoulders. Every instinct urged her on. She wanted him, she needed him. Now. *Dios,* right now.

Easing his hold on her, he let gravity impale her on his cock. She whimpered into his mouth, and his tongue plunged in as his dick hilted inside her. The double penetration made her sex squeeze around his shaft.

A groan reverberated through his chest, and she could feel it in hers. He withdrew and thrust deep again, the friction more amazing than anything she'd ever known before. She tightened her legs around his waist, moving with him as he worked her on his cock. Angling his pelvis, he hit her clitoris every time he entered her pussy.

"Rafe!"

"I like my name on your lips," he whispered. "Teresa."

She liked the way he said her name too, as if she were the most desirable woman on the planet. It turned her on even more. Everything about him did—the way he smelled, the way he tasted, the way their bodies rubbed together when he filled her. "Harder, Rafe."

"I like that even better." He laughed, his fangs showing, his eyes dancing with merriment, and he gave her what she wanted. He slammed deeper inside her, arching his hips to power his thrusts.

She screamed when his cock touched her G-spot, and points of light burst behind her eyes. Any second she was going to come. Contractions built in her pussy, and she could hear how wet she was, how his skin slapped against hers. It was carnal and animalistic and nothing like her normal self, which made it even hotter.

Tingles broke down her limbs, and her breath was little more than gasping. Sweat glued their bodies together, made the glide of their skin erotic. Every movement was fucking divine. "I need to come."

"Then come for me." He ground against her clit, shoving deeper inside her than he'd gone before. Then he shuddered and pumped his fluids into her pussy.

It was enough to make her explode. Her sex fisted on his cock, milking him as he flooded her channel. Ecstasy rocketed through her system, and another wave of orgasm gripped her pussy. She closed her eyes, clinging to him as she rode out the storm. His arms held her tight, crushing the breath from her lungs, but she liked the feel of him. Her nipples rubbed his chest, stimulating the too-sensitive tips.

Shivers still rippled over her skin a long time later. She dropped her forehead to his shoulder and sighed. The musk of sex permeated the air, and their combined scents filled her nose as she panted for breath. It smelled . . . right. It felt perfect, and that scared her to death. This wasn't *right*. She knew what kind of pain mating could cause. She'd seen how wrong it could go. Her brother still spent most of his days in a mindless stupor because of his problems with finding a mate.

She didn't want this. She'd never wanted this. It had only been an excuse to come to the summit, and a part of her had been so sure, so absolutely certain that she wouldn't find a mate on her tour. Fate wouldn't do that to her, not after what it had done to Enrique.

But it appeared Fate was a spiteful bitch when it came to the Garcia family.

2

"I need a shower."

Rafe groaned and eased his weight from where he was crushing her into the wall. It had been mind-blowing. His fangs had extended to the point that they scored his lower lip. He'd damn near bitten her, marked her as his. The urge had been so powerful, it still made him shake. He'd known his share of lovers, but this possessiveness was totally foreign to him.

Teresa looked everywhere except at him as she scooted around him to walk toward the bedroom. He narrowed his eyes at her retreating back. Should he give her space now to try to sort through this insane connection? He'd have given anyone else space, but the Panther in him flatly refused to be separated from its mate so soon after their first time together. "I'll join you. I could use a shower myself."

She shot him a fulminating glance over her shoulder, but what could she do? Kick him out right after sex? Her scent was all over him, and if she hoped to be discreet, she didn't want him walking around this way. He agreed with discretion. The imperative for mating and breeding new Panthers to save their race from extinction meant there was enormous societal pressure once news circulated that mates had found each other but remained unclaimed. Her reactions so far said she didn't want that kind of attention any more than he did. So, she had to keep him around a bit longer. He grinned at her and followed her through her room and into the bathroom.

The room was plush, which befitted her status as a visiting Pride heir. Good. After Diego and Ric's behavior, Rafe had thought they might stick her in a basement closet. His Pride leader, Antonio, had always struck him as a sensible man, and Rafe was glad that had won out over rancor for the European Pride.

Cold tile made his toes curl when he got to the bathroom, and he watched her sort through a small basket of toiletries Eva must have provided. Teresa unwrapped a new bar of soap and plucked out a few bottles of what he assumed were shampoo and conditioner. She carried everything toward the shower, reached in to spin the knobs, and turned on the hot water. It was a pleasure to watch her move. She was a beautiful woman, curved in all the right places.

"You really are lovely, Teresa." The words were out of his mouth before he thought better of it.

He caught a glimpse of the surprise in her gray gaze as she glanced over her shoulder at him. "Thank you. I like the way you look, too."

"I guess that's how it's supposed to be with mates."

Her shoulders hunched a bit. "We aren't mated."

"Yet." He couldn't help a smile at her low hiss. She threw him a narrowed glance, and something about that struck him, but he wasn't sure what. Her body positioning, the look in her gray eyes. Something. "I've seen you before."

She arched an eyebrow and gave him a look reserved for

simpletons. "Before when? We just saw each other in the bedroom, the car, the airport . . ."

"Oh, funny girl." He rolled his eyes and watched her struggle to hold back a grin. Good. He wanted to see her smile. "I meant I've seen you before *today*. I visited Spain once before when I was about eighteen."

Dios, that had been nineteen years ago. Teresa would have been maybe ten or eleven—not even old enough to shift yet, since that ability hit right around puberty. It explained why he hadn't sensed who she was to him then.

Tilting her head, she squinted at him. "Yes, I think I recall the incident. You didn't even stay long enough for dinner, but we didn't get a lot of foreign visitors. Not teenagers, anyway."

"It was my only trip to Europe until Antonio came to power." The memory crystallized, and he remembered walking out of the Pride leader's office and glancing up. The gray-eyed urchin had been peering over a balcony to get a peek at him. She must look like her mother, because he would never have guessed that the little girl was related to the man who'd spent an hour grilling him about what the trip to European territory would accomplish.

"Oh? Why is that?" She stepped under the shower spray, holding the door open for him to come in with her.

The honest curiosity in her expression warmed him. He was used to people being interested in what he did—travel writing was an unusual career for humans and unheard of for Panthers—but considering how she'd avoided even looking at him after they'd had sex, it was nice that she was intrigued by him. He sure as hell wanted to know everything about her. "Antonio's father, Esteban, was less than approving of what I do for a living."

"Travel journalism. I've read your collections of stories."

She shrugged and leaned her head back to let the water run through her ebony hair. "They were good books."

He smiled down at her. She'd read his work. She'd *liked* it. "I'm flattered."

Shrugging, she turned her face into the shower, and he stepped close behind her to catch some of the spray. The hot water made him sigh. When was the last time he'd had a bath? A bed big enough to fit his height? Months, probably. He didn't mind roughing it, but that meant he treasured the modern conveniences and comforts when he could get them.

"It's strange for a Panther to go as many places as you do, to live outside the Prides, but not be an outcast." Her expression turned considering. "Most wouldn't choose that life."

"It's what I love. I did a year of foreign exchange in England, which is why I visited your Pride, and then I took a road trip around the U.S. after I finished my senior year at Stanford. The travel bug bit me, and I haven't stopped since." He grabbed the bar of soap, working up a lather between his palms before he handed it to her. Her slick skin sliding against his, even in so innocent a touch, made his body react, and he had to focus to keep up the thread of the conversation. "Esteban was willing to negotiate one extended trip to each continent for me, but for the most part I've spent all my time in Africa."

"Because he didn't have to negotiate when Africa had no Pride to rule it." Her response was immediate. Of course, the politics would catch her attention. She was an heir.

"Right, and since then Antonio has been willing to make a few concessions to other leaders in order for me to travel everywhere." He'd loved it, too. Going wherever the assignment offers took him, no longer having to limit himself for the sake of complex Panther policies that his very human editors didn't understand.

Her brows drew together as she absentmindedly rubbed

shampoo in her hair. "I've enjoyed my trip to each Pride, but I doubt I'll get to do much travel outside of the Panther world. Heirs don't have those luxuries."

The water raining over her breasts, through her hair, down her naked flesh broke any concentration he had in the conversation. He stepped forward, well into her space, and lowered his voice to a purr. "I could show you places that would blow your mind. Haven't you ever wanted to see the sun rise over the Himalayas? Swim naked in Tahiti?"

Her breath caught and her pupils dilated as her gaze focused on his lips. "I . . . I . . ."

Reaching out, he let the tip of one finger follow the trail of a single droplet of water, down her neck, dipping into the hollow at her collarbone, slipping between her lush breasts. "You'd be as wet as you are now. Wetter. Just for me. Wouldn't you, Teresa?"

"We shouldn't . . ."

The steam in the shower surrounded them, caressed them. Her eyes blazed to silver, then swirled with the pure gold of her feline side. He could smell how damp her sex had grown. It made his cock hard enough to throb with the need to be inside her. He let his finger slide down into her navel, over the lower curve of her belly, and into the soft thatch of hair between her legs. "What shouldn't we do? Isn't this what you came here for? The twins said this was your mating tour, disguised as an ambassadorial visit."

She laughed and moaned at the same time as he pushed his fingers into her wet cleft, teasing the slick lips he found there, the hard little clit. "No, this is an ambassadorial visit disguised as a mating tour."

"I don't understand." He paused for a second, trying to push the lust away long enough to sort that out in his head.

She killed any hope of that when she wrapped her fingers

around his cock and pumped him in her hand. "The distinction is family politics rather than Pride politics."

"Okay." He'd figure it out later. Right now, he had more pressing matters to contend with. Like having his mate as often as possible.

Dipping forward, he licked along her bottom lip. Her grip on his cock tightened, and she moaned. He took her mouth, shoving his tongue inside to capture her flavor. Sweet, so sweet. At the same time, he pinched her clit and she squirmed in response. He liked making her squirm. He liked it a lot.

One of her hands stroked up and down his shaft, while she ran the thumb of her other hand over the head of his cock, pausing to rub the sensitive underside. A purr soughed from his throat and he shuddered, thrusting his hips forward to add to the sensation. The water pouring over them only increased the intensity of the moment. It felt like hundreds of hot fingers slid down his skin, and her touch on his dick made him groan.

Twisting his hand, he forced her thighs farther apart and delved deeper into her sex. The plush lips were swollen and soft, slick with a moisture the shower hadn't made. She whimpered against his lips, shoving her tongue into his mouth to twine with his. Her hips moved with his hand, and he moved with hers, locked together in a carnal dance with only one end. Her wetness coated his fingers as he pushed three digits into her pussy. The scent of her was addicting. He had to have her, craved that connection with her in a way he'd never craved it with anyone before. Mate. The recognition of it roared through his blood.

He jerked away from her, pulling his fingers from her channel. She hissed, her eyes now pure gold. "Don't stop!"

Grinning at her feral reaction, he grabbed her shoulders and spun her to face the tiled wall of the shower. Pressing himself to her back, he shoved his thigh between hers, widening her stance so his cock could slide over her pussy from behind. "Stop? I wouldn't dream of it."

"Good." Her voice was clipped, her low feline growl almost drowned out by the pounding shower spray.

He reached around her, slipping his palm down her wet flesh until he could toy with her clit again. She cried out when he stabbed his cock deep into her pussy. *"Dios."*

The feel of her was as close to heaven as he'd ever been. It was as terrifying as it was intoxicating, how just being near her reached into his soul and grabbed onto something he hadn't even known was there.

Flicking his fingers over her clit, he made her writhe against him. He trailed his free hand up to cup her breast, squeezing the soft curve. The rain of hot water over them sealed them together, increased the friction everywhere their skin met. He could feel her responses deep within, the subtle clench and release of her pussy each time he caressed her most sensitive flesh. She twisted in his embrace, a scream ripping from her when he thrust his cock to the hilt and pinched her nipple hard.

He bent forward to kiss the nape of her neck, holding her tighter to him, loving the feel of her, the steam, the shower. All of it. He savored this experience, this moment, as he did with everything in his life. It's what made him so good at his job, and that level of revelry in the unknown was nothing compared to this. Fucking her hard, he trailed kisses across the back of her shoulder and up the side of her throat to her ear.

Sucking the lobe between his lips, he flicked it with his tongue and nipped at it with his teeth. Her hips shoved back to take him deeper, and he could feel her grow slicker. She liked this, and her pleasure made him burn. She moaned, tilting her head to give him greater access. Taking advantage, he released her ear and moved his mouth down her neck to the tender spot at the base of her throat. The sounds she made when he suckled the tendon there made his fangs erupt from his gums. God, it was all he could do not to come then and there. His mate brought out his basest and most animal instincts. Mate. Yes. He dug his fangs into her flesh, a rough request. He wanted to mark her. The Panther within him made the need nearly unstoppable.

"No," she gasped, shrugging her shoulder to try to push him away.

He growled, his fangs scoring deeper, but some small bit of human sanity held him back, refused to let him take what was not freely offered. He would never, *could* never, do that to her. Not his mate. Releasing his grip on her skin, he groaned.

To distract himself from what the Panther wanted, he focused on the sheer physicality of their joining. The way her wet sex clung to his harder flesh, the glide of water over their bodies, the way they moved together. Her moans when he fucked her pussy. The building tension in her body that told him how close she was to orgasm.

"Rafe!" Her voice went high and thin, and he rolled his finger over her clit, knowing she needed more to go over the edge.

He wouldn't disappoint her.

Slamming his cock deep, he ground his pelvis against her and roughly fondled her clitoris. A Panther's shriek jerked out of her, and her inner muscles flexed on his dick. Over and over again as she came apart in his arms. He loosed his own reaction, letting the feline free only as orgasm dragged him under. His fluids jetted inside her and he shuddered as something deeper than ecstasy ripped through his system.

He let his forehead rest against the back of her skull, water raining down on them, dripping from their hair, their faces, their limbs. His heart pounded, his breath bellowing out. It took a long time to come down from that high, and he held her as he enjoyed those moments. She twitched in his arms, and he forced himself to ease his weight away from her.

"We've just killed the point of this shower." She sighed and reached for the soap, scrubbing off quickly. Tossing the bar toward him, she let him do the same.

Leaving him to rinse himself and turn off the water, she stepped out to dry off with a thick terry cloth towel. Frowning, he stepped out and dried himself as well, then hooked the towel around his hips. Just as she had after their first time, she didn't even look at him. He had a feeling if he let her get away with it, she'd scurry out of the room, dress, and be gone without saying another word to him.

Not that he had a lot of experience with this kind of thing, but this didn't seem like the normal reaction of a woman who'd just found her mate. He strolled over to the bathroom door while she brushed her hair and planted himself on the threshold, keeping her from leaving.

"Can I ask you something?" He folded his arms across his chest and saw her gaze turn wary as she faced him. She nodded, set down the brush, picked it up, then dropped it again. Her fingers shook a bit. Nerves? Or something more? He took in the odd reaction, adding it to the list of other reactions that didn't seem to fit. "Why wouldn't you let me mark you?"

"We've only just met, Rafe." She bunched her fingers in the towel she had wrapped around her. "It's hardly unreasonable to want to get to know you before I . . . before we . . ."

"Before we're mated?" He leaned a shoulder against the door frame, still effectively blocking her escape. "Sure, that's reasonable, but you can't even say the word. That tells me something else is going on here. So, let's try this again. Why wouldn't you let me mark you, my mate?"

"I don't want a mate," she burst out, then covered her

mouth and closed her eyes. She shook her head. "I'm sorry. I shouldn't have said it that way, but . . ."

"But you don't want a mate." He finished the thought for her, and it shredded that fragile connection between them. God, it hurt. She was right, they didn't know each other, but that didn't seem to stop the ache that spread like a bruise inside him. He felt like he'd been sucker punched. "I see."

"I'm really sorry." She knotted her fists in the towel. "It's not you. I just . . . I have my reasons for not wanting to mate. I honestly hoped I didn't have one. I'm sorry."

"What are your reasons?"

"My brother. I'm sure you've heard about him. Everyone has." Her gaze hit the top of the vanity, and her face smoothed of all emotion.

She was lying. Or at least not giving him the whole truth. Years of observing human behavior told him so. Every Panther instinct inside him confirmed it. There was far more to the story than that. "And that's your only reason?"

"Isn't that enough?" She lifted her chin, but her expression remained blank.

If he pushed her now, she'd never tell him. He knew it down to his bones. So he just nodded and stepped aside to clear her path. The look of intense relief that crossed her face only justified his suppositions. There was something she didn't want to talk about, which meant she was hiding something—something that made her not want to be mated. He shoved aside how that stung him. His mate was upset enough to deny what every Panther hoped to find. If he focused on how that pained him rather than rooting out what had turned her against the very idea of mating, then he'd never change her mind.

While he'd never really thought to find a mate himself, and had forgone the traditional mating tour at thirty in favor of his career, he wasn't set against it the way she was.

Time for a strategic retreat. He could break through her reserve slowly. She was in San Francisco for the two weeks of the summit, so he had some time, and he'd use that to his advantage.

They both dug through their abandoned bags for clean outfits. His was a pair of well-worn khakis and a fleece pullover. Hers was a silk shirt, skirt, and heels. When it came to the differences in their positions in the Prides, that just about said it all. He lived out of a backpack while on assignment, so he didn't even travel with a spare pair of shoes. He'd have to go barefoot until he cleaned up his boots.

She brushed an invisible piece of lint off her blouse. "I have to go present myself to Antonio. I'm sure the housekeeper informed him of my arrival."

"Eva is the butler, not the housekeeper, but you're right. She's very efficient." He threaded his belt through the loops on his pants, buckling it in place. "If Antonio didn't sense your arrival in his domain, he's been told by now."

He plucked his wallet and cell phone from his old pants and transferred them to his new ones. Then he shrugged into his backpack, scooped up the dirty clothes and blood-spattered boots, and opened the door to let both of them out. Her face held that same calm she seemed to have perfected, but her hands were balled at her sides. It was the hands that gave her away, and he knew to watch for that now.

He didn't think he'd let her in on the fact that she had a tell. She'd likely train herself out of it and into even more control, and he liked having some insight into the woman who was his mate. They stood in the hallway outside her room—he was reluctant to leave her, and he'd bet she was even more reluctant to deal with the leader of a Pride unfriendly to hers.

"Good luck with Antonio. He's a fair man, a *good* man." He

offered a reassuring smile, hoping she'd relax a little. "I trust him."

Her gaze searched his face for a long moment. What she was looking for, he couldn't guess, but she must have found it, because she let her breath ease out. "Okay. I'll keep that in mind."

"Do you want me to go with you? I can introduce you." Most of the time, Rafe didn't deliberately throw himself into Pride matters, but he found himself wanting to do anything to break the tension that seemed to be screaming through her body. "It might make it easier to have a third party in the room."

"No, no." She shook her head, making her still-damp hair fly around her face. "I can do this myself. I *will* do this myself. Antonio's a fair man, so I'll be all right. Thanks for the luck. I hope I don't need it. Good-bye."

Staying where he was, he watched her walk away until she disappeared down the stairs. He tried to assure himself that they were both right, that she'd be fine, that she didn't need his help, that Antonio was a good leader and he'd treat her with respect, no matter what he thought of her father or brother.

She *would* be fine. He tamped down on any concern that might be niggling at the back of his mind.

"Rafe!"

He turned, already prepared to be wrapped up in the huge bear hug by Ben Aguilar. "Benedicto, my man!"

To say Rafe welcomed the distraction was an understatement, and the chance to see one of the people he was closest to in the world was one of the best reasons he'd had for coming home.

They slapped each other on the back, laughing. It had been too long since he'd seen the younger man. Holding him by the shoulders, he pushed Ben away. "Let me look at you. Damn, I think you've gotten even taller."

"Maybe." His sandy hair curled over his forehead, his blue eyes far too old for his age. He grinned and shrugged out of Rafe's grip. "It's good to see you. How was Cairo?"

"Good, good. Always interesting, you know."

Yeah, Ben did know. They didn't talk about how Rafe had found the underfed sixteen-year-old boy wandering through Africa, working where he could, and occasionally hawking a few photographs from his one and only real possession in the world—a camera his mother had given him before she'd watched him be turned out of the Australian Pride for being a non-shifter.

Now twenty, the kid had grown into a young man whom Rafe was damn proud he'd had a hand in helping get where he was. A few more years and the kid was going to be one of the most recognizable photojournalists in the business. Rafe had yet to see something Ben couldn't get a sellable picture of, from wildlife and warfare to fashion and sports.

At first, Rafe had made sure that Ben had food to eat, but the boy's pride had balked at taking handouts. So, Rafe had dragged the kid along with him on assignments, letting him take the pictures that went along with his travel writing. It hadn't taken long for magazines to start offering Ben assignments of his own—he was just one of those rare talents that people couldn't help but notice. Perhaps it was just a natural gift, but Rafe thought the boy's experiences had given him a keen view on the world that translated to his photos.

Ben sniffed the air a bit, his eyes glinting with good humor. "Man, you stink."

The frank speaking wasn't something everyone got from Ben, and it was nice to see him smile. It had taken months after they'd met before the boy had cracked a grin. Rafe shrugged. "Eid al-Adha."

"Well, that explains the blood. Nothing like the Islamic

Feast of the Sacrifice to make things exciting." The young man pointed to the stained clothes Rafe carried.

He chuckled. "Exactly. This is going to turn into a great story."

"Can't wait to hear everything, but I'll let you get over the jet lag first." Ben angled his shoulder to point down the hall to Rafe's room.

The younger man didn't mention that Rafe was standing in a hallway outside a room that wasn't his, carrying dirty clothes, and obviously fresh from a shower. The scent of sex might have washed away, but it didn't take a genius to figure out what he might have been doing.

"I don't think I can sleep yet." Rafe shook his head and started toward his room to drop his stuff. Ben guessing what had been going down was one thing, but the rest of the Pride was another matter. "So tired, I'm wired."

Meeting Teresa, touching Teresa, had done nothing to help him wind down enough to sleep. He'd thought he'd crash when he got to the mansion, but now he wasn't sure when he'd be able to stop his mind from running like a crack-addled gerbil on an exercise wheel.

"I've been there." Walking alongside him, Ben slid his hands into his pockets. "Isabel's got something good coming out of the oven. I've been smelling it for the last half hour."

Food was always something that interested Ben, no doubt from the years where a full belly had been rare. It was no surprise that he'd made friends with the Pride's chef.

"Let's eat, then."

After Antonio had come to power and mated with a woman who had also been thrown out as a teen for being a non-shifter, Rafe had gone to the leader and asked if Ben could join the North American Pride.

It had broken Rafe's heart to see one of his own kind abandoned for a supposed flaw he had no control over. There was no way he could walk away from the young Panther, regardless of his ability to shift or not. Rafe had roamed the world for years, seen all manner of superstitions and what they did to people, but his own race's fear of non-shifters was one he would never understand. He hoped it changed someday, but he was glad Ben had a place in the Prides again.

Tossing his gear on the worn leather couch in his room, Rafe turned to lead the way down to the kitchen. When they reached the ground floor, he got a whiff of Teresa. That captured his attention, made the concern he'd been pointedly ignoring rear its ugly head. She was in Antonio's office, and when they passed the double doors, he dragged in a deep breath, trying to sort out all the scents in the den to see if fear was also floating on the air. No. He sensed no fear, no anger or unrest. He forced himself not to stop, not to knock and go in.

He glanced at Ben. "When do you leave on your next job?"

Ben's gaze went from the office doors to Rafe, no doubt catching the same female scent that had also emanated from the room Rafe had stood outside with his dirty clothes. One of Ben's eyebrows quirked upward, but he didn't comment on it. "Not for a week or so. I'm doing a shoot this week for Andrea. She's got a new line launching."

A grin broke across Rafe's face and he threw an arm around Ben's shoulders, dragging him into a headlock. "Sounds perfect for you. Haute couture and free food from catering services."

"You have no idea." A short laugh burst out of Ben, and he slapped Rafe's belly. "Babes in bikinis this time. It's a rough life, man."

Rafe chuckled, letting the younger man go as they stepped into the kitchen. "Sounds like it. Have fun with the models."

"Yeah, I have my eye on one of them. Should be . . . interesting."

Ben didn't say it, but Rafe knew most Panthers still refused to associate with him. The Pride accepted him, but there was acceptance as a Pride member and then there was ridding oneself of old prejudices enough to want to get close. Panther females avoided him, and most tried not to touch him—as though his condition was some sort of contagious disease.

It was a damn shame, but Rafe always made a point of hugging Ben, ruffling his hair, and accepting any kind of affection he was willing to reach out and offer. It wouldn't surprise Rafe if he was the only person in the world Ben was completely comfortable offering even a simple hug to.

They were greeted by the scent of fresh-baked sweets as soon as they entered Isabel's domain. Rafe's mouth watered, and it hit him how many hours had passed since he'd had a real meal. Burning energy the way he had with Teresa probably hadn't helped, but given the choice, he'd do the same again.

"Welcome back, Rafe!" Isabel grinned from where she stood icing cinnamon buns. He brushed a kiss to her cheek and helped himself to the buffet along one counter that was always loaded with food for Pride members who might want a bite. As good as the sweets smelled, he could probably use something besides sugar.

He set his food on a bar that overlooked Isabel's workstation and sat on the stool beside Ben's. The other man looked inordinately pleased with himself to have a steaming cinnamon bun in front of him.

"So, tell me about Egypt." Isabel glanced up from her work and grinned. "Sing for your supper."

Rafe laughed and regaled her between bites, while Ben interjected his own observations about Cairo. They had the blond woman cracking up and putting down her tube of icing to sit with them. She brought them all a cup of coffee, and they whiled away the better part of an hour just catching up.

"Oh, damn!" Isabel jumped up and bustled around the kitchen, loading up a silver serving tray with cinnamon buns and a carafe of coffee. "I'm going to take this in to Antonio and the Spanish Pride heir, and I'll be back." The blonde offered a dimpled smile that didn't quite hide the trepidation in her eyes. "Don't tell any good stories without me."

The mention of Antonio and Teresa brought Rafe to his feet. He had the tray out of Isabel's hands before he'd even put a coherent thought to what he intended to do. He flashed a grin he hoped was charming. "Ah, why don't you let me do this for you? You've got a banquet to cook at every meal during this summit, and grumpy politicians who aren't getting their way during the negotiations."

He was already backing toward the door while she stared at him as if he'd lost his mind. Maybe he had, but he'd lay blame for it squarely at Teresa's feet.

But relief crossed Isabel's expression. She didn't want to deal with anyone from Spain, and Rafe didn't blame her. He, however, had suddenly gained an immense interest in all things Spanish.

"Okay, well. Have fun." The look on Ben's face was more knowing and amused than anything else. "Try watching where you're going—you're less likely to fall flat on your face."

Fall flat on his face by making an idiot of himself over a woman, which is what Ben didn't say. Rafe threw him a dirty look. "Thanks a lot."

Shoulders shaking with silent laughter, Ben toasted him with his coffee mug. "Anytime, brother."

Rafe turned his back before he started defending his bizarre behavior. That would take an explanation he didn't want to make.

Then again, considering he had no idea what the hell he was doing, he had his own doubts about whether he'd fall flat on his face. This was not how he'd expected things to go when he'd gotten off the plane today.

Good thing he liked the unexpected, right?

3

She'd had to wait almost an hour before Antonio had showed up. The twins had joined her in the leader's office but had spent most of the time watching her with thinly veiled suspicion in their gazes. She tried to relax, tried to take in the comfortably worn decor of the office. If she ignored the men, then she'd imagine this was a room one could be at ease in.

A sigh slipped from her. It wasn't as if she didn't understand the suspicion. Her father had made it very clear that he didn't want anything to do with this peace summit. They had to be asking themselves why she was here and how she'd changed her father's mind about sending a delegate.

But how could she *not* be here? Something of this magnitude had never happened in the Prides before. There were three-day sessions on a variety of topics and the whole thing spanned several weeks. Trade rights would be hammered out, peace treaties would be signed, new Seconds would be selected for three different Prides—there might never again be such an opportunity to sway Pride politics.

Ric cocked his wrist to look at his watch. "Antonio will be

out of his meeting with the Australian delegate soon. He'll be in to greet you shortly."

It was the longest speech either of them had made since she'd met them at the airport. Either their reputation for being gregarious was wildly exaggerated or they didn't think she was worth the effort to be polite. She was fairly certain she knew which option was the correct one.

A small commotion sounded from a side door to the office. That would be Antonio, she assumed. She lifted her chin and squared her shoulders, preparing to meet the Pride leader who had the greatest reason to dislike her, just for being a Garcia.

The door swung open and a man walked through who looked enough like the twins that there was no doubt about his identity. Teresa rose from her seat and offered a formal nod befitting a Pride leader.

"*Hola,* Antonio." She offered him a hand to shake, made sure her grip was firm. She was grateful he didn't try to show off his machismo by squeezing her hand hard enough to break it. He wouldn't have been the first Panther male to try, and she refused to back down and start flinching and crying from the pain. They'd have to try a lot harder than that.

Instead, Antonio's demeanor matched hers, brisk and professional, with no unnecessary power plays or shows of dominance. It made her suspicious. Felines were well-known for playing such games, and she had no idea if he was just toying with her before he struck. She had to stay on her toes and keep her guard up.

"It's good to meet you, Teresa. Have a seat." He arched his eyebrows at his younger brothers. "I think we can take it from here, gentlemen."

Diego opened his mouth to protest, but Antonio held up his hand. The twins frowned, but obeyed and exited in short order. She drew in a deep breath, ignored the knot of anxiety in her chest, and assumed a relaxed pose in her chair. It wasn't entirely natural, but she could fake it well enough that no one who didn't know her would be able to tell.

Antonio sat behind his wide wooden desk. He examined her for a moment, tapping his fingers against an ink blotter. "I don't think I need to tell you that the success of this summit is important to me."

In other words, if she hadn't come to play well with the other kids on the playground, then she could go home. She settled back and crossed her legs. "I'll be blunt, sir, if you don't mind."

His brows rose, surprise crossing his face. He waved his hand. "I prefer it."

"Good." Of course, she'd heard that about him, and she'd done her homework on how to deal with every person who was scheduled to attend this summit. She'd made certain to meet all of them while on her tour of the Prides, learned what made them tick. She was the new kid on the block, and on many levels she was working at a disadvantage. The only thing she hadn't anticipated was actually finding a mate. She hadn't seen Rafe coming. She stuffed that thought away, and the shiver of awareness it caused. That was a problem for another time. "I'm here to play a part in what I believe could shape the Panther world for decades to come. I'm not going to cause problems—in fact, I think this summit is a brilliant idea."

"Thank you." He narrowed his gaze as if reassessing her. Good, she wanted to keep people on their toes. He blew out a breath. "I'm honestly surprised your father allowed anyone from his Pride to come here."

She folded her hands in her lap. "I support my father's leadership and policies, but my views are somewhat different on certain issues."

Namely, anything that had to do with the African or North

American Prides. Discomfort twisted inside her when she thought about why the bad blood had developed between her Pride and theirs. She didn't like to think about that time or of what had become of her brother. She hadn't been present at the event, but it had changed her life forever.

Because now she was living the life that should have belonged to Enrique. She quashed the thought, stuffing it deep down inside of her soul. Dwelling on what couldn't be changed was pointless. Best to focus on what was in front of her.

Antonio watched her silently, and she forced herself not to fidget, to meet his gaze as if she were his equal rather than some second-rate leading-family lackey. He steepled his fingers together under his chin. "Most of the delegates are a bit older than you are."

"Experienced, you mean."

A small smile curved his lips. "Yes, that's exactly what I mean."

"It was me or it was no one." She could only hope she did well enough that "no one" wasn't the better option.

"Cesar Benhassi is representing his own Pride. He didn't send a delegate." His gaze pinned her in place, his intent stare one that only a feline could manage.

"The African Pride was the first stop on my tour of the various dens." She shrugged delicately. "It seemed sensible, as it's the closest geographically to Spain."

She'd also done it to make a political statement about her intention to end the tensions between her Pride and any other. Her movements were always watched, analyzed, and she knew it. They had been when she'd just been Fernando Garcia's second child, and even more intensely now that she was his heir. So, she'd used that to her advantage.

"I see." And it was obvious Antonio did see exactly what she'd done. A glint of what might have been respect sparked to life in his gaze. "Well, you missed the ball last night, but the major negotiations don't begin until sundown."

"I understand, sir." She'd need to get some sleep today and be in top form. Any misstep could be a disaster for her people, and she felt that knot in her belly twist tighter.

Panther politics were often vicious and deadly. There had been times when infighting had wiped out Prides completely. Most leaders worked hard to establish a clear line of succession in order to be certain the transfer of power from one generation to the next went smoothly and caused no bloodshed. Even that didn't always work. At one time, it wasn't unheard of for a younger child to kill off the heir in order to become leader.

Now, things were typically more civilized, or at least less bloody. But even in the last century, they had all had a clear view of exactly what happened when the transfer of power didn't go smoothly. The African Pride leader had died without an heir, after killing off those who contested his authority, and when he passed, every member who had even the slightest claim to leadership made a bid for power. The result had devolved into civil war, killing most of the Pride and sending the survivors fleeing for asylum in other Prides.

It had only been in the last six months that Benhassi had reformed the nucleus of the African Pride, and he'd had to negotiate in order to get his claim recognized by the other Pride leaders. He'd had to convince those who had once been in the Pride to come back, to lure their children away from the other Prides.

A short knock sounded on the double doors behind her, and she fought a groan as Rafe's scent intensified. She could sense him in the mansion, and she'd been steadfastly trying not to think about him and what they'd done together in her suite. How she was going to sleep in there without going mad with the memories, she didn't know.

"Antonio, Teresa." Rafe came in balancing a tray on one palm. He slid it onto the desk that dominated the room. "I talked Isabel into letting me bring you some sustenance."

Isabel. The woman Teresa's brother had attacked. The woman now mated into the leading family of this Pride. Teresa had grown up in the same Pride with her. They'd *both* grown up in the same Pride as Antonio's wife, Solana, but Teresa had never been close with the older girls. Neither of them had been well-served by the Spanish Pride, Teresa admitted, and in Isabel's case, she bore part of the blame. Relief washed through her that she didn't have to deal with that on top of everything else today. She would need to eventually, but not now.

"You should try the cinnamon buns. I'm sure after all the energy you've expended today, you could use the sugar boost." Rafe's smile held just a hint of wickedness when he handed her a plate with a huge bun smothered in white icing. "You know, from the long flight."

"You flew in from Egypt," she pointed out. "That's not a short trip."

"Well, I'd love a cinnamon bun, too. Thanks for the invitation."

Antonio rubbed a hand over his mouth to hide a grin when Rafe snagged an extra coffee mug off the wooden sidebar and served himself along with everyone else.

"Thanks, Rafe." Antonio's gaze flicked between the two of them. "The twins mentioned you met our roving goodwill ambassador at the airport."

Rafe chuckled, and even the sound of it was warm and inviting. Some part of her relaxed in a way that hadn't unwound since she'd left his side. She didn't like to admit it, but it was reassuring to have someone there with her. Rafe gestured with the hand holding his coffee. "Hardly. I leave the politics to others and just focus on my job. Travel writing is the best of all worlds. I trot around the globe and then I get to tell stories about it."

"Sometimes exaggerated stories." Antonio sipped his drink. "And they always leave out the part where you occasionally shift into a cat."

"A little artistic license to fine-tune my narrative. It's a necessary evil." Rafe shrugged, the good humor in his expression inviting everyone to let go of any tension and just enjoy the moment. She had a feeling that was how he operated on most days. She was curious to find out if she was right, and scolded herself for wondering about him at all. They'd had sex, that was all. Panthers were highly sensual beings, so this was hardly a first for either of them. She didn't want to be mated, so the best idea would be to go no further than she had already. If they never marked each other, they could still live apart. If they never claimed each other, this was no more than a simple affair. They could avoid the madness that came from losing a marked mate.

The Panther inside her shrieked in denial at the very concept. *Mate.* The instinct clamored again, demanding she acknowledge what her mind didn't want.

Antonio shook his head at Rafe. "And they say you write nonfiction."

"I just tell the story as I saw it." He popped a piece of the pastry into his mouth. "That *is* nonfiction."

"Yeah, yeah." The Pride leader flapped his hand. "The truth, but not the whole truth."

"Coming from a politician, that admonishment is rich." Rafe stretched out his legs and crossed them at the ankle. "The problem with travel writing is you have to frame the story in an engaging way. If I gave the whole truth, right up to and including what I have for breakfast each day, I'd bore the crap out of myself . . . *and* my readers. Only so much detail needs to be in there, just the parts that are important to the one incident I'm talking about. Plus, I can use those other details in different pieces. One trip can give me fodder for a half a dozen stories."

"Fascinating." The word was out of her mouth before she thought better of it. But it *was* fascinating. This man's life was just so far outside her realm of experience. He had a point in that politicians did frame the truth—or bald-faced lies—to suit their own ends, but other than that, their jobs were nothing alike. She disliked writing anything longer than a brief or memo, and she certainly had no desire to do it for a living, but his ability to travel on a whim was enviable. Even before she'd been heir, she'd had no such freedoms. She'd even gone to university in Barcelona instead of another city in Europe in order to remain close to the den.

Rafe's gaze moved over her face. "I'd be happy to tell you anything you want to know about me."

She flinched, looking away. There was no way she could offer him the same promise. Anything he wanted to know? No. There were family secrets that had the power to make her heart wrench in her chest. Things no one who wasn't a Garcia should know.

And no matter how loudly her instincts howled at her, those secrets were what would keep her from mating with anyone.

Ever.

Something had made her sad.

Rafe could sense her lowering mood, but he didn't know what had caused it. And he wasn't in a position to be able to ask outright. Frustration crawled through him that he couldn't delve deeper, faster. Patience was usually one of his strong suits, knowing a good story would come to him if he could school himself to wait. But he didn't want to do that with Teresa. He found himself wanting to pounce, to take and claim and ask questions later.

It was nothing like him, and that worried him.

What worried him more was the forceful reminder of exactly who and what she was when he'd walked in and seen her coolly eyeing Antonio Cruz. The man had the charisma of John F. Kennedy and the iron will it would take to overhaul the world as they knew it. He was a force of nature, and seeing her with him brought home exactly the kind of person he was dealing with.

The cell phone he had clipped to his belt began vibrating, and he set down his coffee so he could turn it off. "Sorry."

"No problem." Antonio motioned with the curl of cinnamon bun he held in his hand.

Rafe flashed an apologetic grin and glanced down. The number belonged to one of his editors. Damn. "And now I'm even sorrier, because I need to take this call."

"Interruptions are the name of the game in our line of work, Rafe." The Pride leader shrugged. "Don't worry about it."

"Hello, Kevin." Stepping outside the office door, Rafe closed it behind him.

"Santiago, good. I'm glad I caught you." The man's characteristic clipped New York accent broadcasted loudly through the receiver. "I had a last-minute cancellation, and I need someone to cover a travel writing conference for the magazine."

"Where?" He asked it out of sheer curiosity—he couldn't help himself.

"Barcelona."

It took all he had not to laugh. Normally, he'd be all over this kind of assignment, but everything he wanted in Spain was right here in San Francisco. "Sorry, Kevin. You know I'm taking some time off to stay at home."

"Yeah, I figured." The human sighed. "Couldn't hurt to ask, though, right?"

"Nope, not at all." He shook his head at the irony of the situation. "Thanks for thinking of me, Kevin. Sorry I couldn't come through for you this time."

"Enjoy your vacation. Or whatever you call it." Kevin chuckled, and Rafe grinned. Most people traveled to go on vacation, and Rafe went home.

Even then, he had to wonder if this place was really home. He hadn't lived there full-time in close to two decades, and he doubted he'd return as often as he did if it weren't for Ben being here. Was this really where Rafe belonged? Perhaps. Perhaps not. This thing with Teresa pointed toward the latter. Would that shake the restlessness that had plagued him for so long? Or would it cost him far more than he could afford to give up?

He didn't know, and he was too tired to figure it out. The fatigue that meeting his mate had held at bay caught up with him in a painful rush.

"Talk to you later, Kevin." He flipped the phone closed and turned to reenter Antonio's office only to find Teresa exiting.

She looked as haggard as he felt. Unlike him, she had to attend the summit that started at dusk, while he could sleep in. He attached his phone to his belt. "Hey, what are you up to?"

"Apparently, I passed inspection." She spread her hands. "I called my father when we were taxiing on the runway after I landed, but I should probably update him about how things went with Antonio." The prospect seemed to exhaust her, and her shoulders sagged for a moment before she pulled herself up and lifted her chin.

He hummed in his throat and walked with her as she headed up the stairs. "You could probably use sleep more than anything else. I'd imagine you're dealing with some killer jet lag."

"I can sleep as soon as I'm done."

They reached the door to her room and he stopped to look down at her. "How long do you think the call will take?"

The skin around her mouth tightened. "An hour. Maybe more."

He shook his head. "That's no good. You need to be rested for tonight. Everyone who'll be there besides Antonio is already asleep. You're going to need your A-game with these Panther delegates. The ones I've met are man-eaters."

She rubbed a hand over her forehead, the motion both weary and annoyed. "I know that."

"I'll worry about you if you don't go to bed soon." He had no idea if that would affect her at all, but it didn't hurt to try. It wasn't even a lie. He *would* worry about her. Just leaving her alone to face Antonio—a man he trusted—had worried him. These were some heavy hitters she was dealing with, and she didn't seem like the type to take her duties lightly. In fact, from what he'd seen, she was far too serious. He'd like to see her laugh more, but this was no laughing matter. Panthers made human politicians look like amateurs in their games of cat and mouse.

"I—I don't know what to say." Her expression softened, and she blushed a little, rubbing a finger over the bridge of her nose.

"You can say you'll wait to call until after you've gotten at least six hours of sleep. Or as long as you can."

"I really should call."

Just as he'd suspected. She had an overdeveloped sense of responsibility. He narrowed his gaze at her. If sympathy didn't work, glib sarcasm was always a good fallback.

"Well, you can use me as an excuse for why you didn't call a *second* time to let them know you're fine." He grinned at her when she lowered her hand to give him an incredulous look.

"You think we should be sleeping together?" She shook her head. "I told you I don't want—"

"And I heard you." He steered her into her suite, through the sitting room to the bedroom. "I'm talking about getting some sleep, not marking each other."

She frowned up at him as he lifted her out of her heels. "That's a bad idea."

"Well, I'm open to marking, if that's your preference for how to pass the time." When she hissed at him, he smiled at her, stripped her down to her panties, and set her in the middle of the bed.

Opening her mouth to speak, she froze in place and stared at him as he shucked his shoes, shirt, and pants. No, *stared* wasn't the right word. She *devoured* him with her eyes, that pale gray gaze roving over every inch of his bared flesh. Whether she wanted to mate with him or not, she definitely wanted him. His cock went hard in an instant, his body more than ready to satisfy the interest on her face.

He crawled onto the mattress beside her but refused to let himself touch her. Covering his erection with the thick bedspread, he turned on his side and propped his head in his hand. She eyed him warily. "What are you doing?"

"Sleeping. That's what I said I was going to do, and that's what I'm doing. Someday you'll trust me when I say something, but we have time for that." He ignored her low snarl, settled against the pillows, and closed his eyes. "I'd probably sleep better if you were in my arms, but that's up to you."

There was a long pause while she fidgeted next to him, then she lifted the covers to slide under. A few minutes later, her warm body fitted against his side, her arm draping over his chest. "This doesn't mean anything."

"Yes, it does." He opened his eyes to meet her pale gaze.

She wrinkled her nose, and her claws lightly raked down his ribs. "Yes, it does."

He brushed a kiss over her forehead. "Don't worry, I won't tell anyone you like me."

Snorting on a laugh, she dug her talons in and made him jolt away from the sting. "Don't let it go to your head."

His reflexive movement brought him into fuller contact with her half-naked body. He bit back a groan at how good it felt.

"Wouldn't dream of it." He stroked her hair back from her face, drifting his fingers through the silky strands. "I want you to know, I'm not going to try and force the mating issue. Yeah, I want to get to know you, want to know why destiny says we're mates. But I'm really not going to tell anyone about us, not going to help anyone pressure you. We don't know each other yet, but you *can* trust me."

"Thank you." Her lashes brushed his chest as her eyes fluttered closed. "I don't have a choice except to believe in you for this, but . . . I do anyway. For no good reason, I do anyway."

Being mates was a good reason, but he didn't point it out as she slipped into sleep. She snuggled into him, the innocent trust in the gesture more revealing than she probably wanted. Far more revealing than her words had been.

He shifted around on the bed, and she rolled with him until her back was to his front. He wrapped her in his embrace, and the floral scent of her hair filled his nose. The sweetness of having her smooth skin against his went beyond a mere physical touch. It was something deeper, something far more fundamental to his well-being.

But the nagging thought came back to him . . . what would it cost him to win her?

She was an heir, and his career made him a political anomaly.

Panthers didn't like those, but he'd gotten away with it because he had no political power at all. He wasn't in line for leadership. His family had never had any real influence in the Pride—his parents had met and mated very late in life. Their advanced age made his birth nothing short of miraculous, but it meant he'd lost his parents to old age when he was in his last year of high school. He'd been drifting ever since. Entering another Pride's territory was tricky to get approved under any circumstances, and if he were in a leading family? Doubtful.

So, the question became what was more important to him—his career or claiming his mate? She didn't want to mate, so the second option was not only viable, but easy.

Unfortunately, he'd never been one to take the easy route. His work involved long hours of hiking through inhospitable territory, being harassed by locals, struggling with foreign languages, and occasionally doing something dangerous and stupid for the thrill of it. Swimming with great white sharks off the coast of South Africa was one such particularly brilliant idea, especially when one had tried to bite him. His Panther speed had been all that had saved his left arm, because even his advanced strength was nothing compared to one of those finned beasts.

He hadn't done anything that death-defying in years, but he still liked the thrill of ice climbing and BASE jumping. The Cruz twins had gone with him on a few of the trips he'd taken in North America.

Would he have to stop that kind of travel, except in Europe? He'd restricted himself to Africa for years, but the kind of writing people did about Europe was much different. It would mean a big switch in his career, regardless. His chest tightened, but change was something he dealt with every day. He was as much writer as traveler—could he focus on the first and tone down the second?

Hell, he didn't know. He thought if the reward was big enough, he might be able to, but he'd expected that the decision to stop his extensive traveling would be made when he was around the age of retirement. He wasn't even forty yet, and with the excellent health being a Panther ensured him, he was a long time away from that.

A soft purr soughed out of Teresa, and she mumbled in her sleep, cuddling into him. The tightness in his chest loosened and he curled his arm around her, holding her nearer. Something close to wonder unfurled inside him. A mate. He'd honestly never thought he'd find one. He was thirty-seven and he'd been to all the Prides at least once, even if he hadn't done the usual mate-seeking tour, so he'd just assumed he'd spend his life alone. Or as alone as anyone could be who made his living talking to exotic people and writing about the often-hilarious and sometimes dangerous adventures that ensued.

But this? This was an adventure that would never come around again. If he walked away, if he took the simple escape she'd already offered him, he might regret it for the rest of his life. And he'd never been one to collect regrets. Life was for living, not for hiding from fate.

Wherever fate led him, he'd go along. He was too damn curious not to find out what might happen next in this story. The thought made him grin, and he sighed, letting sleep take him as swiftly as it had taken her.

4

His fingers were buried deep in her sex when she woke up. Her nipples were tight, her pussy so wet she whimpered before she opened her eyes. His arms held her back tight to his chest, but she twisted around as best she could to look at him.

Only to find that he was still deep in slumber.

She snorted, dropping her head onto the pillow. *Madras,* the man was seducing her in his sleep. If she weren't so painfully aroused, it might have been funny.

"Rafe," she breathed.

He groaned, his hand moving within her. She couldn't hold back a hiss, arching her hips to get more friction on her clit. Any resistance, any rational part of her that might think this was a bad idea, was shredded by the insistent demand of her hormones.

She felt him jolt to awareness, and he sucked in a startled breath. His big body froze against her back. "Um . . ."

"Good morning." Her voice was remarkably even, which she was a bit proud of, until he twitched his fingers inside of her and made her moan.

"You're wet," he growled. He ran his thumb over her clit and she clutched at the sheet wrapped around them. One of his arms was trapped underneath her, and it flexed each time his hand delved into her pussy.

She gritted her teeth, only to find her fangs had extended from her gums. "I thought you were only here to sleep."

"I was. I slept. You slept. Now we can try something new." His top hand tugged the sheet away, and the cool air made her shiver, her nipples peaking tighter.

Grabbing his free hand, she dragged it to her breast and curled his fingers around her curves. "Try this while you're at it."

He laughed. "Damn, but I do like you, Teresa."

She liked him too. Liked the way he'd cared that she got the sleep she desperately needed, liked that he'd worried about her enough to find a way into Antonio's office to check on her, liked that he'd addressed her concerns about their relationship being exposed, liked that he even knew she needed the reassurance. He was doing everything right, and he wasn't even trying.

And she more than liked the way he touched her. Which was far more than she should. How long could she keep this up before she gave in to the instinct to mark him? It was madness, how she craved a man she barely knew.

He plucked at her nipples, one at a time, twisted them with slow precision that made her squirm. More fluids surged from her sex and he purred, sliding his fingers in and out of her channel, slipping her moisture up to swirl around her clit, and then reversing the hot circuit.

"Oh, God," she breathed. Her claws raked down the mattress in front of her when he thrust three big fingers inside of her. "Fuck me. Right now. I want you inside of me."

He jerked his hand away from her sex and used it to shove her top leg forward. She arched her body, lifting her hips to open herself to his penetration. She felt the blunt probing of his cock and then the exquisite pressure of him working his long length inside of her.

A rough sound burst out of him when her pussy spasmed around his dick. "Damn, you feel good."

"Hurry." She shoved her hips back, taking him as deep as possible.

He used the fingers on one hand to tease her nipple, and the other circled her clit while he thrust his cock into her. The rhythm was just fast enough to have her on the screaming edge, but not fast enough to allow her to fly over. The pleasure of it was so white-hot, she thought she'd burn. He touched her everywhere she wanted to be touched, fed her every craving.

The way he filled her made her writhe to get closer, to get more. He pinched her nipple hard, and she hissed. Her fangs scraped her lower lip, but his every stroke within her only frayed the tethers she had on the wildness inside.

"How do you want to come, Teresa? Hard and fast?" He flicked her clit just that way, and every muscle in her body jolted. His chuckle sounded more like a purr. "Or do you want me to make it last for you? Tease you until you can't stand it anymore?"

"*Dios,* you want me to *decide?*" She choked as the tip of one of his claws teased her clit oh-so-gently.

"Mmm-hmm." He nipped at her shoulder but didn't bite her. Still, the Panther within her writhed in excitement at the very possibility.

Two of his claws scraped over her wet, sensitive flesh and she cried out. "Fast. Hard. That's . . . that's how I want it."

"See? That wasn't such a difficult decision, was it?"

As a response, she swung an elbow back and caught him in the belly. His breath whooshed out, but he sputtered on a laugh. She snorted and then couldn't help the giggle that burst out. When was the last time she'd laughed during sex? Playful wasn't normally her way, but she had to admit she enjoyed it.

His pelvis slapped her ass as he powered into her pussy. The swiftness of it caught her off-guard, left her gasping at the intensity of the way he filled her to the limit. She wrapped her hand around his forearm, holding on for dear life as he picked up speed and force, giving her exactly what she'd asked for.

"Yes, yes, yes!" She moved with him, taking all of him. Her inner muscles flexed around him with each hard entry, and she could feel orgasm building.

It was too good to last, ecstasy this perfect.

And that was the worst knowledge in the world; it flayed at her soul. She couldn't keep this. Sadness swamped her soul, and she had to swallow a lump in her throat. She barely knew this man, and she couldn't let herself get to know him. The instincts that rode her like the devil himself would make it far too easy to give everything without thought to cost or consequences. Those impulses went against everything she was as a person— meticulous and in control.

His claws raked over her nipples one at a time, and the sting was as sweet as the pleasure, each of them feeding the other. He snarled when her pussy spasmed around him. "Are you close?"

She nodded, unable to trust her voice. Her breath came in ragged gasps, and she could feel his chest bellowing as he panted. Sweat trickled down their skin, and the bedsprings squeaked underneath them. The sound of their flesh slapping together when he thrust into her, their mingling cries and groans, all combined in a carnal symphony that drove her higher and higher. Any moment, she would fall.

Reaching back, she grabbed his ass, urging him faster. He complied, racing her for orgasm. "Teresa!"

Her name on his lips, the sound half guttural demand and half reverent prayer, was enough to break her. She screamed, slamming her hips back to meet his next thrust and everything inside her shattered into a million little pieces. Her sex pulsed in waves on his cock, and his continued strokes only pushed her orgasm onward, kept her channel flexing around him.

Digging her claws into his arm, she tried to keep from sobbing at the endless ecstasy. "Come with me, Rafe."

He groaned, his strokes faltering. Then he pushed inside her once, twice, three more times before he shuddered against her. His come pumped inside of her, flooding her sex.

His arms wrapped around her, holding her close as they came down from the high. She sighed and let her eyes drift shut while she enjoyed the feel of being in his embrace. She shouldn't let herself linger, shouldn't even admit how much she liked it. Just another few minutes, she promised herself. Then she'd get up and walk away. Then she'd get on with the work of the summit.

Anxiety and anticipation fluttered through her. There was so much riding on how well she did at this political meeting of minds. These were the most powerful people in her world, and she had to prove she was their equal, without any support from her family. Her father should be here. Hell, her brother should be here. This was supposed to be his destiny, not hers.

She pinched her eyes closed tighter and pushed away thoughts of her family. Father had empowered her to make decisions here, and he trusted her not to let him down, not to let the entire Pride down. This was what she needed to focus on, not having wild sex with a virtual stranger. It didn't matter that the stranger in question was her mate, or that she found him irresistibly attractive, or that he seemed genuinely concerned about her in a way no one had been since she was thrust into her brother's place as heir.

"I have to get ready and go downstairs." She tugged at his arms.

"I know." He kissed her shoulder and let her up, no fighting with her, no annoyance over her work interrupting their post-coital cuddling.

She liked that, as she liked so much about him. Which was something she shouldn't think about. She'd made her decision about mating before she ever met him, and her motivation for avoiding it hadn't changed. Crawling out of bed, she fished a robe out of the suitcases she still hadn't managed to unpack.

He rose to his feet, pulling his shirt over his head. It was a shame to cover all that taut male flesh. She had to force herself to look away before she jumped him. He stepped into his pants and fastened them. "I'd like to see you when you're done today."

"I don't know when I'll be done." She belted her robe tight around her waist, taking comfort in the thin protection it offered. "This sort of event is unprecedented and therefore unpredictable."

"Well, I have a lot of writing and research to do, so I'm more than capable of keeping myself entertained. I still want to see you when you're done, even if it's just to hold you while you sleep."

She bit her lip, uncertain. There were so many reasons why that was a bad plan. She was usually one who planned everything ahead of time, examined every angle, tested every flaw before she made the best decision possible. With Rafe, she wanted to make a decision she knew wasn't a good one. She should say no, should refuse to be alone in the same room with him until she left for Spain.

The Panther within her sank its claws deep into her soul, a protest that such a thought would even surface. She ignored the feline instincts that warred with her rational mind. "It would be a mistake to get to know each other."

He flinched a bit and a part of her ached inside that she'd

brought him any pain. She bunched her fists and ruthlessly reminded herself that it was better to face the pain now than deal with the endless suffering that her brother was going through. That was not something she wanted to deal with, not something she wanted to inflict on a man she *liked*.

Rafe's dark chocolate gaze held hers. "I want to know you, my mate."

"We'll never *be* mated, Rafe." She crossed her arms and hunched her shoulders. "Trust me when I tell you it's better this way."

"Why should I trust you when you won't tell me the whole truth about why you're so afraid of mating?" The words were soft, but implacable, and they made the guilt she always tried to ignore come screeching to the surface.

She wanted to insist that she wasn't afraid, but it wouldn't be true. The truth was she was *terrified* of mating. The truth was far more complicated than anyone could guess. The truth was a tangled web of lies and secrets that weren't entirely hers to tell. She shook her head. "I've told you everything I can."

He reached out and cupped her chin, running his thumb over her bottom lip. "Someday you'll trust me with everything, Teresa. Not just your body, but your heart and soul as well. Until you give me a reason that's good enough, I'm refusing to believe we can't work through whatever is holding you back. I can wait for you to be ready, but I'm not going anywhere."

A shiver went down her spine, and she jerked away from his light touch. She couldn't give him what he wanted. She *would not*.

But that didn't stop her from wishing things were different, that she were different. That she hadn't seen what she'd seen, that she didn't know what she knew about what happened when mating went wrong. Her heart squeezed in pain at the reminder. The plan had always been to never mate. That was the *only* plan where she avoided the kind of misery and madness her brother lived with every day. That was the only plan she could trust.

Normally, he'd have avoided this cocktail party like the plague, but it was an opportunity to see Teresa and to watch her in what would be her natural environment. They were almost a week into the summit, so she'd had some time to settle in. He straightened his tie and tugged down the cuffs on his jacket. It had been a few years since he'd worn this suit—not since Antonio and Solana's wedding. He spent his time in hiking boots, not Italian wool suits.

Sweeping the Panther gathering with a look, he saw the entire Cruz family circulating through the crowd, and a few North American Pride members were also in the room, but most of them cast surreptitious glances at the celebrities of the Panther world. Antonio was deep in conversation with the South American Pride leader, the African leader heatedly debated with the Asian delegate, and the Australian emissary chatted with the South American heir and Teresa. She said something and the other two laughed.

Rafe had already gotten the impression of the savvy politico when he'd been in Antonio's office with her, but he was too fascinated not to try to uncover more. He knew already that she was a passionate lover and a stubborn female when she believed in something. She'd refused to even speak to him about why she didn't want to be mated since that first conversation—a fact that made the journalist in him chafe. The bullheaded fortitude to see an idea through would serve her well as a Pride heir and someday-leader, but wouldn't be as desirable in a mate. Relationships required people to bend, to change. Was her uncompromising outlook strictly related to marriage or did it spill into all areas of her life?

This was his chance to find out.

He greeted a few of the Pride members, moving through the crowd with the ease of someone who spent his life talking to strangers. He'd found that no matter what country he was in, no matter if the people were rich or poor, educated or not, they were still just people with an interesting story to tell. Keeping that in mind had always made it a little easier to deal with Panthers who outranked him by a mile.

Eventually, he worked his way into the same group as Teresa. He fought a chuckle when he found the Australian ambassador had apparently had one too many servings of scotch. She slurred her words a little and gestured grandly with her glass. He met Teresa's gaze and winked, which made her lips twitch as she struggled with her own laughter.

"So, when're you going to come Down Under again, Santiago?" The Australian hiccupped quietly and squinted her eyes as if concentrating. "Loved the little things you wrote the last time you were there."

Tomas, the Brazilian Pride heir, coughed into his fist. "Yes, I . . . quite liked the *little things* you wrote about your last South American expedition. Machu Picchu, wasn't it?"

"It was." Rafe smiled, noting how often the other man's gaze strayed to his wife, Ciri. It wouldn't surprise him if the two disappeared soon. The pheromones were thick enough to cut with a knife. He'd heard the couple had had some issues lately, made worse by her attack from an outcast. It seemed those problems had been cleared up. He was glad for them—he didn't know Ciri well, but he'd met Tomas a few times and liked him. "Ben was with me on that trip as my photographer. He got some great shots."

"Ciri says Ben's work is amazing." Tomas dragged his gaze away from his wife and gave an unashamed grin when he noticed he'd been caught staring at her. "I'm afraid I leave knowing anything about art to her, but she has excellent taste, so I'm sure she's right."

"I'm right, am I? Can I have that in writing?" Ciri slipped in beside her mate, and he wrapped an arm around her waist and bent to brush her lips in a quick kiss. The smile she gave him was so intimate, Rafe felt he was intruding.

He looked to the Australian emissary. "I'm glad you enjoyed my stories, ma'am. I'm not sure when I'll get down there again, but I'd love to go back. You have a wonderful country."

"We do." She nodded, and he thought it was supposed to be a crisp movement, but with her silver hair up in a topknot, it ended up looking something like one of those wobbly headed dolls. She focused on Teresa. "How rude of me. I forgot to ask how your brother is. I haven't seen him since—"

Her eyes widened as she realized what had come out of her mouth. Teresa stiffened beside him, and he set a supportive hand on her back. She lifted her chin. "He's as well as can be expected. Thank you for inquiring."

The older woman was saved from responding when a child's piping voice cut through the low burble of the gathered adults.

"Are you *really* a non-shifter?"

Rafe jerked around and watched Ben freeze outside the doorway. He was in jeans and a T-shirt, a cup of coffee in one hand. Since he avoided Panther gatherings like the plague, Rafe guessed he'd been passing by on his way from the kitchen to the main staircase.

"Marisol!" Ciri voiced the child's name as an admonishment. She gave Rafe an apologetic glance. "Tomas's niece. She's only eight."

She was small for her age, a tiny fairy with a carrying voice. She looked confused as she stood there in the doorway. "What?"

A flush swept up Ben's face as he realized every person in

the room was now focused on the tableau with the non-shifter. His flesh mottled red, but his gaze was steady when he met the child's eyes. "Yes, I'm a non-shifter."

Her brows scrunched. "My *avô* says you're a curse on our people and you shouldn't be allowed to stay in a Pride."

Rafe's fists balled at his sides and it was all he could do not to walk over and punch the South American Pride leader in the face. This was the kind of bullshit that had left Ben a homeless, starving *child*. Teresa's hand curled around his forearm, and he wasn't sure if she meant the gesture as reassurance or a way to hold him back, but it snapped him back to logic. He was so angry, he was shaking, and he latched on to her hand and squeezed.

Ben's shoulders straightened, but he didn't back down from Marisol's comment. "It's fortunate for me that your *avô* doesn't make decisions for this Pride. Antonio Cruz believes there's more a Panther can contribute to a Pride than the ability to shift and breed. There are too few of us in the world to turn anyone out in the cold."

Too bad the Pride he'd grown up in hadn't felt the same. Sickness curdled in Rafe's gut. He took a step forward to go to Ben, to give him a show of support, but Ben met his gaze briefly and shook his head, telling him to stay where he was.

Teresa squeezed his fingers and breathed in his ear, "You'll hurt his pride if you don't let him stand on his own two feet now."

"I know. Damn it." So he stayed and let Ben suffer alone, his chest tight with too many emotions.

The little girl tilted her head in thought, biting her lower lip. After a long moment, she nodded decisively. "I think you're right. Families should be together, and Panthers are all family."

A slight, bitter smile curled Ben's lips. "I wish it were that simple."

"I understand that adults make things more complicated than they are." Marisol's face looked far too old and wise for her years. She reached out her hand and tucked it in Ben's much larger one. "I understand that I like you. Don't you like me too?"

The young man looked stunned by the child's open gesture of friendship. Rafe knew there had been very few Panthers who willingly touched Ben after his non-shifter status had become apparent. He'd been treated as though he had leprosy. He swallowed hard, his voice emerging in a rasp. "Yes, I do."

"Good. We'll be friends, then." Her smile was brighter than sunshine. "Aunt Ciri said you go all over the world and take pictures."

"I'm a photographer, yeah."

"I want to travel, too, but *avô* says because I'm in the leading family that I won't be able to go to other Panther territories."

"I'm not in the leading family."

She nodded sagely. "You're lucky, then."

He snorted. "You're the only person to ever say so."

"Will you take my picture? I look very pretty in my dress." She held out the edge of the deep blue skirt. "Aunt Andrea made it just for me."

"It's a nice dress." A tentative smile curled his lips at this pint-sized whirlwind of energy and enthusiasm. "I'd be glad to take your photograph."

"Okay, let's go now!" She started down the hall, towing Ben along in her wake. He flashed Rafe a relieved look before he disappeared from view.

"Is it safe for her to be alone with him?" The Australian ambassador turned to Ciri and Tomas.

A muscle ticked in Rafe's jaw and for the first time in his life, he seriously considered doing damage to a woman. "Ben is a good man, which you would know if your Pride hadn't thrown him out."

Teresa's grip on his hand became bone-crushing. He snapped his mouth shut and glared down at her. Did she agree with this woman? Did she think non-shifters were cursed and should be discarded like so much trash? Everything in him recoiled at the very thought.

"Australia did nothing that every other Pride hasn't done in the past." The older woman flushed, her mouth tightening.

"That was the past, and we must look to the future. I think Antonio is giving us an excellent example to follow, both with this peace summit and with his policy of non-shifter acceptance." Teresa's voice was cool and smooth, but loud enough for every Panther in the room to hear. "This Pride has suffered no ill effects from taking in a non-shifter. No curse troubles this den. And I, for one, believe that destroying others of our kind through feuding or prejudice is counterproductive. We must preserve the Panthers we have, regardless of their ability to shift, and use every resource at our disposal to thrive."

The Australian emissary snorted. "You're as crazy as your brother if you think one leader can make everyone accept non-shifters. They aren't normal Panthers—they can't give a Pride what it needs most, and that's more Panthers."

"A non-shifter *is* a Panther, and their financial contributions to a Pride help support Panther children. Even mated Panthers have no *guarantee* of breeding more of our kind—if they don't, does that really make them less worthy?" Teresa shook her head. "It's unfortunate that your bigotry has blinded you to what's truly valuable."

The older woman's gaze narrowed to dangerous slits, an enraged hiss erupting from her throat. "Your father will hear of how insolently you've spoken to me this evening."

"I'll be certain to let him know about the disparaging remarks you've made about my brother. Be certain your Pride leader *will* hear of it—from my father. I can assure you he will be most displeased." Teresa's chin rose, a gesture Rafe was beginning to associate with her. Her gaze swept the room. "If you'll all excuse me."

He kept her hand in his, squeezing tight as they both strode from the room. A few people noted his gesture, but there were more important things to contend with. Like his mate. She stopped at the foot of the stairs, her gaze glassy with shock. She looked around as if she had no idea where to go now. He urged her up the steps, gently leading her down the corridor to his room. Tonight, he wanted her in his space, not some guest suite.

"Thank you for defending Ben." He drew her fingers to his lips and kissed them.

Teresa shook herself out of her stupor and met his gaze. "He'll be all right. Marisol seems like the kind of kid that could make anyone laugh."

A growl was the best he could manage while he pulled her over to sit on his couch. It was beat-up and comfortable, like everything else in the large room. "He's been through too much already."

She squeezed his fingers, kicking off her heels to curl her feet underneath her. "He seems more than capable of fighting his own battles. You can't save him from what he is."

He grunted. "He shouldn't need saving."

"I agree with you." She sighed, brought his hand to her mouth, and kissed his palm.

It was in that moment that he realized *why* she was his mate. He could handle the stubborn streak as long as their fundamental beliefs were the same, and her actions today had told him more clearly than anything else could that she was the kind of woman he could respect.

Her self-deprecating grin crinkled the corners of her eyes. "Though I'm afraid my lecturing the Australians about persecuting one of their Pride members will just make me look hypocritical considering what happened to Isabel."

He pulled his knee up and propped his elbow on it. "No one here holds you responsible for what Enrique did to Isabel."

The smile disappeared, and something dark and painful flashed in her gaze. "They have every right to do so if they want to."

"Why? You didn't do it." He tightened his grip on her fingers when she tried to pull away. "Even by our own culture, the Pride leader is held responsible for the actions of his people. Other members are not."

Her throat worked, and she swallowed hard. "I played as much a part in what happened as my father did."

"I can't believe that." He shook his head at her. No way. A woman who valued people's lives so much wouldn't have let Isabel be mauled. It just didn't fit with what he knew of Teresa's character so far.

"You should believe." Her mouth firmed, and that horrible pain flickered in her eyes again before she masked it. "I'm not perfect, Rafe. I've done things you wouldn't approve of, things that would make you think badly of me."

"I'm sure I've done the same. No one is perfect, least of all me. But you can tell me anything, and I promise not to judge."

She glanced away, saying nothing more, and he felt a frustration he was becoming familiar with. It was one step forward, two steps back with her. "Okay, time to call Father. I'm afraid jumping into the fray tonight means I have to explain my actions to him. No talking me out of it this time."

He waved his free hand at the cordless phone sitting on a side table. "Feel free to use the line in here."

"Thank you." She rose, picked up the handset, and dialed.

He was glad she didn't protest and insist on going back to her room. Even when he wanted to shake her, he liked having her here, liked watching her wander around in her bare feet while she explained to her father what she had done, her scent spreading and mingling with Rafe's. It felt good.

He snagged a notebook from the coffee table and started jotting down a few notes for a story he was writing. If she was working, he could always occupy himself. Toeing off his shoes, he propped his feet on the low table—something he couldn't do in her fancy suite.

The sound of her voice was a soothing murmur in the background as she spoke to her father. That her voice never rose and remained calm told Rafe that everything was fine, and he settled in to get as much done as he could.

"What are you doing?" She replaced the cordless phone and stood there looking at him.

"Just getting some stuff out for a story before I forget it." He wrote down a few more lines before he set the pen and paper aside.

When he glanced up he saw her moving toward her discarded heels. There was no way he was letting her leave now. Using the extra speed his Panther side gave him, he was on his feet and had her in his arms in under a second.

She startled, but molded her body to his when he slanted his mouth over hers. He teased her lips with his tongue, and she parted them for him. The taste of her was sweet. He caught her hands, drawing them behind her back as he continued to kiss her. Long, slow, drugging kisses that made her sag against him. He tightened his grip, and he felt her stiffen the moment she realized how neatly he'd captured her. She jerked her mouth away from his. "Let go, please."

"What's the matter, beautiful?" He knew his grin was as much mocking as teasing, and her muscles tautened further. "Do you need to be cool, calm, and in control that much?"

"I'm supposed to be." He watched passion and logic war for dominance in her gaze. She licked swollen lips and his cock jerked in response. He'd love her mouth on him. Next time. This time, he wanted his cock in her hot little pussy.

"Hmm. Is that right?" He squeezed her wrists tighter, just to let her know who was in command of this situation. Then he brushed her lips in a quick, hard kiss. "You don't have to be in control around me, Teresa. I won't tell anyone if you let your guard down. You can trust me."

Her gray gaze searched his face. "I know that. I barely know you, but . . . I can trust you."

He grinned. "Instinct versus logic—the curse of being a Panther."

Shadows danced in her eyes. Secrets and pain she wouldn't share with him. "That's not the biggest curse."

"Oh? What is?"

She shrugged. "There are a lot of them."

That wasn't the whole story. Again. As usual. He ground his teeth together as the annoyance lanced through him. But he squelched the anger. Patience, he reminded himself. He could push her to tell him and get nothing for his effort, or he could push her in other ways.

Sitting down on the couch, he reeled her in by the grip he had on her wrists. Flipping her over his knee, he had her across his lap before she'd finished gasping in surprise. He tossed her skirt over her head and stroked his fingers down the soft globes of her ass. "So, you trust me, don't you, Teresa?"

A shiver passed through her and she tugged at her hands. He held fast, waiting for her to adjust. He wasn't above tipping the scales in his favor, so he eased his hand under the edge of her thong panties and slid his fingers up and down her wet slit. And she was wet. Every passing moment made her wetter. *Dios*, but he loved the way she reacted to him.

She moaned, clutching at the leg of his pants for balance as she lifted her hips to meet his touch. "Please, Rafe."

"Please, what?" He withdrew his fingers from her sex, trailing her wetness in circles over her ass. Then he smacked her lightly. She choked, and he felt her claws rip through his trousers. "Please, what, Teresa? Is this what you want?"

He hit her again, harder this time, so there'd be no mistaking his meaning. She squirmed on his lap, and her hot scent reached his nose. "Yes. Please. Whatever you want. I want you."

Swatting her thigh made her jolt, and he grinned. "I want you too. And I want this."

He peppered slaps across her backside, increasing in speed and force until her flesh was warm and red under his hand. She moaned, undulating against his legs. The crack of his palm on her ass sounded loud in the room, and his cock became a steel rod in his pants. He didn't know how much longer he could hold out before he had her. Pausing, he cupped one buttock in his hand, just so she could feel the sting. She hissed, her back arching like a cat in heat.

He slipped his fingers inward, teasing the slick lips of her pussy. Her panties were soaked with moisture, and he plunged two digits into her sex, fucking her with his fingers. Her inner muscles spasmed, and he could tell she was already close to orgasm. He pulled away, not wanting her to go over that edge yet. Not yet.

"Please, Rafe!" she cried out, wriggling to get free of his hold, but he gripped her wrists tight and spanked her harder.

Lifting her ass to meet each stinging swat, her claws dug into his thigh. A Panther's scream burst from her, and it called to the basest part of him, the feline that craved her as he'd never craved anything in his life. He had to have her. Now.

Groaning, he jerked her upright. She straddled his lap, reaching between them to rip open his belt and pants. She jerked aside the inset of her panties, and then he was inside her, and she rode him while he shoved his hips upward to fuck her. Her wet sex hugged his cock, and it was so good he thought he might explode from his skin.

His lungs heaved for breath, and sweat slipped down his skin. Sliding his hips out to the edge of the leather couch, he positioned them for a deeper angle.

"Rafe!" She leaned backward, bracing her hands on his knees and the angle was even better, her slick sheath even tighter on his dick.

"I love the feel of you on my cock, Teresa. All sweet and tight and wet." He gritted the words out between clenched fangs.

She shuddered, her face flushed, and she worked herself on his dick faster. "I like how you feel inside me."

Now it was his turn to shudder, pumping his cock as quickly as he could. His muscles burned from the strain, and he could see how her eyes had burned to gold. She smiled down at him, her fangs flashing. They went wild on each other, everything in perfect sync. The Panther inside him struggled for control, and his talons scrabbled across the leather sofa. He fought the urge to rear up and bite her, mark her as his. He held back, but just barely.

His hands reached out to bracket her hips, sliding around to squeeze the punished flesh of her ass. She hissed, the cat within her shimmering just below the surface. Her pussy flexed around him, her moisture glistening on his hard flesh when she lifted off of his cock and slammed herself back down.

Firming his grip, he pulled her tight on the base of his dick while he ground his pelvis against her clit. She threw her head back and shrieked, the gold of impending change flickering over her skin. Her channel closed around his cock, milking him until he couldn't hold out any longer.

Jets of come spurted from him, and still he thrust into her, wanting that contact, that friction, while he emptied himself inside of her. They shuddered together, the orgasm never ending. She swayed in place and he pulled her down to his chest. She collapsed forward, whimpering.

"Rafe," she whispered.

He trailed his fingertips through her sweat-dampened hair. "Teresa."

That was it. Just their names. A warm, comfortable silence fell as their bodies cooled and their breathing and heart rates slowed to normal. She nuzzled her nose against his chest. "I'm getting cold."

"Okay." He stood up and set her on her feet. In under a minute, he had them divested of their damp clothes. Then he lifted her off her feet and walked to the bed.

Yawning catlike, she curled against him. "That was fun."

"It was, but I'm betting you're glad that Panthers heal when they sleep, or your ass would be stinging tomorrow."

She chuckled. "So undignified for an heir to squirm."

"Except when said heir is with me. Then she can act however she wants." He settled them both in the bed and kissed the top of her head.

Cuddling against his side, she threw a leg over his thigh. Her hand stroked up and down his torso and he broke into a purr. He felt her lips curve in a little smile against his chest before she kissed his skin. Propping her chin on his shoulder, she met his gaze.

"What?" He rubbed a lock of her hair between his fingers, then tucked it behind her ear.

She shook her head, her eyes crinkling at the corners. "Nothing. Just looking at you."

"Well, then. Look as much as you want for as long as you want." He ran the pad of his thumb over her high cheekbone. For a moment, he let himself envision being able to look at her, touch her, any time he wanted, as often as he wanted. It was an intoxicating thought. He, who'd never spent more than a few days or weeks with a lover who happened to catch his fancy, wanted to have the same woman. Over and over again. For years. Forever.

Just like he had her now, soft and warm and satisfied in his arms.

He could imagine coming home to her for the rest of his life, could see himself looking at her across a dinner table, could picture them as an old married couple, with her just as bull-headed as she was now. He wanted to be there for all of that.

The breath eased out of his lungs as he watched her drift to sleep. Yes. This was right. Having her was right. A bit of the disquiet that had plagued him for so long crumbled. He wasn't sure where this road would end, but the journey was what mattered to him. Whatever issues they had, they could work them out. He'd found what he wanted, and he didn't intend to let anything get in his way.

Not even her.

5

Only a few days remained in the summit, and while it had been long and trying so far, exhilaration pumped through Teresa when she walked out of the conference room. She felt as if champagne fizzed in her veins, as if she were floating. It wouldn't last, she knew. She'd had defeats along with her victories, but this confidence booster was amazing.

She passed a window and realized that the sky was beginning to lighten, misty fog rolling over the San Francisco Bay. They'd worked all night and into the morning, debating trade policies in the various territories. Servers had brought food, which they'd eaten while continuing the deliberations.

Even though the sun was beginning to rise, she didn't know how she'd sleep. Like most cats, Panthers were nocturnal. Their day started around sunset, but with the different time zones that each Pride occupied, it sometimes meant being up at all hours of the day and night to take a phone call or answer an e-mail. It was a pain in the backside sometimes, but she was finding she liked what she was doing. Before she'd become heir, it had often felt as if she were ... unneeded.

Now, she was more than needed, she was required. It was both terrifying and invigorating. She'd expected to spend her life serving her brother, not making decisions for the Pride herself. Even her father had listened to her when she'd told him they'd set a good precedent with her confrontation with the Australian ambassador. He'd respected her opinion, and spoken to her the same way he used to talk to her brother when they'd planned their next move for the Pride. She felt as if she were living Enrique's life and not her own, and it confused her that she liked it more than she'd enjoyed the life that was supposed to be hers.

It was wrong to think this way, and she felt her good mood evaporate like the San Francisco fog. She shook her head, turning in the direction of the kitchens. If she went to her suite, Rafe would want to know what had upset her. There was no way to hide it from him—the man had the uncanny ability to see through any subterfuge. And there was no way she could sleep now, not with the horrible guilt that she'd tried to ignore creeping in to poison her happiness. Because she *was* happy with what she was doing. It was as if she'd stolen her brother's life away, and now he was suffering, locked alone in his own mind.

"Good morning, Ms. Garcia."

"Good morning, Benita." She smiled automatically at the wrinkled old woman—one of several chefs who worked here. In every Pride, the kitchens were always busy, always ready to feed the entire den. Even on another continent, it was a comforting place to be.

She poured herself a cup of coffee and picked up a croissant from the buffet. "I'm going out to watch the sun rise. I'll bring the dishes back when I'm done."

"Of course, of course." Benita grinned. "My wrap is hanging by the door. Take it with you—it's cold out there!"

Setting her food down, Teresa obediently put on the wrap. "Thank you."

"Enjoy the quiet." The old woman made a little shooing motion with her hands. "I know I do at this time of day."

Teresa found a small bench at the edge of the property to sit on. From here, the tall hedges that formed a maze blocked the view of the house. No one could see her, no one could hear her unless she screamed. She was alone. It was the most privacy she'd had in a long time.

Swallowing, she let her head rest against the tall stone wall that rimmed the property. It hurt, feeling so ashamed of how she loved stepping into her brother's shoes. He should be the one attending this summit, not she. Not the second child. Even thinking of Enrique, how she'd seen him last, hurt her. He hadn't even recognized her, he was so out of his mind.

"Teresa."

She laughed softly, and the sound emerged close to a sob. Of course he'd tracked her down. "Rafe."

He came to her through the fog, stepping out of the bushes. The way her heart fluttered just seeing him should have made warning bells go off in her head, but not once in the last week and a half had she been able to quash the reaction.

The heat from his big body enveloped her when he sat beside her, and she leaned into the warm comfort he offered. His arms went around her and he pulled her sideways into his lap. "Did the negotiations go badly today? Is the Australian ambassador giving you problems?"

"No, her Pride leader was pissed that she was drunk at the party and said tasteless things about my brother. Apparently, Antonio was also unhappy about her making comments about a member of his Pride. He called Australia about her behavior, too."

"Yeah, Ben mentioned that to me."

"That woman is never going to be a friend of mine, but she'd be a fool to start anything right now. She's in enough trouble as it is." Teresa sighed. "And negotiations were very successful today. I'm close to opening up freer trade between Europe and Asia."

Meaning their Prides would have more leeway in investing in companies in each other's territories. The added layer of politics for Panthers made business technicalities and legalities even more complex than in the human world. She yawned and rested her head in the crook of Rafe's neck.

"But something's bothering you." He stroked his fingers through her hair, the low rumble of his voice relaxing her.

"Yes." It was no use denying it. He'd learned to read her remarkably well in the days they'd known each other. His persistence in being with her whenever they weren't working was playing in his favor and they both knew it. Meals together, hours spent talking and then making love, or making love and then talking had whittled away at her resistance. Her heart was softening toward him in ways she knew she shouldn't allow.

"Tell me." His voice was soft, coaxing. It invited her to intimacies that she couldn't grant anyone.

So, she told him as much as she could, because she couldn't stop that traitorous, weak part of herself that insisted she was safe with him, that he would never betray her. "I like doing this."

"Doing what?" He massaged the back of her neck, and an involuntary purr slid from her throat.

She waved a hand in the direction of the mansion and then down at herself. The movement made cold, damp morning air slide under her wrap, and she shivered, tucking her arm back in. "This. Being heir. It should be Enrique who's here."

He was silent for a long moment. "You feel guilty."

Cringing at how neatly he hit the nail on the head, she turned her face into his shoulder. "I don't want to talk about it."

"It's not going to stop bothering you if you ignore it."

"Talking about it won't make it stop bothering me either." She swallowed. "It won't change that I'm the heir and my brother is not."

His hand cupped the back of her head, urging her to look at him. "You feel guilty because you *want* to be Pride leader. You *like* the work, you like the challenge, the political bickering, the wheeling and dealing." He shrugged. "Sure, there are days you wish this weren't your life, but there aren't that many of those days, are there?"

"No," she choked out. God, it sounded even worse when he said it aloud. Almost every day, she was *glad* that she was heir, glad that she would be the leader someday.

His arms tightened around her, refusing to let her hide from the truth. "You love this and you feel guilty about it."

"Leave me alone." She tried to struggle upward, but he was a Panther male and easily stilled her motions.

"Never." His face fell into uncharacteristically solemn lines. "Just admit it. Admit that your life is exactly how you want it."

"Fine." Hissing, she shoved at his arms but couldn't budge him. Rage whipped through her, and even though she knew it wasn't fair, she was angry at him for making her discuss this. Tears glutted her eyes and she blinked fast to keep them from falling. She loved her brother, but she was happy with *his* life. "I admit it. Are you happy now? I usurped my brother's title and I'm relishing every second of it while he wallows in madness and despair. Aren't I a wonderful sister?"

"You feel guilty," he repeated, quietly, implacably.

"Hell, yes, I feel guilty!" she burst out, swiping at the rebellious tears on her cheeks. "Wouldn't you?"

"In your place, perhaps." He held her closer, cradled her to his chest. "But you didn't usurp his title, Teresa. He went mad. Your father was *forced* to make you his heir."

"Exactly! All of this is supposed to be his. Not mine."

"You didn't steal anything, Teresa. You couldn't do that. It's not in you."

"I could hurt someone if it protected a loved one. I've done so in the past." And that was a truth that skated far too close to things no one should ever know.

His eyebrows drew together and he searched her face. "I could do the same."

"It's not always an admirable or understandable thing to do." The shame of it poured through her, and it shamed her even more that part of her never wanted him to know what she had done, what she had let happen, because she'd hate to have him look at her with anything less than the respect she saw in his gaze now.

"Is taking your brother's title the imperfect thing you thought I wouldn't approve of?"

She licked her lips and tried to find an honest way to answer, without saying more than she should. "It's part of it, and that's all I can tell you."

"I hate when you don't tell me things." He sighed and rested his chin on the top of her head. "In general, I'm glad that you love your work. I love mine, so I want that for you, too, my mate. I'm glad to help you in any way that I can."

"You don't mean that." She turned her face away, tried to make herself turn away from the temptation he presented. It would be too easy to learn to rely on him. And that was *not* part of her plan.

"Of course I do, you just don't believe me. Yet. But you will." He slipped his hand into her hair, tugging on it until she was forced to tilt her head back to look at him. "Talk to me about why you feel so responsible. You didn't do anything to make this happen. You shouldn't spend your life feeling terrible about enjoying your work."

"This wasn't supposed to be my life." It was that simple, and that complex.

"But it is your life, now." Confusion reflected in his gaze, but she could see he was trying to understand the depth of her guilt. He couldn't because there were still so many secrets he didn't know, things her family didn't want people to know. He ran his thumb over her cheekbone. "Your brother isn't going to suddenly regain his sanity, is he?"

"No, never." She huffed out a laugh, fighting the need to lean into his touch.

"Then this is *your* life." He shrugged. "For whatever reason, no matter how painful, this is your destiny. Being Pride leader is *your* destiny, not his, whether he was born first or not."

She swallowed, biting back the words that would give him all of the truth about her part in the sordid affair. "He was raised to do this."

"And you're going to do a magnificent job at it." He gave her a small smile, his fingertips stroking her skin.

"He would have done better." If Enrique had never felt the mating urge, he might still be doing it better. It was a good reminder, a harsh reminder, that the same urge now rode her.

"Better?" Rafe arched an eyebrow. "This from the woman who's going to break open trade with Asia? I disagree with you that your brother would be better at this, but I'll compromise and say you'll do as good as he would have done."

"No."

"Yes."

She poked him in the chest. "You don't even know him."

"But I know you." He looked down at her prodding finger and lifted his brow higher.

213

"Do you?" She narrowed her gaze at him. "After nine days?"

"Yes. I do know you." He glared down at her. "You can deny it all you want, but we both know that there are parts of you that no one will ever understand as well as I do. My mate."

"Stop it." She crossed her arms over her chest. "You said you weren't going to push me."

"I'm not pushing you, and I don't know all your secrets, but I *have* gotten to know you. When I look at you, I see *you*. Not just a Pride heir or Enrique's little sister or Fernando's daughter." He shook his head. "You can't run from the truth forever—not about me, or your brother, or yourself."

"I can if I want to."

"Stubborn." He grinned and it made her want to smack him and kiss him all at the same time. "I'm sure there are many things that a Panther in a leading family can do, but altering reality to fit his or her whims is not one of them. That's not part of the magic of our kind."

"You are a pain in the ass, you know that, right?"

His smile grew wider. "Well, then, we're well-matched in that as well, aren't we?"

"Dios mio." She rolled her eyes but couldn't help her answering grin. A laugh bubbled out of her, and she shook her head.

He seized her mouth, catching her laughter and replacing it with a moan. Passion burst inside her, an instantaneous reaction to her mate. It was like a match to kerosene—explosive, consuming. She thrust her tongue between his lips and untangled her hands from the wrap to shove them into his hair. The soft feel of it against her palms contrasted with the hardness of his erection digging into her hip.

He slipped his hand up her thigh and under the wrap. Squirming, she tried to part her legs for him, but the skirt she wore hampered her movements. He skimmed his fingers past where she really wanted them, over her midriff, and up to her breast. The sensations were incredible. They always were with him. Her body jolted when he scraped a claw over her beaded nipple.

Ripping her mouth from his, she gasped. "Rafe, I want you."

"I know. I can sense how hot you are for me." He nuzzled his nose into her neck, nibbling at the tender flesh there.

"Then what are you waiting for?" She slid one hand up his chest, circling a small nipple through his shirt. The other hand she trailed down to his zipper, fondling his hard sex and the softer sacs beneath. "How much incentive do I need to give you?"

In answer, he tumbled them both onto the soft, damp grass. She landed on her back, with him on his knees between her thighs. He arched an eyebrow, shoved her skirt up to her waist, popped the elastic on her panties, and tucked them into his front pocket. "That's about enough incentive for me, thanks."

The clink of his belt unbuckling sent tingles running down her skin. He yanked off his shirt and tossed it aside, then unfastened his pants and freed his cock. Her sex clenched, utter want shivering through her. "Fuck me, please."

Pulling her hips up to rest on his thighs, he brought her legs up to drape over his shoulders and dipped his fingers into her sex. Her hands fisted in the grass when he toyed with her clit. Moisture gushed in her pussy, and he stroked her from one end of her slit to the other. Then he parted her buttocks and teased the tight pucker of her anus. Her heart tripped, and she closed her eyes, her breath shallowing out to nothing. Heat flushed her skin, so hot she thought she might burst into flames.

"And what if I wanted to fuck you here, my mate?"

She opened her mouth to remind him—again—that they

weren't mated, but the words ended in a groan when he pressed two thick fingers into her ass. The pressure was intense, but so was the pleasure. Every nerve lit up, agony and ecstasy twisting in a white-hot sensation that screamed through her entire body.

His hand began an endless circle, where he drew fluid from her pussy and used it to ease his passage into her ass. Scissoring his fingers, he stretched her for his penetration. His other hand played with her clit, and her muscles contracted and loosened. A shudder rippled through her and her legs flexed against his shoulders, raising her hips.

"Shh." He turned his head and kissed her ankle, her calf. "You can take me. Just relax."

Shock seized her lungs when he plunged his fingers in and out of her anus, pressing her farther open with each pass. Then he pinched her clit. Hard. Her mouth formed a silent scream as orgasm slammed into her, a dark wave of pleasure that overwhelmed her and dragged her under. He worked her with both hands until she screamed, the clench and release of her inner muscles making her arch off the ground.

She panted, and the scent of rich, crushed grass filled her nose. It mixed with the smell of sex and *him*. He didn't let her rest, didn't give her a chance to recover. She had no control to hold onto or hide behind. It was raw and powerful. He forced her to *feel*, to react and respond. Oh, God. She couldn't survive this. A moan bubbled forth from her throat when his fingers left her ass. Then he lifted her hips until his cock nudged her rear entrance. Her claws scrabbled at the soft earth beneath her when he pushed his big dick into her ass one slow inch at a time.

When he was embedded deep inside of her, he stopped. He kissed her ankle, stroking his fingers up and down her legs. "See? I knew you could take me."

"You're a pain in the ass." She stuck her tongue out at him.

"Literally," they quipped together.

She chuckled, and it only emphasized how full she was. Her inner muscles spasmed around him, and he groaned. One hand dropped to rub over her clit, and her thighs jerked. He clamped his other arm down on them, holding her legs against him.

Then he started to move. He withdrew from her ass as slowly as he'd entered, and the tension wound tighter inside her with every passing moment. He pushed forward a little faster, his flesh slapping against hers. The air rushed out of her lungs at the pleasured pain that sliced through her. His fingers danced over her swollen clitoris as he began to piston his cock in and out of her anus.

Her muscles squeezed around him every time he entered her, her pussy clenching on nothingness. She watched the lust play over his handsome face, and it only turned her on more to see how aroused he was by what they were doing.

"I want to mark you, Teresa. I want to make you mine," he whispered.

Jesus, the temptation to just let him do it was so powerful, she had to bite her lip to keep the *yes* from breaking free. The Panther within her writhed in need, shoving her toward giving in and allowing her mate to claim her. She opened her mouth to speak, but the breath whistled out of her lungs when he changed the angle of penetration, stretching her ass even more.

His fangs grazed her skin, a question, a demand. Logic kicked in just in time. "N-no. Don't do it, Rafe."

She shook her head to emphasize her point. Whatever time they had, she would savor it, but she would never mark him. *Dios,* that made her heart sting even more than the animalistic side of her screeching a protest.

He released her flesh, air gusting over her wet skin as he sighed. "As you wish."

Arching his hips, he slammed into her, taking them both

over the physical edge even if they denied the emotional, instinctual possibilities in their joining. His fingers played over her clit, working her in time with his thrusts, and they both shuddered into orgasm. Her inner muscles pulsed around his cock and he jetted come deep into her ass. Her heart pounded, her lungs burned from lack of oxygen, her body shaking with the overload to her senses. He threw back his head, his fangs bared as golden light danced over his skin. The feral display called to the feline within her and she hissed as another wave of climax rolled over her. She twisted against the grass, shivering at the contrast of the cool morning air on her flushed skin. When it was over, she relaxed, boneless and utterly spent.

The shadows of dawn gave way to sunshine, bathing them in light. He slid out of her, making them both moan at the friction on over-stimulated flesh. He collapsed facedown beside her, one arm flung over her midriff to hold her near. The gesture was sweet and possessive all at once, neither of which she should tolerate, but she stayed where she was anyway. He was getting too close, breaking down her resistance, just by being himself. Wasn't that how it was supposed to be with a man fashioned just for her? The question nagged her again—how long would she be able to resist him *and* the animalistic part of her nature?

She didn't know. Everything was so confused lately, and she didn't know what she wanted anymore, what was right or wrong. He had her in a tailspin, where logic and emotion warred with each other.

Nothing was as clear or simple as it had been before she'd met him.

"Good work tonight, Teresa." Tomas rose from his seat beside her, collecting the papers he had scattered over his portion of the long conference table. The scent of stress and sweat permeated the room, and she sensed that most of the people here were grateful for the end to another day.

"Thank you. Your Pride is doing well for itself, too." She smiled at the man who'd helped her come up with the excuse she'd needed to get here in the first place.

"I'll see you tomorrow." He glanced down at his watch. "If I hurry, I can meet Ciri for dinner."

"Have fun." She waved him off, and took a moment to chat with a few other delegates on her way out of the room. She had a rendezvous of her own to get to. Rafe would be waiting, working on his next story.

She climbed the stairs to the mansion's second floor, following his scent. It lured her as nothing else ever had or would. He was in her room. But his room or hers, it didn't matter. They'd spent multiple nights in both rooms. The layering of their scents, their essences throughout the spaces was the most perfect and most tormenting thing she'd ever experienced. Perfect because it felt so right, tormenting because she knew it would fade into nothing but memory after she was gone from this place.

Time was running out.

She could feel the moments slipping through her fingers. She would leave in a matter of days. There was no reason for her to stay.

No reason she could admit to publicly, though she was fairly certain no matter how discreet they'd been that the Panthers in this den had figured out she was having an affair with Rafe.

That didn't mean anyone had discerned the true nature of their relationship, but it pained her to have to deny what was becoming so important to her. That was nothing to the pain she'd feel when she was forced to part with him, but the understanding that to lose him after they'd mated would be so much worse an agony kept her from acting on any impulse to mark him.

When she entered her room, she found him naked in her bed, his broad shoulders propped up against her headboard while he read a book. His dark brows drew together in concentration, and he made occasional notations in a leather-bound journal he always kept handy. She found the habit endearing, and stood there watching him for a moment. He was so handsome, kind and understanding, but strong enough to fight for what he believed in. He would have been the perfect mate for her, and her soul railed at fate for taunting her with something she couldn't keep.

Tears welled in her eyes, and she blinked them back. She wouldn't waste the little time she had left on sadness. "Good book?"

"Mmm, yes." He turned a page. "Flaubert."

"*Madame Bovary?* I think I read that at university."

He glanced up and met her gaze. "No, it's a collection of his letters from his trip to Cairo. I'm reading it to add a different angle to the story I'm writing. Would you like to hear about his impressions of Egypt?"

The idea charmed her. She smiled, stepped out of her shoes as she walked, and sat down on the end of the bed. It had been years since anyone had read a story to her, perhaps not since she was a child and her mother was tucking her into bed for the night.

His grin was a teensy bit mischievous, as it always seemed to be. Just being near him began to relax her after the long hours of political maneuvering. The fact that he was nude only added to her enjoyment of the moment. "Yes, please."

"One of my favorite parts is on page 117, so I'm just going

to skip right to it. It's about watching a woman dance the Bee." He cleared his throat and began to read. "'Kuchuk shed her clothes as she danced. Finally she was naked except for a *fichu* which she held in her hands and behind which she pretended to hide . . . after repeating the wonderful step she had danced in the afternoon, she sank down breathless on her divan, her body continuing to move slightly in rhythm.'" Rafe glanced up, his dark gaze gleaming. "Flaubert also talks about making love to the dancer, 'She is very corrupt and writhing, extremely voluptuous. . . . Her cunt felt like rolls of velvet as she made me come.'"

Teresa swallowed, stunned by the sensuality of the reading, and how his voice purring the words made her body burn. Her nipples tightened to the point of pain, and her breath rushed into panting the longer he read. She also couldn't help but notice that his cock grew harder by the second, flushing a deep red and pulsing with a life of its own. Licking her lips, she wondered what he would taste like. She'd never taken him in her mouth, never sucked him. The thought sent a wave of heat through her. She swallowed, staring at him, listening to the low growl of his voice. Squeezing her legs together, she savored the ache between them. Her body flamed out of control for him. Only for him.

Scooting forward on the bed, she reached for him. Her fingers curled around the hard shaft covered in soft skin. He groaned when she licked her way around the head of his cock. A glistening drop of pre-cum slipped free and she caught it with her tongue. The salty tang of his flavor filled her mouth. Her sex flooded with cream, and her hips moved as she struggled to contain the lust building in her body.

When she sucked him deep, he wrapped her hair around his

hand and pulled. "Sweetheart, I'm going to last about ten seconds if you keep doing that."

She let him slide out of her mouth, but gave a last lick as he popped free. "Well, we can't have that."

"No, we can't have that." He kept tugging on her hair until she was upright. "I have other ideas in mind."

"Oh? Care to share?" Her scalp stung, and her body throbbed with unquenched longing.

"Absolutely." The flash of his white teeth was the only indicator she had before he shoved her forward. She landed on her hands and knees, and he urged her down into a prone position with her cheek pressed to the mattress.

"Grab your ankles."

Her eyebrows drew together and she twisted a bit to look back at him. "Why?"

"Because it's fun." He bent forward and nipped at her ass cheek, making her jolt. "Let loose a little, Teresa. Have fun with me."

The wicked delight in his gaze was irresistible. She wanted to try whatever put that gleam in his eyes. So, she complied with his request, wriggling around until she could reach back and wrap her fingers around her ankles. It stunned her how exposed she felt in the position, her face against the bed, her thighs opening until she knew he could see all of her. Her swollen, slick lips, the pucker of her anus. Everything.

A shiver passed through her when he circled one finger around her clit and drew it up her slit to her ass, teasing every millimeter of her aroused flesh, allowing cool air to touch her most intimate places. He purred softly. "Don't you like this, Teresa? Giving me everything? Letting me pleasure you?"

She shouldn't enjoy the lack of control, shouldn't admit to anything. "Yes."

"Good girl."

Before she could retort, his mouth was on her. She screamed as rapture hit her in a swift rush. He sucked her clit between his teeth, bit down on it lightly, and flicked it with the tip of his tongue.

His mouth moved up until he could feast on her sex, drinking her juices. Her breath clogged in her lungs when he slid upward and teased her anus, pressing his tongue into the tight hole. No man had ever done this to her before. Dark, wicked pleasure twisted through her. It was so forbidden, and that made it even more decadent.

"*Rafe,*" she cried. Her hands tightened on her ankles, pulling her legs wider for him.

Every inch of her skin tingled, and her breath burst out in ragged gasps against the sheets. His fingers teased her sex and manipulated her clit, while his tongue continued to torment her ass. The blood pumped so fast through her veins that she could feel the beat of her heart in her face. Little whimpers spilled out of her, a desperate, needy sound she didn't even know she was capable of making.

Orgasm beckoned, close enough that she could feel it quivering through her muscles. "More, Rafe. I want more."

He pulled his hands and mouth away from her body, but before she could protest, he slid his cock into her soaking pussy. She arched at the full sensation. He was so big, he stretched her so perfectly. Her fangs extended and she hissed into the mattress as he began thrusting into her. The glide of his sex in hers made goose bumps break over her limbs. *Dios,* it was good.

Then he worked his finger into her ass, which was still wet from his tongue.

"Rafe!"

He just laughed, the sound wild and free. Sliding his finger deep into her ass put pressure on his cock to hit her in just the right place with every rough thrust. The double penetration meant she could feel every inch of him—his cock, his finger, and the thin wall of tissue that separated the two. She screamed when the head of his cock made hard contact with her G-spot.

Her back bowed, every muscle in her body clenching as she came. "Oh, my God!"

The only response he gave was to groan and hammer himself into her pussy until they were both screaming in orgasm. Her claws dug into her ankles as her sex fisted again and again, milking his length. He hilted his cock inside her, flooded her pussy with come, and shuddered over her.

She let go of her ankles and collapsed to the bed, his cock slipping free of her body. Sweat streaked down her skin, making her shiver. Sleep beckoned, euphoria fizzing through her veins. She yawned, more relaxed than she remembered being in her life.

He sprawled beside her, dragging in ragged breaths. "See? Didn't I tell you it would be fun?"

The smug grin on his face cracked her up. "Yes, dear. You were so right."

He rolled to his side facing her, his chin propped in his hand. "I'm right about us, too, you know."

The pain hit so fast it made her head spin, slicing through her heart. "Don't."

"Why won't you bond with me, Teresa?"

"Have you even thought about what that might mean for *you?*" She closed her eyes, unable to look at him as she pushed him away. Again. "Your career isn't conducive to a Pride leader's mate."

She expected him to stiffen, to get angry. He didn't. "Are you asking me to quit?"

"No, I would never do that." She opened her eyes and sighed. "I want you to have a life that makes you happy. You're content in the career you have now. I just don't know how that would work out if you mated with me. I don't think you're considering all the consequences."

"You do that enough for both of us. And I *have* considered it, I've just decided that if we can both compromise, everything will work out. So, if that's not holding me back, it shouldn't hold you back. Now, let's try this again . . . why won't you bond with me?" He ran a finger down her arm, his touch gentle. "You want to, I know you want to."

Yes. *No.* A picture of the last time she'd seen her brother exploded through her mind. His eyes blank and dead, rocking and humming to himself in a chair in his suite. She shook her head wildly, covering her eyes. "No, I *don't*. I don't want to bond with anyone ever. I was hoping I didn't have a mate."

"Everyone wants a mate." Rafe's tone remained quiet, but the edge of hurt that was there made tears burn her lids.

"Not everyone. Not me."

"Why not?"

"Because . . . because of my brother." A sob caught in her throat and she swallowed to stop it from escaping. Her jaw clenched so hard she thought her teeth might crack.

"That's not the same as us at all." She heard him sit up, and forced herself to look at him. Then she wished she hadn't when she saw the pain she felt reflected in his dark gaze. "We *both* sense this. We're both sane and cogent of what we're doing. Your brother was definitely not."

"You don't know *anything* about my brother." The words exploded from her, a dam that burst within.

His words were still gentle, but relentless in their insistence. "He attacked Isabel, a member of his own Pride. Tried to force her to mate with him and claimed they were mates despite her denials, despite her mating into the Cruz family. He's mad,

225

Teresa. Everyone knows it. He showed it during the confirmation ceremony for Cesar Benhassi's leadership."

She shook her head. "That's not what I'm talking about."

"Then what are you talking about?" He made a frustrated gesture. "Just *tell* me why you fear mating so much. Help me understand why you're refusing to do what we both want."

A tear streaked down her cheek, and she swiped it away. "Enrique is mad. *Now*. He wasn't always."

"I've heard these things aren't always apparent in childhood, that they grow over time." He ran a hand through his hair, leaving it in furrows. "You can't know that this wasn't an inevitable outcome of an unbalanced mind."

"Yes, I *can!* He wasn't always mad, he wasn't destined to be mad." She bolted upright, angry words of defense she knew she shouldn't say pouring from her mouth. "You all think you know so much, but you don't. You only know how it ended, not how it began."

A muscle in his jaw flexed, and he took a deep breath before he spoke. "You're right. No one knows that story. Tell me."

Her mouth worked for a moment, her mind telling her to keep her family's confidences, her instincts insisting she could trust this man with everything. "He had a mate."

"Isabel was *not* his mate."

"No, Isabel wasn't his mate." She shut her eyes, another tear slipping free. Sadness crashed through her, and guilt followed on its heels. "But she looked like her."

"What?" He straightened, his gaze sharpening.

"Isabel *looked* like his mate, Lupe. Their coloring was very similar." Close enough that there might have been some relation between the two families way back in their bloodlines. It wouldn't be surprising considering the size of the Panther population.

Rafe shook his head. "Then why the hell did he claim—"

She lifted her hands. "Because Lupe died just after he mated with her. Isn't it obvious?"

"Shit."

"Yeah." Her hands wilted to her sides as the confusion and terror of that time pummeled at her. "They say Panthers can go insane if they lose a mate, and he did."

"I'm sorry."

A laugh straggled out, more tears sliding unchecked down her cheeks. "So am I."

"Why didn't you tell anyone?"

"Father didn't want it. Neither did Enrique. It's family business, and there were no excuses we could make for his behavior that would make it better. The Prides had vilified my brother, and there was no making up for what he did. He was wrong, I know it." She shook her head, wishing things were different, but knowing it could never be. That past couldn't be undone. "He did horrible things to Isabel, and he is insane. I don't deny any of that. What I do deny is that he was a festering time bomb of insanity just waiting to go off. He was a good man, a wonderful brother. He was so *happy* when he found his mate, and she was happy with him. He wasn't always the way he is now."

Rafe caught her hand in his. "Why did you try to hide it after she died?"

"We hoped that he would recover. We hoped that he would eventually come to grips with the pain of his loss. Grief is a natural thing." She sighed and looked away, unable to bear the thought that her mate would think less of her for her complacency in what happened. "And in the end, it was denial on my father's part. On all our parts. Father was wrong, and he should have protected Isabel. I think he even hoped that she *was* Enrique's mate, that she could bring him back from the edge."

"But he already had a mate. No one has ever had a second mate."

"Except Isabel, with her twins." The irony of that had never escaped her.

"Those are *at the same time,* not a replacement of a dead mate."

"I know." Her shoulder jerked in a helpless shrug. "I make no excuses for any of us. I was as much to blame as anyone else. None of us wanted to admit Enrique had lost his mind, and by the time the Benhassis' ceremony debacle took place, it was far too late to save him."

"I'm sorry. Sorry for Isabel, sorry for your brother, sorry for you and your family. I'm so sorry." He squeezed her hand until she looked at him. The sympathy in his gaze was her undoing, and a sob bubbled up in her throat.

"He's not a bad man, no matter what anyone says. I know it's hard to make the distinction for other people, but that madman is *not* the brother I knew. The Enrique I grew up with would have been a great Pride leader." She shook her head, pushing away those thoughts. Nothing would stop her guilt over reaping benefits from her brother's pain, her shame over not stepping in to force her father to take action when Enrique spiraled out of control. She met Rafe's gaze. "So, now you understand why I don't want to mate. If I lost you . . . I'd end up like Enrique."

He brought her fingers to his mouth and kissed them. "You're assuming you would lose me."

"Everyone dies."

"Eventually, yes." He turned her hand over and kissed her palm. "You're assuming I would die first. You could just as easily leave me alone."

"Don't you see? If we never mated, that wouldn't happen to

us." Her tone went pleading, and she hated herself for weakening on what she knew was right, but everything in her cried out for this man. Woman and Panther both wanted him, and only the woman held back. "We could avoid that fate."

He squeezed her hand between both of his. "Do you really think it would be that simple, now that we've met each other?"

"It could be."

"No. No, it couldn't be, Teresa." His mouth flattened into a line. "Maybe if we had never known about each other, and mating had always just been a theoretical concept you avoided, it would have been simple, but we *know* each other now."

"It hasn't even been two weeks." She recited all the justifications she'd used in her own mind every day since she'd met him. "We've both had affairs last longer than this. We can just . . . go our separate ways and we'll be fine."

"We won't be fine, Teresa!" He threw his hands in the air. "We won't be together. We're mates, that's what we're supposed to be. *Together.*"

She twisted her fingers in her lap so tightly, they tingled with the lack of blood flow. "You promised you wouldn't force me into mating with you."

Eyes widening, his mouth dropped open and a flash of outraged hurt crossed his face. "When have I forced you to do a damn thing, Teresa? When have you ever *not* had a choice in what we did?"

"Rafe, please." That pleading note entered her voice, and tears closed her throat. Why did this have to be so hard? Why did it have to hurt so much? "I thought you would understand."

"I do understand. I understand that you're so twisted up over what happened to Enrique that you can't separate his problems from yours."

Her lips trembled when she spoke. "Tell me it's not true. Tell me I'm wrong. Tell me that Panthers don't ever go insane when their mate dies. Tell me there's some guarantee it wouldn't happen to us."

He shoved his hands into his hair, gripping the strands tight. He shook his head, a harsh laugh bursting from him. "Stubborn woman."

"I'm trying to protect us both." She wrapped her arms around herself, holding on to keep from crumbling. "I couldn't bear it if I did to you what Enrique's mate did to him."

And that was the worst part. It wasn't just about saving herself anymore, it was as much about saving Rafe too. Somehow in a few short days, he'd wormed his way into her heart. She had to hold fast and keep them both whole. Someday they would recover from this in a way that Enrique never could. Someday they would be all right. This pain would only last so long.

"His mate died, Teresa! I doubt she did it on purpose." The look in Rafe's eyes was enough to rip her to pieces. He stared at her for a long time, as if she'd brought his entire world crashing down around him. For a moment, she almost thought she saw tears sheen his eyes. "You're never going to give in, are you? You're never going to mate with me."

"No," she said, but it sounded like a sob. "I was honest with you from the beginning. About this, anyway."

"Honest, right." He nodded, then scrubbed a hand down his face. "Fine. I won't push you, just like I promised. I hope you're happy alone. My mate."

With that, he shoved himself out of the bed, gathered his things, and disappeared.

She clamped a hand over her mouth to keep from calling him back. Sobs wracked her body, and she curled up on sheets that were still warm from their bodies, still smelled of sex.

Shards of agony pierced her. She tried to tell herself this was the right thing, that she was keeping them both from a fate worse than death.

The thought was small comfort as the scent of her mate drifted farther and farther away.

6

Rafe dragged in a deep breath as he stepped out of the airport, taking in the scent of the city. Barcelona. For as long as he lived, if he had his way, this would be his home. No matter where he might roam, this place would be the one he came back to, but only if Teresa changed her mind. Thinking of her made his chest tighten.

It was a blow to the heart to remember her sobbing when he'd left her bedroom the night before. A phone call to his editor had revealed the magazine still needed someone to cover the travel writing conference in Spain, and Antonio and Fernando had been more than willing to let him go. He didn't question why they'd made it so easy for him, he'd just needed to get away.

There had been times he'd wanted to turn back, to rail at Teresa for not having even the smallest amount of faith in them. The fact that she didn't burned like acid in his skin. His mate didn't want him. She might never want him, and he would spend his life regretting that he hadn't found her before her brother's breakdown, that he hadn't claimed her before she even knew she wanted to run. But regrets got him nowhere. He lived in the here and now, not a land of dreams.

And the reality was, he felt as if he'd been flayed open and left to die. Alone.

The long plane ride and dealing with the usual hassle of international travel had given him time to clear his head and think past his own pain. Teresa would have to return to Spain soon, and some time apart might give her the chance to rethink her position. She wouldn't have him pressing her to give in to him, and he wouldn't have the opportunity to lose his cool over her obstinacy. He wanted her willing or not at all.

Not at all was the option he didn't want to face, but many sleepless hours of staring out a small airplane window had provided him time to wrap his mind around the yawning emptiness he might feel for the rest of his life. He snorted. What he wouldn't give to have every bit of his restlessness back.

But, no. No matter what happened, he couldn't regret meeting his mate. He just wished he could keep her.

His first stop in Barcelona was the European Panther Pride den. He had to meet with Fernando Garcia, the way he met with every Pride leader before he wandered through their territory. The Pride's chauffeur met him at the airport and drove him through the city to the mansion. They passed the incredible spires of Gaudí's cream-colored Sagrada Família cathedral, and the dramatic lights at night made him understand why people said it was built of bones.

The macabre thought reflected his mood perfectly. He had little hope that Teresa would reconsider anything. She had yet to yield anywhere except in bed, and he could handle her stubbornness, gladly, if she was willing to be that tenacious about making their relationship work.

But she wasn't.

The weight of that pressed down on his chest, strangling the breath out of him. Unfortunately, he could understand her terror now all too well. Watching a brother she adored dissolve into insanity, assault an innocent woman, and be forced down from the role he'd been born and raised for, all because he'd found a mate, would scare anyone. Being Teresa, she'd assessed the problem and found a way around it. Or so she thought, until she'd met Rafe.

He could understand her side of things, and that just made it harder to be angry. Instead, he just felt . . . exhausted. Hopeless. Helpless. And frustrated by all of it.

It was not the best mind-set with which to meet his mate's father.

When the car pulled up to the elegant mansion, Rafe drew in a deep breath and schooled himself to calm. He used to be good at that, before Teresa. Stepping out, he dragged his backpack out behind him and slung it across his shoulders. The butler took it from him when he entered and directed him toward the leader's office. Rafe recalled the location from his last visit.

The man sitting before a crackling fire was older than he remembered, lines digging deep grooves beside his eyes and mouth. Time hadn't been kind to Fernando Garcia. He motioned Rafe into a chair opposite him.

"So, you're my daughter's mate." Dark eyes pierced him, and whatever time had done to his appearance, Rafe understood that nothing had affected the older Panther's mind.

Somehow, he was unsurprised that the leader had figured out who he was to Teresa. They'd been discreet about their sexual relationship, but the extra senses of Panthers made secrets like that difficult to keep. It explained why it had been so easy to get permission for this trip. "We aren't yet mated."

"And why not?"

He decided not to pull his punches. This man needed to respect him and understand that he would stand firmly beside his mate when she became Pride leader. "She's afraid to mate be-cause of what happened with Enrique."

Fernando winced and glanced away. "Nasty business. My poor boy."

"I'm sorry, sir." On the one hand, this man's inability to see his son's condition for what it was had left a woman defenseless when she should have had her leader's protection. That was an unforgivable offense. On the other hand, the agony of watch-ing your child lose his mind would be enough to bring any par-ent to his knees.

Fernando nodded, a deep sigh heaving out. "People think . . . he's a monster, but it's not true." The desperation in the older man's eyes reminded Rafe so much of Teresa that he reached out to squeeze the man's shoulder.

"Teresa told me. I understand, and I'm sorry." He settled back into his chair. "But that excuses Enrique, to a certain ex-tent. It doesn't excuse you."

The leader's dark gaze turned flinty and his mouth worked for a moment. "I know it doesn't. I failed in my duty to Isabel. I failed in my duty to my entire Pride by leaving Enrique as my heir until I was forced to make a change. I'm a father, not a complete fool."

"Good. I'm glad that you recognize that." Rafe hitched his ankle onto his opposite knee. "However, I'm not a father, so I'm not going to pretend I know what you've been through."

And it was good to see that the man was fully cognizant of his failings. That kind of ongoing behavior in a leader was something Rafe wasn't sure he could live with. He'd spent enough time under a totalitarian ruler with Antonio's father.

Fernando grunted. "Your career is a problem."

He flashed a feral grin as he neatly turned the tables on who was in the defensive position in the conversation.

Rafe tilted his head in an acknowledging nod. He'd figured

this was going to come up, and he was glad they were laying all their cards on the table now. "So help me make it *not* a problem."

Eyebrows drawing together, Fernando stroked his fingers down his chin. Then he gave Rafe an incisive look. "It's occasionally necessary to send emissaries to other Prides. This summit is an example of such things, but it's not always that intensive and not with that deep a need for resolving political matters. It's more . . . maintaining a positive presence in the other Prides."

"And you'd want me to do this for you?" He thought about that. If he weren't closing some sort of deal, it might be workable. He wasn't a politician and didn't intend to become one, but he could make nice with anyone. That skill was one of his current job requirements.

"I think it's plausible."

"What would it cost you—and my mate—to have them let me loose in their territory?" It was a question he didn't want to ask, but he had to know. If it became too much of an issue, it could make them less likely to let him do his job. He'd chafe under the restrictions, so it was best to know what he was dealing with upfront.

The older man narrowed his gaze, rocking a hand back and forth through the air. "It's hard to say. I think it's feasible that an emissary on a goodwill mission be shown the high points of the culture influencing the Pride he's visiting."

Rafe snorted. "Okay, I can see that."

"We'll see how it goes, but only after you've mated with my daughter."

"I understand." He tapped his fingers against the arm of his chair. "She may never decide she wants to complete our mating." He met Fernando's gaze directly, making sure there was no doubting what he had to say. "I won't force her, and I won't allow anyone else to force her either."

The leader grunted. "Of course you're as stubborn as she is."

"She gets that from somewhere, sir."

That got a rusty chuckle. "Touché."

"I'm in the city for work, and I need to get some sleep so I'm ready for it." He rose to his feet, extending his hand to shake. "It was good talking to you."

"Yes, it was." Fernando stood and took the proffered hand. "I hope you sort things out with my Teresa, but I won't interfere. Unless you hurt her, in which case I will tear you to pieces. Slowly. Do I make myself clear?"

"Very clear." A small smile crossed Rafe's face. "I hope we sort things out too."

But he knew the hope might be futile. This entire conversation might well have been pointless. Coming here at all might mean nothing other than another assignment.

The summit was over.

Thank God.

Teresa's concentration was shot. She hadn't slept since Rafe had disappeared to God knew where. Antonio had stonewalled her subtle attempts at questioning, and no one else seemed to know anything. Not even Ben, which concerned her more than a little.

And now she was hours away from leaving and had no idea where her mate was. She had no one to blame for that except herself. Misery wrapped around her soul, and if she could have crawled out of her own skin to escape herself, she would have.

It hurt worse than she'd ever have imagined, and she didn't

even want to know what it would be like if they'd been mated. Could it get worse than this? Best not to ask the question.

Skirting the staircase, she walked toward the kitchens. Anything to avoid rooms that reminded her of her time with Rafe. That time was over, and she couldn't wait to get back to Spain. Or anywhere else that didn't have the scent of Rafe fading slowly from her suite.

She drew to an abrupt halt when she saw who sat working at the kitchen counter. "Isabel."

It was the hardest thing she'd ever done, getting on the plane to San Francisco, knowing she'd eventually come face to face with this woman.

Her stomach twisted as she saw fear flash through the woman's golden eyes, then she lifted her chin and faced her squarely. "May I help you, Ms. Garcia?"

"Hello, Isabel. You've known me long enough to call me Teresa." She forced herself not to twitch nervously. A Pride heir was not supposed to show weakness, but she hadn't been raised as an heir. She was just the heir's baby sister. Or she was before he became obsessed with this woman. That one event had changed so many people's lives forever. Isabel's, every member of the Garcia family's. The entire power structure of the Prides had shifted, a new potential ruler with new alliances to be made. It was a confusing, painful mess. "How are you?"

"I'm well, now that I'm not in the European Pride."

Teresa winced, but acknowledged it was a fair statement. Isabel hadn't been treated well by the Pride or its leading family, Teresa included. "I'm glad you're happy here. Congratulations on your matings."

"Thank you." The words were stiff and Isabel's lips compressed for a moment. Then she withdrew into her professional role as a chef for the North American Pride, any emotion locking away. A pleasant, distant smile crossed her face. "Can I get you some tea or coffee or . . . something to eat?"

"Some coffee would be lovely, thank you. I'll take it with me to my room." She could use the caffeine if she was going to stay awake for the long trek through various airports she had to deal with today. The lack of sleep and constant strain to outthink her political opponents was starting to wear on her. She was more than happy to get the trip over with.

With a cup of liquid ambrosia cradled in her hand, she turned to leave the room. Then she paused and looked back at Isabel. "For whatever it's worth to you, I'm sorry for what my brother did to you. Father should have interceded on your behalf. I should have insisted that he do so. We were wrong, and you were hurt because of it. I will always regret my part—or lack thereof—in what happened."

The blond woman stared at her for a long moment and then nodded. "I've made my peace with it. I'm happy with my mates, and I'm not sure when or if I would have met them if Enrique hadn't pushed me into running." A sharp smile crossed her face. "I was also really glad when he got punched out by my mates."

Teresa snorted. "I don't blame you. He'll never apologize and neither will my father, but I *am* sorry."

"Thank you." Isabel swallowed. "I forgive you. My mates never will, but . . . I appreciate you doing what your family won't."

Teresa nodded and left, something loosening in her. In the end, she hadn't told the whole truth. It could have hurt her Pride if she'd admitted how negligent they'd been by denying Isabel wasn't Enrique's mate, when they'd known he'd already had and lost his true mate. She had to think of what was best for her people, and creating more scandal and upheaval just to assuage her guilt wasn't fair to anyone. So, she'd done what she could to make things right with Isabel, though there was really no making any of it right.

If Rafe had been there, he'd have hugged her and told her she'd done her best. He'd have understood, and God, but she needed that now. Just his understanding of others, whether he agreed with them or not.

She missed him so damn much. She could understand as she never had before exactly why her brother had gone crazy. More than ever, she feared she might share his fate. Without even mating with Rafe, she felt the fogging grief of his absence. The pain would have been so much easier to bear if she knew *where* he'd gone. But she had no right to know—she understood that; she just hated it.

And she hated herself most of all for never having the guts to tell Rafe she loved him. Even if she couldn't have him, he should at least know that he owned her very soul.

She owed him that much. If only she knew where to find him—she'd tell him.

7

He dreamed of her. Just as he had the night before. He knew it was a dream, but there was nothing he could do to stop his mind from playing tricks on him.

This time, she came to him in Panther form, her jet-black fur rippling in the lamplight.

Her movements were fluid, the pure grace of a cat. His hands were propped behind his head, and he lay naked in bed, waiting for her.

She was beautiful, no matter what form she was in. The Panther within him purred at the sight of her. Her golden gaze locked on him, a predator stalking its prey.

He grinned, flicking his fingers to beckon her forward, welcoming the challenge. Stepping up onto the mattress, she continued toward him, her gaze never wavering. She set a paw on his upper thigh, just below his hardened sex, and flexed her muscles to dig her talons into his flesh.

"What exactly are you planning to do with those claws, sweetheart?"

She ran her tongue down a long fang, stepping forward until

her front paws were on either side of his hips. Bumping her head against his chin, she purred. He chuckled and stroked her silken fur.

She shifted to human form, her body dissolving into a warm glow of golden magic. When she re-formed, she was naked with her arms curved around his thighs, her body between his legs. Glancing down at his cock, she licked her lips.

He shuddered, groaning when she flicked her tongue out to trace the crown of his dick. Every muscle in his body grew taut as she took him into her mouth. He laced his fingers through her hair, holding her in place. Her lips closed around him, sliding down to take all of him.

The air in his lungs froze at the intense sensation. His grip tightened on her hair, his hips thrusting upward to fill her mouth as she suckled him hard. Sweat broke out on his skin when her fangs grazed his shaft. "*Dios mio,* Teresa!"

Her only answer was to soothe the sting with her tongue. It was all he could do not to lose control, and her hot sucking did nothing to help him in that arena.

"God, I love fucking your mouth."

She choked, her body beginning to writhe where she lay between his legs. Soon, he'd pull her over him, slide into her sweet pussy, and possess all of her. The thought was arousing enough to have him skating on the very edge. Then she worked her tongue down the underside of his dick, glanced up so she knew he could see that she'd taken all of him, and then purred, sending vibrations down his shaft.

"Teresa!"

Rafe ripped himself out of the dream, her name on his lips. He panted for breath, still hot and hard and shaking like a teenager in the backseat of his dad's car.

He gritted his teeth and grabbed hold of his cock, pumping himself roughly in his fist. It took only a few strokes to explode. His come spilled over his stomach and on the sheets. He shuddered, flopping back against the pillows. "Jesus Christ."

He wasn't sure if he wanted these erotic dreams to stop, or to never stop. God, he missed her.

A sigh heaved out of his lungs. He needed to get up and get to the conference. He had a panel to sit on today, a reading from one of his books, and a presentation to give on adventure travel. A busy day was good. He'd found that packing every single minute with activity helped to keep him from thinking of Teresa.

Unfortunately, he had no such control over his sleeping hours.

The hollow feeling in his chest expanded, and he had to clench his teeth to keep from howling with the building agony. It throbbed at the base of his skull, an ache he couldn't escape. The Panther within him constantly pushed him to go after his mate and force the issue between them. The insistent, gaping loss tattered any optimism he might have been able to muster.

The longer he was away from his unclaimed mate, the more it hurt. He wasn't sure if this was something that would get worse before it got better, or if it would just always be . . . worse. The only thing he could do was put one foot in front of the other and get on with what had defined his life for so long—his work.

As much as he still loved what he did, it was no longer *everything* to him.

He didn't know what he'd do if Teresa didn't change her mind. He tried not to think about the fact that her flight should arrive this evening. Fernando had given him that information, expectation in his gaze that Rafe wasn't sure he could meet. He would see his mate again soon, and then he'd know one way or another what direction his life was about to go.

His fate was in her hands.

* * *

She could smell him.

The ghost of Rafe seemed to linger around her, haunting the halls of her Pride's den. Teresa shook her head and ignored the tricks her senses were playing on her. It was just the loneliness, which she'd brought upon herself.

After she unpacked, showered, and changed into fresh clothes, she found herself walking toward her brother's suite. Sometime during the long flight to Europe, she'd come to the realization that she needed to talk to him, to resolve this horrible guilt that wouldn't stop eating at her soul, this fear that held her back from . . . everything. Some of it had been allayed by apologizing to Isabel, but the rest? She needed to see her brother.

Tapping on his door, she poked her head in. The room was clean and bright, rich silver tapestries covering cream walls. A wide window looked out on the Pride's property and the city beyond. She could see her brother sitting in one of the chairs grouped by the window, his back to her, his dark head bowed. She coughed into her fist to get his attention. "Enrique?"

He seemed to startle when she spoke, as though waking from a dream. Then he smiled and bounded out of his chair. "Teresa!"

He pulled her inside, lifted her off the ground, and twirled her around, much the same as he'd done for most of her childhood. She closed her eyes tight and tried not to cry. He still smelled of Enrique, still felt like her brother.

"Sit and talk to me." He waved her into a chair opposite his, and she sank into the soft upholstery. He poured them both a cup of coffee. "Hardly anyone stops by anymore. Mother, of course, and a few old friends, but . . ." He shrugged, a bashful grin curving his lips.

She took the cup he held out and sipped the strong, slightly bitter liquid. Just the way she liked it. "I've been away, or I would have come."

"Have you?" He tilted his head. "Yes . . . I think Mother said something about that."

"I found my mate. His name is Rafael Santiago." She said it boldly, baldly, and waited for him to react.

His face paled, his chin jerking to the side as though he'd been slapped. He choked, swallowed hard. "Con—congratulations, *hermana.*"

"I'm miserable."

His gaze came back to her, and he looked utterly dumbfounded. "But, why? Isn't he good to you? Doesn't he want you?"

"Yes, he's perfect for me." She laughed, and the sound was bittersweet even to her ears. "And I've pushed him away."

He looked at her for a long moment, searching her face. "Because of me, because of what I've become. You're scared."

"I'm terrified, Enrique. Terrified to move forward, terrified of where I am." Moisture burned at her lids, and she closed her eyes. Two tears streaked down her cheeks and she shook her head. "You should be the one with the mate. You should be the one who's heir. You should be the one who's away on political missions. I stole your life, Enrique."

"No." He set his coffee aside, reached out to grab her shoulders, and shook her a bit. "Don't be an idiot. My life was over when I lost Lupe. You aren't me, and she wasn't your Rafael. Your life together will be different."

"But . . ."

"Stop. Just stop." He released her and flopped back in his own seat. He scrubbed a hand down his face. "Don't throw away what I've given everything for. My life, my sanity. You have the chance to be happy, to do what I wish I could have done."

"If I mated with him, I could lose him like you lost Lupe." And go insane, but she didn't say it out loud.

"Would it hurt any less than having lost him by pushing him away now?" His gaze bored into her, refused to let her run from his question.

She swallowed and faced the horrifying truth. "No."

Spreading his hands expressively, he arched his eyebrows. "Then what are you waiting for?"

Reining in her spinning wits, she tried to focus the conversation on what she'd come here for—absolution. Or resolution. Or something that would give her the excuse she needed to move forward and stop looking back. "Don't you resent me?"

"No. I wish things could have been different for me, but they aren't. Your life isn't my life. You'll be a wonderful Pride leader, and you'll restore the honor I cost our people." He held up his hand when she opened her mouth to protest. "It's true. You know it is. My crazed behavior cost a great deal."

She swallowed. "You don't seem insane now."

"This minute? Yes. Five minutes from now? Perhaps not." His brows drew together as if perplexed. "I can . . . feel myself going in and out. I know when I'm right and I know when I'm not, but I can't control it. I'm slipping further and further away. The time I lose is more than the time I remember now." He closed his eyes. "It's to my shame that I'm glad."

"Shh, *hermano*." She caught his hand with hers and squeezed, her heart contracting in pain. "Don't speak like that."

His head rolled on the back of his chair and he opened his eyes to meet hers. His smile was sad. "It's the truth. We pretended for far too long, didn't we? All of us pretended."

Oh, God. She wanted to sob, wanted to scream and cry for this brother she'd adored her entire life. Her lips shook when she spoke, and her voice quavered. "I love you, Enrique."

"I know." He squeezed her fingers tight. "I love you too,

but you have to move on with your life. You have to live, *because* I cannot. I'm not strong enough. I should be, but I'm not."

"Enrique . . ."

He shook his head, and his grief radiated from him. "Do better than I've done, little one. Destiny's done well for you."

A sob lodged in her throat, threatening to strangle her, and she tried to force it down before it could burst out. "It's not fair, that I should get so much, and you should have so much promised to you, and have it all taken away."

He laughed, and it had an edge of mania to it. "You think I haven't thought of that? You think I haven't railed against the world, and fate, and destiny about that?" A hysterical giggle spilled from him. "I have. I thought of everything I could have done that might have saved her, saved myself, but it's not to be." His laughter cut off abruptly, and the silence sent a chill down her spine. He released her fingers and seemed to calm. "I'll be with her again soon, and the less I remember between now and then, the better off I am."

Soon. His word made her insides twist. The implication was one she didn't want to accept. She didn't ask how he knew he'd be with Lupe soon. She didn't want that question answered.

"I'm sorry, Enrique." For perhaps the first time, she didn't feel guilt when she looked at him, just sympathy. Losing a mate was terrifying, horrifying. There was no escaping that, but she couldn't escape that she *had* a mate. Even if she lost Rafe, her life wouldn't be nothing to her. She didn't think his would be nothing to him if she died first. For Enrique, nothing had mattered except Lupe. Not their people, not his duties. He'd gone so far as to try to replace his mate. She could understand the agony of loss, but everything else? No. She couldn't make those same decisions. That wasn't who she was as a person. Did that make her better or stronger than her brother? Maybe.

Maybe not. It just made her a different kind of person, and the only thing she could do was make the best of what life had thrown at her.

Just as Rafe had wanted her to do.

Enrique rubbed a hand across his mouth. "Life isn't fair— take from it what joy you can. Every moment is precious. Plan for the future as best you can, but there are no guarantees. Anyone who tells you otherwise is lying."

He'd just given her exactly what she'd thought she needed when she came in here. Absolution. An excuse to go after what she truly wanted. In the end, it didn't matter what her brother said. *She* needed to make the choice to move forward, and no one could do that for her. On every front, she needed to accept her fate and face her fears. She needed to find Rafe and beg his forgiveness for hurting him.

Rising from her seat, she bent to kiss her brother's forehead. "Thank you."

8

An intense whiff of Rafe's scent hit her when she exited Enrique's room. It was disorienting, and harder to dismiss than it had been when she arrived.

"*Benvinguda,* Teresa."

The Catalan greeting caught her attention. Like other Prides, Panthers spoke Spanish and English, but in Barcelona, they also spoke the local language. She turned to see a maid stepping out of a guest room down the hall. "Thank you. It's good to be home. Who's staying in that room?"

"This room?" The woman looked confused as she closed the door behind her, a vacuum gripped in one hand. "A Mr. Santiago. He's visiting the Pride from North America."

Of course he was. Where else would he have gone, but the one place where she couldn't run from him or from herself? So much of who she was was wrapped up in this home and the people who lived here. A wry grin curved her lips and she shook her head. "Do you know where he is?"

"A conference for travel writing, but I'm not sure where." The maid flashed a grin. "At least that's the gossip in the kitchens. He's very handsome, and the chef says his books are good."

"They are." His scent called to her, beckoned her to follow. Now that she knew he was in the city, she could track him.

It took her over an hour, but she found him in a bar, where he sat in a dark corner with two human men. One was older, with a gray beard crusting his jaw, and the other was around Rafe's age . . . late thirties, early forties. There was something about them that reminded her of him, somehow, but she couldn't put her finger on what. Their body language, the lazy way they savored the drinks in front of them while they talked. The older man made a comment that set the three of them laughing, and she couldn't help but smile. It was wonderful to see Rafe laugh. It was wonderful just to see him at all. The last time she had, she'd been uncertain it would ever happen again.

She stood there for long moments drinking in the sight of him, and though he did nothing to acknowledge her presence, she knew he had to have caught her scent by now. The Panther would have sensed his mate nearby.

But now that she was here, her courage faltered. This was a huge step, a huge risk. Something she'd never imagined she'd do. And he knew that, which was why he would have let her come to him when she was ready. The man understood what she needed before she did. And since she was the one who'd denied their mating, she was the one who had to make it right between them. So many mistakes she'd made, so much doubt and worry. She sighed and pushed herself forward, moving until she stood next to Rafe's chair. "Hello."

"Teresa." He climbed to his feet, and the other men followed suit. He smiled, but didn't look her in the eyes. He gestured to the two humans. "These are my friends, Rolf and Tim."

The older man's blue eyes twinkled with mischief, and she

liked him immediately. He had the look of a man who possessed an endless curiosity about the world around him. It reminded her of Rafe, and she smiled and shook his hand. "It's nice to meet you, Tim. What brings you to my country?"

Tim's gesture encompassed all three men. "We're here for a travel writing conference. That's what we do."

"I see." She offered Rolf a hand to shake, tilting her head back to meet his gaze. The man was *tall*—he topped Rafe by at least an inch or two—so he towered over Teresa. His look was a little more serious than either Tim's or Rafe's, but she could see the same curiosity in his gaze. "And are you enjoying Barcelona?"

"Very much."

Since her mate remained silent, she tried not to let it rattle her. Her stomach knotted, and she rubbed her sweaty palms against her skirt. "What do you like best?"

"It's a beautiful city, and with the Gaudí architecture, you'd never mistake Barcelona for any other place." When she smiled at him, Rolf looked between her and Rafe as if he had no idea what was going on with them, but he gamely returned the grin. "I like it that you can go out at four in the morning, and the street is full of Barcelonans, just as if it were four in the afternoon. The city never seems to sleep and everyone seems . . . casually determined to have a good time."

"What a lovely impression we've made on you. I'm glad you're enjoying your visit." She finally managed to meet Rafe's gaze and could only hope he saw the apology in hers. She let everything show, hid nothing from him. She didn't want to hide from her mate anymore. She wanted that connection, that love that had no conditions. "May I speak with you? Privately?"

He looked at her for a long moment, and whatever he found in her expression seemed to appease him because he nodded and picked up his jacket from where it was draped on the back of his chair. He glanced at his friends. "I'll see you guys tomorrow."

From the wicked smiles that formed on Tim's and Rolf's faces, she didn't need to guess what they assumed Rafe and she were off to do.

Then again, she hoped they were right.

Rafe's gut churned as they rode back to the mansion in silence. What they had to say couldn't be said in front of a human cab driver. The way Teresa looked, the way she smelled, the heat of her slim body next to him—*Dios,* he'd missed her. It had taken everything he had not to grab her the moment she'd walked into the bar tonight.

But he couldn't.

She'd been running from him, hiding things from him since the moment they met. If they were going to make a relationship work, she needed to want it as much as he did. She needed to open up. He'd been trying to convince himself that she could let go of her fear of mating, but it didn't matter what he believed. She had to believe it. And he needed the assurance that she did. The days apart had proven that he could only beat his head against a wall for so long.

"I spoke to my brother."

He stilled, turning to look at her as the cab pulled to a stop in front of the house. She'd spoken to the brother whose actions, however inadvertently, had done so much to put a barrier between them. Was talking to him a good thing or a bad thing? Rafe wasn't sure. "Oh? What about?"

"Me. Us. Everything." She paid the driver. *"Gracias, señor."*

She slid out and he followed her into the den and across the foyer to an office not far from the front door. It smelled like her and held light, curvy, feminine furniture, so he assumed it was her office. "And did your brother say anything interesting?"

"Many things, actually." She closed the door behind her, clasping and unclasping her hands in front of her. She was nervous. Good. It meant she cared, that she was uncertain, not stubbornly entrenched in her viewpoint. "He was having one of his more lucid moments. They . . . aren't as frequent as they used to be."

"I'm sorry." He wanted to take her in his arms, reassure her, but he didn't. Setting himself up for more rejection and pain wasn't something he was interested in.

She hugged her arms around herself, but her jaw set in a firm line. "He said he'd be with his mate soon. And I think . . . he may kill himself to make that happen. Or become completely vegetative."

"*Dios.*" He couldn't remain aloof from her. Not from his mate, not when she was hurting. He reached for her, and she threw herself into his arms, wrapping her arms around him.

"It's a mercy, really." But he could hear the suppressed sob in her voice. "He's in misery right now, and he wants to be with Lupe. I can't begrudge him that."

"No, I can understand that." But he couldn't understand the selfishness that could lead a man to cause so much suffering in those he was supposed to care for. Teresa would never have done those things, and neither would Rafe. More than anything else, that fundamental comprehension of their character gave him a spark of hope that they could move beyond Enrique's fate.

"He told me I was a fool if I let my own mate walk away and didn't hold on to whatever happiness I could find for as long as I could keep it."

That surprised Rafe into a chuckle. "Your brother is a smart man in his lucid moments."

253

Tipping her head back, she gave him a wan smile. "I know. He used to be that way all the time, but now . . ." She shrugged helplessly. "He told me I'd make a good Pride leader and that I was stronger than he was. I don't know if I believe that, but I hope he's right. I hope I can restore honor to my people."

"You can." He had absolutely no doubts. Her dedication to her family, her sense of fairness, her dutiful nature meant she'd do whatever it took to succeed. He wished he had such absolute faith in her willingness to be mated.

She pressed her face to his chest, her shoulders shaking. "Thank you, Rafe."

"Of course." He slid his hand up and down her back.

"Seeing my brother just brought home so many things." She swallowed audibly. "I'm so sorry, Rafe."

For what? He wanted to ask, but the question froze in his throat when he saw her grief and guilt-ridden expression. His chest tightened to the point where he couldn't speak, couldn't breathe. This was it. She'd end it now, ask him to leave the den, tell him that talking to Enrique had only reinforced her desire to never mate. That place he'd hoped to belong, that final end to his restlessness evaporated.

"I should never have let you leave San Francisco. I should never have let my uncertainties get in the way of . . . of everything. My whole life. I was afraid to be the heir, so I kept telling myself it shouldn't be me doing it. Even though I loved it." Her lips shook, but her gaze was clear. "And I was so in that mindset, I did the same thing with you. I was afraid to have a mate, so I pushed you away. Even though I wanted to mate with you. Even though I love you."

He laughed; he couldn't help it. Heady relief exploded deep inside him. He'd been waiting for this since the day they'd met—some indication that she wanted to mate with him. He laughed until tears filled his eyes, and he squeezed her tight. "I love you, too."

Her arms looped around his neck, and she held on for dear life. "I'm so sorry, Rafe."

"Are you sure?" He pulled back to look at her.

She nodded. "There's always going to be the chance that we lose each other, though I hope that's not for many, many years, but . . . it struck me that no matter what my brother has done, the one thing he doesn't regret is loving his mate. Why would I fight against the things he *does* regret and not try to hold on to the things that he doesn't? I don't want to repeat his mistakes, and that's been my whole motivation since I was shoved into the heir role." She sighed, shook her head. "All my doubts ended up spilling over onto you, and that hurt you."

"That hurt us both."

"Yes. That hurt us both." She took a deep breath. "I won't say that I'm not scared. I am. Scared I'll fail at being a leader and being a mate, scared I'll lose you and lose my mind. But not even *trying* and living with the regret of letting everyone down, letting you down, letting myself down scares me more. I don't want to regret my life."

He cupped her cheeks in his palms. "I'm not a fan of regrets."

"I want to be the Pride leader, and I want to mate with you. There are so many things that could go wrong, things I watched go wrong with my brother." She covered his hands with hers. "I hope everything works out well, but most of the bad things are beyond my control. I can only do my best, hold on to what I love, and . . . that's it. I know what I want, and no matter how scared I am, I'm not running away anymore."

"That's all I can ask for. That's all I can offer you in return. I promise to do my best, and I promise to be as stubborn as you are about holding on to what I love." He stroked his fingers over her smooth skin, something giving way inside his chest. A final kernel of doubt.

"You walking away was what made me realize what I stood to lose."

He grinned. "Yeah, well. You have your way of making a point and I have mine."

"I got the point." She stood on tiptoe and kissed him. "I love you."

"Prove it."

Her eyebrows arched. "Prove I got the point or prove I love you?"

"Both." He let his smile widen, become lascivious.

Her grin matched his, and she slid her fingers into his hair, pulling him down to her. He devoured her like a man starved. His tongue thrust into her mouth, groaning when her sweet flavor burst over his taste buds. Her grip on his hair tightened, and she held him closer, pressing herself against his body.

The Panther within him clawed for freedom, and he didn't even try to restrain it. For once, the cat and the man were in complete accord. He growled, ripping at her clothes, popping buttons and shredding cloth. She did the same, her hands urgent on his shirt, his pants. They were naked in under a minute, their bare flesh sliding and hands roving over each other. He pushed his fingers between her thighs, found her slippery with cream.

"I love your hands on me." She moaned, lifting her leg to wrap around his hip and give him more access.

"Good. I like putting my hands on you." He chuckled, slipped two fingers into her sex, and used his thumb to stimulate her clit. Her claws dug into his scalp, and she sucked his lower lip into her mouth. He groaned, sweat beading on his forehead as their kiss turned rough and demanding. Stroking his fingers into her, he felt the wildness within breaking loose when she made hot little noises. Her reactions made him pant, and her palms sliding over his skin did nothing to help him hold on to any restraint.

Her hands dropped to his cock, and he ripped his mouth away. He backed her up against the desk, trapping her so she couldn't escape him. Then he shoved his fingers into her sex, hooking them to hit her right where he knew it would make her scream.

She didn't disappoint. "Rafe! Please, Rafe."

Snapping her hips forward, she kept up that friction he knew would send her over the edge. But he had something else in mind first. Catching her hand, he brought it to his lips and kissed her palm. He worked his way up to her wrist, licked and nipped at the tender flesh there. Meeting her gaze, he let the Panther show. His eyes would have burned to gold, and his fangs were deadly points.

He let her see exactly what he planned to do, but still thrust his fingers deep in her wet pussy. She whimpered, twisted to get closer, her tight nipples rubbing against his chest.

Then his fangs sank into her flesh, marking her as his. Forever. His. Flicking his thumb over her clit, he licked the bite mark until she cried out.

"Rafe! *Rafe!*" Her body arched as she came with sudden force. Her pussy gripped his fingers tight, her hips undulating to meet his hand. She grabbed his shoulders when her knees buckled, and she laughed and sobbed at the same time.

He dragged her down to the floor, rolling so that she was on top of him. "Ride me."

"Gladly." She grinned and he watched her fangs gleam. She moaned when he licked her moisture off of his fingers. "Jesus, Rafe."

"Mmm," he groaned, rolling his eyes in exaggerated ecstasy,

sucking the last of her juices from his skin. "Ride me, sweetheart. Now."

"Yes." She grasped his cock, her talons scraping the flesh a bit. He shuddered, gripping her hips and jerking her into position over his cock. She sank down and he shoved up, impaling her on his dick.

Her fingers wrapped around his biceps, her sharp claws digging into the flesh and muscle. The sting of pain ratcheted up his pleasure, made him hiss, the Panther rising even higher to the surface until there was no differentiating the two. Man and beast claimed its mate in a taking that was powerful enough to shake him to the core.

Her breasts bounced, and he couldn't resist them. He cupped them in his palms, tweaking the tips with his talons. She rode him hard, lifting and lowering her sex on his until he couldn't tell where he ended and she began. The blending of them was as close to nirvana as he'd ever been. Feline and human, bonded together for life. Mates.

Almost. It would be perfect once she completed the circle.

"Mark me." He gritted the words out between clenched fangs. Yes. He wanted that final, unbreakable tie. He wanted all of her, wanted to give her all of him.

She hissed, ground her pussy down on his cock, and bent forward to bite his shoulder. A Panther's roar ripped from him, his hips arching until he lifted her off the ground. She clamped her thighs on him and held on, sucking at the mark on his flesh until he pumped his come into her pussy.

Her inner muscles pulsed around him, and she released her fangs from his flesh to throw her head back and scream. "I'm coming, I'm coming. *Dios*, Rafe! Yes, yes, *yes!*"

The words rushed out of her mouth, tripping over each other. Her gaze locked with his, the intense orgasm gripping both of them. They moved together, dragging it out as long as possible. Neither of them wanted this to end. She was his mate, finally his. The thought burned through him, and another jet of come jerked from his body. They worked themselves against each other until there was nothing left, until she collapsed against him, and he held her close. Sweat glued their bodies together, and they shuddered, gasping for breath, hearts thundering in their chests.

They calmed slowly, overheated bodies still shaking as ripples of pleasure passed through them.

"My mate." A fiercely satisfied smile curved his mouth, and he bracketed the back of her neck with one hand.

She stirred a little, sighing. "I love you."

He tangled his hand in her hair, massaging her scalp until she purred for him. He grinned, but then something occurred to him. "You know, my career still isn't conducive to being a Pride leader's mate."

The purr cut off and she stiffened a little, but shrugged. "We'll work it out."

"So it doesn't matter?" he prodded. As much as he loved and supported her, he wanted to make sure they were on the same page about his work. Tilting his head, he looked into her eyes.

A snort burst from her. "It was just another excuse to avoid mating with you, but we'll work out getting you where you need to go."

"Being apart might be a problem." The last few days hadn't been pleasant, but he could make the sacrifice of always missing something to keep both of the things that meant the most to him. If she could.

She was quiet for a moment. "Will you always come back to me?"

"Yes." As if he could stay away.

"Then I can handle being apart when it's necessary." She ran her fingertip across his eyebrow.

He leaned into her touch, savoring the love that showed openly in her gaze. No more secrets between them. "I spoke to your father when I arrived. He'd already figured out we're mates."

She sighed and shook her head. "Figures. Ah, well. If he hadn't known before, he would have after tonight."

"I'm going to serve as a sort of roving goodwill ambassador as I go on assignments around the world." Rafe was actually excited by the prospect. He'd never considered doing anything political, but he imagined with an heir as his mate, Panther politics were going to become much more interesting to him. "He thinks it will work out."

"Will it work for you?" Her eyes were wide and too serious. He liked it better when she laughed.

"Yes." He turned his head and kissed her palm.

"This isn't what you want to do with your life. You love your writing career."

"I love *you* more than anything else." And that was the truth. He doubted he could go without writing, but if it came to choosing between his woman and his career, there'd be no contest. Having both was a blessing. "I can sacrifice some time and energy for the good of my wife and my Pride, especially if it allows me to keep the career that fulfills me. How is that not a good thing? We all get what we need."

"Are you sure?"

"Oh, yes. I'm sure." He brushed his lips over the mate mark on her skin. "Are you?"

She shivered and hissed, arching toward his mouth. "I'm sure."

"And perhaps when your schedule allows you to, I can drag you away from your responsibilities and take you where no one knows you or expects anything from you." He grinned down at her, warming to the idea. "We'd be free to be ourselves and explore without anyone judging you an unworthy Pride leader."

She blinked, a slow smile spreading across her face. "That sounds . . . perfect. Wonderful."

He couldn't agree with her more. There were so many possibilities in front of him, and he wanted to explore all of them. He wanted to develop this new bond with his mate, test all the changes to his role in the Panther world. It was exciting and fulfilling and all of it led back to Teresa. She'd keep him on his toes for the rest of his life, and he looked forward to the challenge.

"I love you, my mate."

Hearing her acknowledge all they were to each other made his chest band with emotion, so tight he could barely draw breath. *Dios.* It was the most perfect moment of his life. "I love you, Teresa."

No matter what ups and downs they faced, he knew they'd make it through. The disquiet that had been riding him for so long disintegrated as every piece of him clicked into place. This was where he belonged. With her, he had the one thing he'd never been able to find, no matter how far and wide he'd roamed—home. Theirs was going to be a hell of a story, one he could never write about in any book.

His greatest adventure ever.